BITE THE BULLET

KARLEY BRENNA

Bite the Bullet

Copyright © 2025 by Karley Brenna

All rights reserved.

No part of this book may be reproduced in any form or by any electronic or mechanical means, including information storage and retrieval systems, without written permission from the author, except for the use of brief quotations in a book review.

This is a work of fiction. Any names, characters, places, brands, media, and incidents are either the products of the author's imagination and used in a fictitious manner. Any resemblance to actual people, places, or events is purely coincidental and fictional.

Do not copy, loan, sell, or redistribute.

Paperback ISBN: 979-8-9888184-5-8

Edited by: Bobbi Maclaren

Cover: Dirty Girl Designs by Ali Clemons

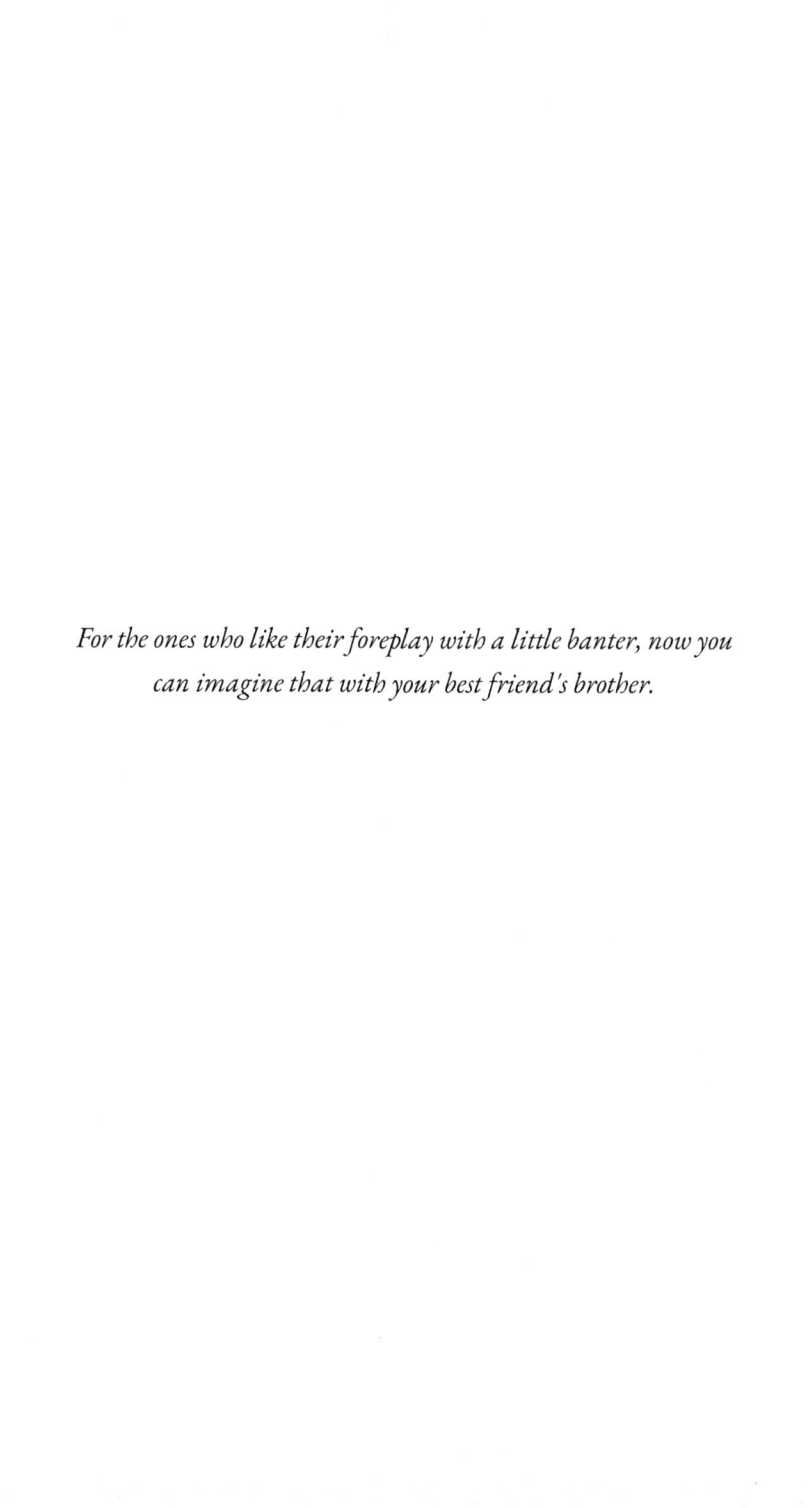

For the ones who like their foreplay with a little banter, now you can imagine that with your best friend's brother.

Important Note

Dear reader,

Within these pages, heavy topics that may be sensitive to some readers are discussed. They are listed below, but please keep in mind that some may contain spoilers to what unfolds in this book. As always, I do my best to handle these topics with the care they deserve. Before you read the list, please remember that, like people, characters are not always perfect. They can be stubborn and hold grudges for various reasons. Without further ado, here are Reed and Brandy's trigger warnings, and their story:

-Distracted driving

-On-page gun use

-On-page minor and major physical assault

-On-page mentions of SA but it does not get that far

-Sibling conflict

-Side character over-indulging in alcohol

-Abusive parent (discussion and some actions shown)

-Very brief mention of fear of infertility from a side character

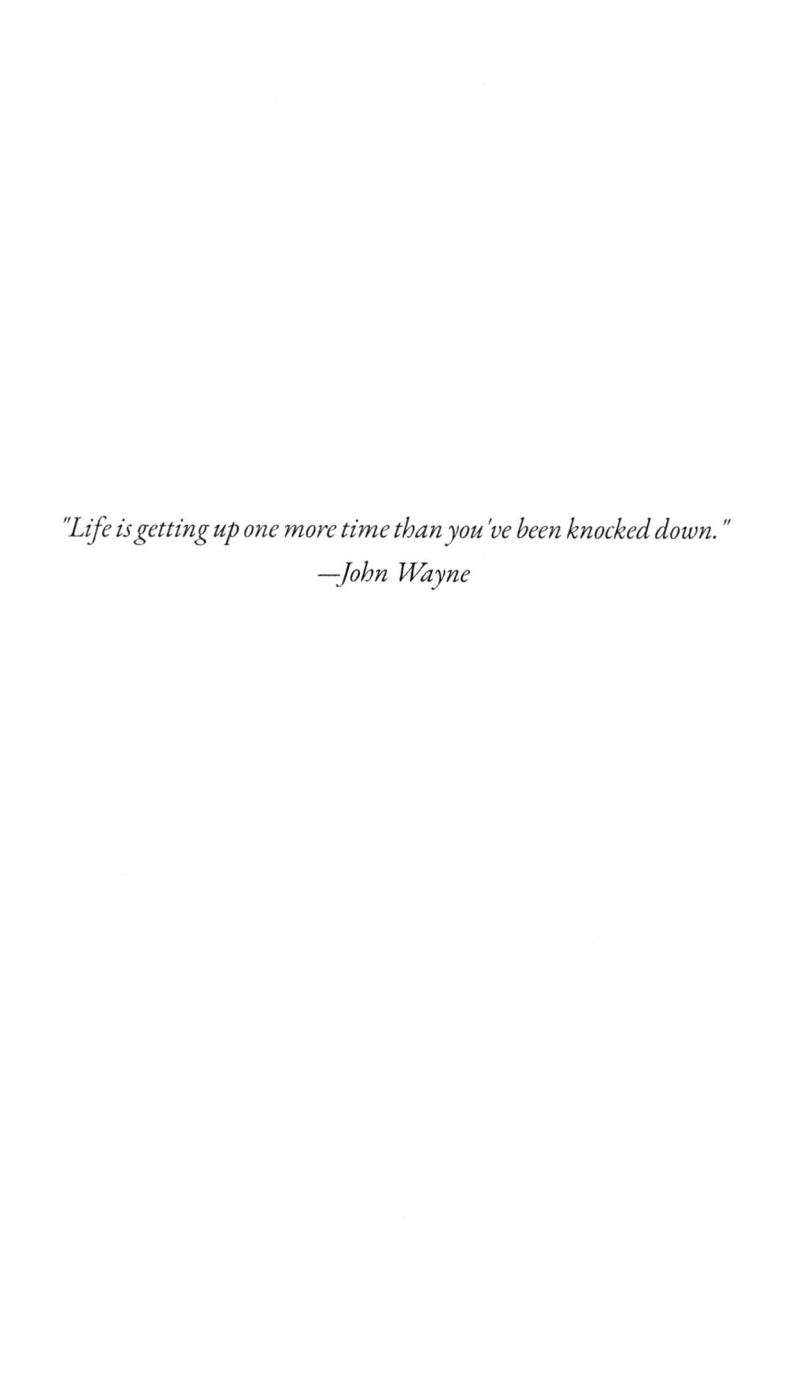

"Life is getting up one more time than you've been knocked down."
—*John Wayne*

1

BRANDY

I told my friends going on a date with a stranger was insane. Not that I was worried about being killed or kidnapped—I'd end them in a heartbeat if they tried anything—but it was more so the idea of meeting someone for the first time at an arranged time and place. That, and the fact that I had no interest in faking it through the evening with forced smiles and half-assed laughs.

Never in my life had I ever had the desire to be set up on a blind date. Honestly, I should have flaked. The guy didn't know me, so he couldn't judge me if I did. Besides, I couldn't give a fuck less even if he did. No fucking way was I going to put myself out there for some random Joe Blow.

And yet.

Here I fucking sat.

The mystery man was already late, by the way. Which, given my reputation, I should have been late as well. Never wait on a man. Make them wait on you.

But again, here I fucking sat.

My hand was fisted around the butter knife that had been gleaming on the table when I arrived. The base of the handle tapped against the surface as my impatience grew, grating on every nerve. The act itself was most likely why the waitress hadn't come to ask for my drink order yet—which, *rude*.

I had no idea why I agreed to this in the first place. All of my best friends were deranged. Maybe not literally, but at this moment, I was starting to believe it. Oakley and Lettie were all high on Sage being pregnant, so of course they wanted me to go on a date with someone. Well, sorry to inform them—not everyone needs to be in a relationship, especially not after how my last one went months ago. Although, that didn't get past the first date, so it didn't really count.

I was beyond fine on my own.

My back was to the door, and I didn't bother turning around to possibly catch a glimpse of the mystery man, if I'd even know it was him, walking through the door. For all I knew, he stood me up and I sat here looking like an idiot.

A hand grabbed the back of the chair across from me, pulling it out so he could slide in.

He, as in Reed *motherfucking* Bronson.

My best friend's older brother who I hated with every fiber of my being.

Still clutching the knife, I glared at him in his typical black cowboy hat and light blue button-up shirt. The fabric even had little diamonds stitched into it. *How fucking fancy.* "Leave me the fuck alone."

Reed leaned back in the chair he'd planted his annoyingly plump ass in, eyeing me. "Whatchya doing here alone?"

"None of your fucking business."

"I see your date arrived," the waitress, who finally decided to show up, said to me. Her glowing smile pissed me off all the more. And the way her cleavage was even more on display than when I'd first seen her, likely showing off the twins for the man unfortunate enough to be sitting across from me. Butter knives may be dull, but they can cause the right amount of damage if you use them properly.

"Not my date," Reed and I replied in unison.

He cocked a brow at me. "You're here for a date, too?"

I rolled my eyes. He was toying with me.

Ignoring his question, I asked the waitress, "Can I get a shot of tequila and the bill, please?" She nodded, but before she could turn to Reed, I added, "Make it a double."

"And for you, sir?" she asked.

"He's not dining here tonight," I answered for him.

"She'll take a single, and nothing for me. Thank you," he said.

"Double," I retorted.

He narrowed his eyes at me, his tattooed arms coming to rest on the table as he leaned forward. I nearly scoffed at the way his sleeves were neatly rolled to his elbows. "Single. How are you going to drive yourself home after a double?"

I pasted on the fakest polite smile as I looked up at the waitress. "Please excuse Satan over here. He's always a bit disoriented when he comes into town." I raised my hand to my mouth, poorly blocking my whisper from Reed. "He's pretty inexperienced."

Reed frowned as he clearly heard my words.

Good. That was my intention.

The waitress darted her eyes between the two of us, but finally got the right idea to walk away, heading straight for the bar. At least she was smart—I'd need that shot and then to get the fuck out of here.

Reed was silent a moment, glancing at my hand still wrapped around the butter knife. "Lettie send you here?"

I did a double take, the realization hitting me. "If this is you trying to interrupt my blind date, you can leave."

He reached forward, gently plucking the knife from my fist, then set it the farthest he could away from me. "*I'm* your blind date."

It was a good thing he'd taken the butter knife. There was no telling what I'd do now.

I found the waitress on her way back with the shot, but I didn't bother waiting for her to reach the table. Standing up, I fished a ten out of the pocket in my jeans as I met her halfway. That's right—jeans. I hadn't dressed up for this, and now I was extremely grateful for that. I grabbed the shot from her, setting the bill in her hand as I downed it, then placed the empty glass on top. "Thanks so much."

Then I beelined for the door.

"Brandy," Reed gruffly called out from somewhere behind me.

I ignored him.

No fucking way was I staying here a moment longer.

I had a bone to pick with my best friend.

As soon as I was out the doors and the cool night air chilled my flaming skin, I shot Lettie a text in the group chat.

> Real fucking funny guys.

Lettie
What's funny?

Oakley
laughing face

Sage
Oh she's mad, she used a period

Lettie
Omg, he showed up

> Fucking Reed?! Seriously? Do you guys hate me?

Sage
We love you

Sage
But do you mean fucking Reed as in you slept with him or like you're mad mad

Oakley
Did anyone record you stabbing him?

> He didn't let me get that far. And fuck no I didn't sleep with him

Lettie
Are you dating my brother now?!

> Not unless he was the last man on this planet. And even then, I'd rather die alone

Sage
Can you pleeease tell us why

Oakley
I will beg on my knees if I need to

Lettie
We just have to get a shot or two in her and she'll spill

I set my phone on Do Not Disturb, shoved it in my jeans, and pulled my key out of my pocket, inserting it into the handle on my '69 Bronco. I was gentle—the car didn't deserve my rage.

The night Reed practically ruined my life was for no one to know but the two of us and those who were involved. Because of course, there were witnesses. Nothing in my life ever went under the radar, aside from what shouldn't.

My foot eased on the clutch as I put the car into reverse, pulled out of my parking spot, then shifted into first. I was not about to stick around to wait for Reed to come out of that restaurant to tell me off. The man was good at nitpicking everything I did.

Sure, I probably shouldn't have downed a double shot of tequila and then gotten in my car, but to be fair, I'd eaten before my date because I didn't want to spend the whole night here with whoever showed up. Because of my pre-date meal that consisted of cold pizza, the alcohol wouldn't hit as hard, and I wasn't starving and angry.

I was just plain angry. With a full fucking stomach.

After ten minutes on the road, a white stream of smoke billowed out from under the orange hood, pulling my attention away from the street.

Just my fucking luck.

Of all the times my friends kept telling me to get a reliable daily driver and to stop driving this antique everywhere, this was the one instance I was kicking myself for not listening to them. Was it the smartest idea to drive a fifty-plus-year-old vehicle every day? No. But I loved this car like it was my baby. There was no way I would replace it.

Thankfully *something* went in my favor and I was able to pull the Bronco to the side of the road before it completely crapped out on me. I shifted into first and pulled the e-brake, then killed the engine. After getting out, I lifted the hood to check to see if whatever was causing the issue might be a quick fix. Given the gaping hole in my radiator that stared up at me, this would take more than just putting two pieces back together.

"Out of all the nights, tonight was the night you chose to overheat?" I asked it, pure annoyance ringing clear in my tone. I was talking to my fucking *car*. "It's not even hot tonight!"

Heaving a sigh, I shut the hood, then pulled my phone out to shoot Lettie a text.

> Can you come pick me up? Bronco took a shit

> **Lettie**
> Reed can't give you a ride? ;)

I glared at the screen as if she could see it, then pulled up Callan's contact. Lettie's older brother was like a brother to me—they all were, aside from one particular asshole—and he always helped when I needed it most.

> Any chance you're able to come pick me up from the side of the road?

I waited for a response, leaning a hip against the front of the car. My phone dinged, but before I could check the text, headlights blinded me from the road as the vehicle pulled off behind my Bronco.

Their headlights stayed on, but as my eyes adjusted, I could make out the vehicle.

I couldn't miss it if I tried.

It was the last fucking truck I wanted to see right now.

Tonight clearly wasn't going to get any fucking better.

2

Reed

I should've known Callan and Bailey would set me up like this. My brother and my best friend were happy with their girls, so naturally they had to butt into my love life. Or attempt to create one, at least. I didn't date.

I had no time for the petty drama on top of everything else going on in my life. Between balancing horseshoeing, my mother's horse rescue, and my parents' ranch, I barely had time for a damn beer at the end of the night.

I'd started learning how to horseshoe long before I probably should have been around those types of tools. I was always intrigued by the farriers that came to the ranch and learned as I went, following in their footsteps. Then, when I graduated high school, I jumped right into it. It didn't take me long to build a clientele, and now it only seemed to grow every month. But for me, that's where my enthusiasm ended. I'd happily go shoe horses all day, break my damn back doing it, just to shut out the world.

You couldn't live a peaceful life if you filled it with nonsense.

It shouldn't have taken me by surprise to see Brandy sitting at an empty table in that restaurant. From the get-go, I knew Cal and Bailey were up to something the moment they brought up the idea. My family was always meddling, but this was the one thing that was off-limits.

Brandy fucking Rose.

I'd left the restaurant shortly after Brandy. God forbid that woman see me following her. She'd blow a damn gasket, telling me off for the hell of it.

Though she'd blame me for that, given I'd supposedly ruined her life.

As I drove, my truck's headlights lit up a familiar orange Bronco, but rather than it being on the road, it sat in the dirt with a certain woman standing beside it.

Speak of the damn devil.

I pulled in behind Brandy's car, not bothering to turn my truck off. I got out to face her standing there, her glaringly demonic attitude aimed right the fuck at me—just like it always was.

"Get in the truck."

Her lips pursed together. "Not a chance."

Given the angle in which we were positioned, I assumed she could barely make me out with the headlights aimed at her, but me? I could see her clear as day, like a goddamn angel standing in front of a midnight field. The stars blared bright in the sky behind her, sparkling just as bright as her damn gold hoop earrings.

"Get in the damn truck."

She uncrossed one of her arms for the briefest moment to hold her phone up. "Callan's coming to get me."

"Is that right?"

She nodded as she returned her arms to their defensive position across her chest.

Good. She didn't need to let her guard down for me, or anyone, for that matter.

"Mhmm," she hummed, her sass still evident in her tone.

"That's funny," I started, mimicking her position by crossing my arms as well, "because he's with Sage in the next town over shopping for baby clothes."

She held her position. If Brandy was anything, it was determined. "Well, they got done early."

I knew damn well they didn't. They were both head over heels for this baby. They'd be shopping until the store closed, and even then, the employees would have to kick them out.

"I'm only going to say it one more time. Get in the damn truck, Brandy."

She turned, planting her ass against the driver door of her car. "I'll wait."

This fucking woman.

"Suit yourself."

I wouldn't stand here all fucking night begging for her to listen for once in her goddamn life. I got back in my truck and pulled onto the street. But because it was Brandy fucking Rose standing on the side of the road in nothing more than a white tank top and those damn flared jeans that hugged her ass just right, I didn't gas it.

Instead, I cruised up next to her and rolled the window down.

"One last offer, or you're standing here all night."

She wouldn't look at me. Just stood there gazing down the road like I wasn't even there. *Oh, how I wished that was true.*

"Jesus Christ, Brandy. If you don't get in the fucking truck—"

She dropped her arms, took two steps, and yanked my passenger door open. She slid onto the black leather seat, slamming the door closed.

I thought maybe she'd cooperate and buckle her damn seatbelt, but no. I waited, and waited, and waited.

I had enough of fucking waiting.

I reached across her, ignoring the hitch in her breath and how her long, brunette hair brushed my arm, grabbed the strap, and pulled it across her. There was no avoiding my fingers brushing her hip, and no overlooking how she didn't scoot away.

She was like a goddamn rock in my boot, both impossible to ignore and irritably annoying at the same time.

Once she was buckled, I straightened and eased my foot on the gas, reaching the speed limit quickly.

"What's wrong with the Bronco?" I asked, not surprised it had yet another problem.

"Not talking to you," she said, her gaze trained out the window.

I pressed my lips together, giving a tight nod. "Great."

The fields on either side of the road were pitch black as I drove, my headlights illuminating only a small strip in front of us.

"I can bring you back tomorrow if you think it's drivable—"

"No, thanks," she interrupted.

My hand gripped the steering wheel harder than it was before. I'd trade places with anyone on this damn planet tonight. *Anyone.*

Brandy reached forward, twisting the knob on the radio to turn up the volume on some pop country station. I fucking hated this new music they claimed was country.

I suffered the rest of the drive until I pulled into Brandy's dirt driveway that led up to her small house. Not many people knew where their little sister's best friend's house was, but I did. I knew too damn much about Brandy. More than anyone else, I reckoned.

But that's what made me and Brandy so toxic. I knew shit she didn't want anyone knowing, and she hated me for it. Granted, I was the reason for some of it, too.

Before I even stopped the truck, Brandy was unbuckling and opening the door to get out. I stomped a foot on the brake right as she swung a leg out.

"Fucking hell," I muttered as she slammed the door behind her.

I threw it into park and pulled a few bills out of my wallet before getting out and following after her.

I caught up quickly, grabbing her arm and twisting her around. She yanked it away, but I'd already let go. "Don't pretend to be the gentleman you aren't and walk me to the door," she spat.

I grabbed her hand, forcing it palm up, and put the cash in the center.

"What's this for?" she asked, doing her best to keep the anger in her tone, yet the confusion seeped in. Brandy never let her guard down, let alone around me. She always kept it fortified in place, each brick caked with so much mortar, not even a jackhammer could penetrate it.

"I was your date, wasn't I? Wouldn't be very fucking *gentlemanly* of me if I didn't pay for your drink."

"Wouldn't be much different from your usual behavior."

I snorted right as she let the bills fall to the ground. Then, she turned on her heel, stomping to her front door. I shook my head as she disappeared inside and turned the porch light off. Instead of leaving, I picked up the money and walked to her door, tucking it under the corner of her doormat. It was fitting that the cursive scrawled across the jute material spelled the words *go away*.

There was no need to knock. She'd find the money tomorrow and hate me all the more for simply leaving it—only for the fact that it gave some evidence that tonight happened and she was my supposed date.

Speaking of, I had a conversation I needed to have with Bailey and Callan.

They weren't getting away with this scot-free.

I walked back to my truck without a single glance over my shoulder. She was home, that's what mattered.

Away from anyone or anything that could harm her.

Just like I made sure of the night I ruined the sliver of friendship we used to have.

3

BRANDY

"You think you can get a tow truck to pick it up this morning?"

I heard shuffling through the phone before Wyatt, Bell Buckle's local mechanic, said, "He can probably squeeze you in around noon."

"And he can bring it to my house, right?"

Wyatt was quiet a moment, the only noise through the line a faint static. "You want me to work on it at your house?"

"I think it's just the radiator, which can easily be fixed here. I'm going to try to do it myself, but I may need you to come by if it's giving me a hard time." Truthfully, I just wanted my car at my house. I didn't like being here without a method of transportation, regardless of it being driveable or not. Feeling stuck was not my idea of a fun time.

"Alright. I'm not free until tomorrow, so if you can check it out today and let me know what I might need to bring, that'd be great." He mumbled something under his breath about the tools being in his shop, but he meant no ill will by it. Wyatt owned North State Auto and never hesitated to drop everything for anyone.

I'd called him about the tow truck because I didn't trust some random guy messing with my Bronco. They had to take care of it the way I did—like it was their most precious belonging.

I treated it better than a lot of people treated their vehicles because it did the same for me. Through all I had to endure with my father, working on that old car was my safe space when I needed to get out of the house but couldn't go to the Bronsons' ranch or see Lettie. Training horses was my true passion, which was why I did it full-time for the Bronsons' horse rescue and ranch, but working on that car was a different sort of therapy. Something about dealing with the intricate parts of a vehicle made you drown out the noise of the world and focus on that one task in front of you. I wasn't a mechanic by any means—I only knew how to work on certain parts.

"Tomorrow will work. I'll keep you posted. Thank you."

"Yep. Just give them a call in the next hour or so, pay the fee, and they'll pick it up." He read off the number for the tow company before we hung up.

I called right away to get it taken care of, thankful it was only a couple hundred bucks.

I had no way of going to the ranch to work some horses, and I didn't want to inconvenience Lettie or call my mother, so I decided to grab my pruning shears from the workbench in my one-car garage to clean up the rose bushes out front.

Years ago, I planted six of them—my lucky number—and ever since, they've somehow stayed alive. My last name was Rose by nature, but my mom named me Brandy because of the brandy rose. It was her favorite flower, so naturally, it was mine as well, if I even had a choice in the matter—I was named after the plant. But she always told me she knew that I'd grow up to be beautiful and strong, but keep that bite to me, like the thorns sprouting from the stems. Beauty couldn't come without a little pain.

I reckoned that's why I grew up in the household I did.

The roses were a perfect light shade of peach, popping against the dark green leaves of the bush. I wasn't a gardener by any means. If I was being honest, I killed every house plant I tried to own. But these rose bushes grew strong every year, getting so out of control that I'd spend hours trimming the unruly branches.

I'd picked up a lot of hobbies growing up as an excuse to get out of the house. Being locked inside with an alcoholic father who liked to hit things when he was drunk—or sober—wasn't my idea of a great time.

People say to fall in love with the little things in life, not to dwell on the bad. So that's what I did. I fell in love with the roses, my Bronco, and training horses.

I lost track of time as I pruned the bushes, snipping away the sprouting leaves to reshape the plant. I wasn't sure if it was hours or minutes that passed when the sound of the tow truck coming up my driveway pulled my attention away from my task. I moved to get up, but in my hurry, my hand caught on one of the thorns, the sharp point tearing my skin from the fatty part of my hand to about halfway up my thumb. I cursed as blood trickled from the spot and headed for the garage to grab a few paper towels. It wasn't deep, as far as I could tell, but it was a bleeder.

"How's it goin'?" I asked the tow truck driver as he hopped out of the cab.

"Another day, another dollar," he replied blandly, moving to unhook the Bronco while barely sparing me a glance.

I held pressure on the cut, and by the time he'd unhooked and lowered my car, the bleeding had stopped.

He gave me some papers to sign, I tipped him the money Reed had left on my doorstep, and then he was off, leaving me staring at my problematic beauty of a vehicle.

I opened the passenger door to grab the bubble gum I always left in the glove compartment and popped a few pieces in my mouth. If the videos I watched last night were right, this may temporarily fix the problem.

After snagging the spare water bottle off the seat, I walked around the vehicle and pulled the hood up. Pouring the water into the radiator to check for any other holes, I watched as the liquid instantly starting leaking out of gaping one. Once the water leaked out enough, I grabbed the chewed bubblegum from my mouth and smoothed it over the hole. With the bottle now empty, I grabbed coolant from the garage and poured it in. None of it got past the gum, so I set the jug in the dirt and came around the side, getting in the driver's seat to start the car. As soon as it rumbled to life, I slid out to inspect the radiator.

I shouldn't have been the least bit surprised when I found the coolant leaking out immediately. I guess the gum wasn't strong enough.

"Fucking hell. Those stupid hack videos never work."

I turned the car off and yanked my phone out of my jeans to dial Lettie.

"Are you calling to give me shit about Reed? Because I wasn't the only one behind the idea," she said as soon as she answered.

I ran a hand through my hair, letting the pieces fan out around my face as they fell. "I need a ride to the ranch. And do *not* offer up Reed."

"Okay, okay. I can be there in ten?"

That was enough time for me to put everything back in the garage. "That's fine. No rush."

"See you soon."

I hung up, pocketing my phone, then grabbed the coolant and shears to put them away. I grabbed one of the plastic buckets from the side of the garage to fill with the clippings from the rose bushes. I'd only gotten through four of them, but I could tackle the other two another day.

After the branches were piled in the bucket, I set it beside the garage to deal with later, closed the door, and headed inside my house to call Wyatt.

"Yello," he answered.

"It needs a new radiator," I told him. "I tried the bubblegum trick and it didn't work."

He let out a small chuckle through the line.

"What?"

"Bubblegum never works, Brandy."

I rolled my eyes, heading down the hall to my bedroom after throwing away the blood-smeared paper towel. "Well, I tried."

"Appreciate the effort. I'll bring one over tomorrow afternoon. I should be done at the shop around two."

"I'll be here," I said dully.

"Wouldn't think you'd be anywhere else. See ya." Then the line went dead.

Tossing the phone on my bed, I changed out of my tank top, opting for a gray hole-filled Coors Banquet t-shirt. Outside, a horn beeped twice, indicating Lettie was already here. I didn't live very far from the Bronsons, the perfect distance between their house and my mother's. This house was perfect for that very reason, giving me the solitude I wanted with hardly any neighbors, and a few minutes drive to see the people I loved.

I pocketed my phone, then headed outside, locking the front door behind me. I got in Lettie's car and buckled myself. The action made me freeze, remembering when Reed had reached across me to grab the seat belt in his truck. I'd wanted to slap him in that moment. Reed and I, we weren't push and pull. It was constantly push. He'd decided that night all those years ago to act like he owned me, and I'd never forgive him for it. But for some fucking reason, last night, I was a little less mad at him and more so irate at the situation my friends had put me in.

They knew we didn't get along, though they didn't know the reasons. But regardless of what those may be, they shouldn't have meddled in that aspect of my life. I'd date other guys all day, any fucking day of the year, if they wanted me to date so badly, but not him.

Reed and I would send a building up in flames if we had to spend more than a few hours together, and that fact would never fucking change.

I crossed my arms, bits of my tan skin peeking out from the holes of my shirt. I should've opted for a neutral colored bra, but instead, I'd left my neon pink one on. No one on that ranch was looking anyway.

"You're scaring me," Lettie said, hesitating in my driveway.

"Good," I clipped. I felt betrayed.

"Brandy, if anything, it was a joke," she started.

I whirled on her. "A *joke*? You don't play around like that, Lettie. You know how I feel about him."

Her face turned sympathetic, her foot plastered to the brake pedal. "I don't understand why."

"You don't need to!" My voice was rising, and I needed to get it under control. I wouldn't yell, especially not at my best friend.

I wasn't a yeller. I grew up with it, and I wouldn't turn into the same person as my parents. "What happened is in the past."

She was quiet for a moment, then asked softly, "Then why can't you leave it in the past?"

I looked out the window at my Bronco, my mind somewhere else. Seven years was a long time, but I remembered it like it happened days ago. "I just can't."

The blood. The crunching sounds. The shouts. It all rang through my ears. But what I remembered most vividly was the leather of his passenger seat under my bare legs.

Though Lettie and I grew up together and told each other everything, this was one thing that I kept to myself.

She finally eased off the brake, heading down my driveway to the main road.

"How's everything going with the wedding?" I asked. She and her fiancé, Bailey Cooper, were having their wedding in just a couple weeks, and I was beyond excited for it.

"Absolutely hectic," she replied. We were both back to our normal selves now. That's what I loved most about us—we never fought. And if on rare occasion we did, we made up within minutes. "Everything is being pushed so close to the date, I'm nervous it all won't be ready in time."

"It will," I assured her. She deserved her perfect day. "If you need help with anything, just call, okay? I'll drop everything for you. You know I will."

While I'd helped plan some pieces of her wedding, she and Bailey had really taken the reins on it, the two of them somehow growing closer in the process, despite having grown up together.

She aimed a smile at me before bringing her eyes back to the road. "I know. I love you all the more for it."

Being an only child from a broken household, the Bronsons had come to feel like a second family to me. Lettie and I had been best friends since kindergarten, rarely apart for more than a day until she went to college. If anyone asked, we were practically sisters.

They made the pieces of my life that had fallen apart feel a little less broken.

And a little more loved.

4

REED

Seven Years Ago

The drive from my house to the barn was always bumpy, my tires rolling over dried hoof imprints and holes in the makeshift trail. I lived on the far side of my parents' property and made this trip daily. It was a routine ingrained in my bones, so much so that I knew where every dip was, which to avoid and which weren't as bad.

The truck jostled back and forth over every divot in the path, dirt kicking up in the wind and blowing inside my old pickup. It was on its last leg, but it was free, so I used it as the work truck on the ranch.

I'd already fed the cows, so next on my agenda was to trim the rescue horses' hooves, something I did about every six weeks. Sometimes we had so many of them that it'd take a couple days to get through the bunch, but right now, we were a little low on rescues with six of them having just gotten adopted out last week.

To get to the barn, I had to use the trail that cut across one of the pastures. The drive was easily the most beautiful, peaceful commute to work anyone could ask for. The meadows of Idaho stretched on forever, butting up to hills and mountains, all of which surrounded Bottom of the Buckle Ranch.

It was why I'd built my house on the other end of their property. Without having to pay for the land, I'd easily been approved for a construction loan and designed the whole place myself. It was secluded, but close enough that if my parents or siblings needed anything from me, I was only a few minutes away.

I got out to open the gate before driving through, making sure to close it behind my truck so no cows escaped. On the rare occasion Bailey forgot to close it, my dad would give him hell. He did it with love, though. We all knew my father, somewhere deep down inside him, was never truly mad at any of us. He was a tough love kind of guy.

Bringing my truck to a stop outside the barn, I opened my door to find my sister beelining it for me.

"Don't bother getting out of your truck," Lettie called.

"What is it today?" I mumbled under my breath, quiet enough to where she couldn't hear it over my exhaust.

"You better not have just said something mean about me," she said, coming within a foot of me before she stopped.

"I'd never."

She rolled her eyes. The concept was true, but she knew her brothers would never stop giving her shit. It was practically our job. She was our only sister.

"I need you to pick up Brandy," she said.

"Can't someone else? I've got work to do." I didn't hate Brandy by any means—she just wasn't the greatest influence for Lettie. She was always talking her into doing stupid shit, and if I had half a mind, I'd think she did it to intentionally piss me off. Brandy was that kind of girl; she'd find out you didn't like something and do it ten times over again just to spite you.

Lettie held a hand up to block the sun from her eyes. "Everyone else is busy."

"Doesn't she have a car?" I knew the one she drove like it was my own. A faded white and orange '69 Bronco with cream rims and a cracked windshield.

"It's not running right now."

"And that's my problem because...?"

"Because she needs to come over."

I shrugged. "Horses can wait for her to work them." Brandy had been coming by the ranch for years to help our mother with the rescue horses, whether it be desensitizing, training, or medicating them. It also came in handy that she knew how to do various ranch chores as well. I had to admit—seeing her fix a fence was pretty cute, if that was even possible. I wasn't a blind man. Brandy Rose was an attractive woman. But that didn't cover up the fact that she was as dangerous as she was pretty.

"Please, Reed. Just this once," Lettie begged.

I heaved a sigh, staring out my windshield with my hand draped over the steering wheel. "Fine. Is she ready now?"

"Yes! Thank you! I'll text her to let her know you're on your way." She leaned into the cab, giving me a quick hug before she pulled her phone out of her back pocket to text Brandy.

"Mhmm," I mumbled, closing the door once Lettie stepped away.

It wasn't too far of a drive to Brandy's mother's house, taking me about twenty minutes until I was pulling up to the curb. I didn't have her number, and honking felt rude, so I waited in the truck. I assumed Lettie had given her an ETA, but after about fifteen minutes of sitting there, I was beginning to think she wasn't going to come out.

After hearing the windchime rustle in the wind for the millionth time, I checked my phone to see that ten more minutes had passed. If I had to hear that twinkling sound again, I'd likely lose my mind, so I tossed my cell on the seat beside me and opened the driver's side door.

My boots hit the asphalt and I closed the door behind me before rounding the front of the truck, heading up the path to her front door. Halfway there, the door swung open, stopping me in my tracks. Brandy appeared as she squeezed through the few-inch gap she gave herself, then quickly closed it behind her. Her eyes were on the doormat, her hand gripped tight on the strap of her bag. She stepped down off the concrete porch, then looked up to find me standing there. She covered up her brief look of surprise easily.

"Impatient, much?" she snapped, brushing past me as she headed for my truck.

Even with those two words, I knew something was off.

Her shoulders were slightly slumped, her usual snarky tone dim. This wasn't the sassy Brandy I knew.

She was already in the passenger seat by the time I turned and headed back for the driver's side.

"Lettie said you were ready to go." I shifted into drive and headed out of the neighborhood.

"I was," she replied.

"She told you I was on the way," I stated.

"Yeah, and?"

"So why'd it take you so long to come out?" Really, I didn't care about having to wait. I wanted to know why she emerged from that house looking like a butterfly caught in a glass jar with no way out.

"I was busy."

I scoffed, shaking my head. "Busy with what?"

I was pushing her buttons, igniting that flame deep inside her. Brandy wasn't herself without that heat.

She whirled on me. "Is it really that important?"

I didn't even have to glance her way to feel her bright hazel eyes on me.

"No need to get defensive," I said, keeping my gaze on the road.

She stared at me a minute, presumably glaring, then turned her focus back out the windshield. She crossed her arms over her chest, leaning back against the seat.

The cab was quiet for a few minutes before she quietly said, "My dad hit my mom."

My boot slammed on the brake, the tires screeching across the pavement as the truck slid to a stop. No one was behind us on the desolate road, but my eyes stayed trained on the side mirror. Every cell in my body raged at what she said, yet I was frozen. I couldn't move a finger if I tried.

She didn't say a word. Just sat there staring out the windshield.

My teeth ground together, my jaw threatening to crack.

"Can you at least get out of the middle of the road?" she asked, still attempting—and failing—to keep that sass in her tone.

I pried my foot off the brake, easing the truck to the dirt pull-off. I didn't put it in park. I *couldn't*. My left hand was glued to the steering wheel, possibly crushing it to bits under my grip, and my other hand was fisted on my thigh so tightly I was surprised a finger didn't crack. I was one second away from turning back and making her father regret he put a hand on her mom.

"Reed, you're scaring me."

Another grind of my teeth. A tick in my jaw. An urge to turn around and beat the living shit out of her dad.

It all ran through me at once.

And I thought she was just taking her time getting ready, doing it to piss me off. Behind that front door, hell had broken loose. How long before I arrived did it happen? Was I sitting there when his knuckles connected with her skin? Or was it his palm?

"I thought your dad left years ago," I managed to get out.

"He did." There was no rise in her tone, no quick breaths from her lungs. She was calm. "But he comes back now and again."

"How often?" I gritted out. My voice was low. So lethally low. And yet, she didn't flinch.

"Every few months," she answered.

"No. How often does he hit her?"

"Oh," she said, a bit deflated, like she didn't want me to ask that. "I don't know."

"You don't know," I repeated. I turned to her then, prying my hand from the steering wheel.

Her eyelids fluttered, but she didn't cry. No, Brandy was too stubborn for tears. "When he comes home."

I stared at her. Just fucking stared as the question I wanted to ask, needed to ask, sat on my tongue like an anchor. If I got the answer I dreaded, there'd be no pulling me out of the sea of rage.

"Does he hit you?"

She looked at me then, and I saw all the hurt. Brandy was laid vulnerable in a way she never wanted to be. "No."

"Are you lying?"

Her mouth formed a thin line. "No."

"If I find out you're fucking lying, Brandy—"

"You'll what, Reed? Go in there and save the fucking day?"

A burst of air flew through my nose as I looked back out the windshield. I ran a hand along my jaw, wishing I could alleviate the ache that had formed with how tense it was.

"Let me guess. Brandy Rose doesn't want saving."

I looked back to her, her eyes darting around my face.

"You need to stay out of it."

"Does Lettie know?"

"No."

"Why not?"

"Because not everyone needs to know what goes on behind closed doors."

I shook my head, not bothering to turn on my blinker as I pulled back onto the road.

Brandy didn't want those secrets coming out, and I understood that. Tough, little Brandy didn't want to be saved, but I was determined to open every single one of those doors she hid behind.

She could ensconce herself behind a damn brick wall if she wanted, but it wouldn't be from me.

5

REED

The hammer clanged against the nail as I fitted the horseshoe on Nova's hoof. Nova was Bailey's horse that he kept here at the ranch. A beautiful black gelding, but his looks were deceiving. He truthfully was a pain in the ass.

He yanked his leg back after I got the last nail in, shifting to the side with his ears pinned.

"Yeah, be pissed all you want. It's done," I mumbled to him as I tossed the hammer in the bag on the tailgate of my truck. I had a separate trailer I used when I traveled to other ranches for shoeing, but I didn't bother moving it around ours. My mom made sure I had a full stock of supplies if I was working on the horses here, whether they were rescues or personal horses. I always told her she didn't need to do that, but she insisted.

"He being an asshole again?" Bailey asked as he came into view.

I grabbed the shoes I'd taken off and tossed them in a bucket. "I was starting to get the feeling you were hiding from me, Cooper."

He picked at the finger of one of his gloves he was holding as he leaned a shoulder against the side of the barn. "Why's that?"

I sucked on my teeth, staring at him. "Bein' an airhead doesn't look good on you."

He shrugged. "It got me your sister."

My stare turned into a glare as he smiled. *Cocky Cooper.*

"As you've reminded me time and time again," I muttered, shoving the bag further into the bed so I could close the tailgate. After it was shut, I set the bucket beside the bag, then faced Bailey with my arms crossed.

"How'd your date go?" he asked.

My teeth ground together before I asked, "How did you think it was going to go, setting me up with her?"

"Well, you're not dead in a ditch somewhere, so I'd say it went pretty well."

"You and Callan are on my shit list."

"Is that any different than before, or..."

My glare deepened as the sound of tires on dirt came rolling up the driveway to the right of us. I didn't have to look to know it was Lettie with Brandy in her car. I'd known where she was going when she passed me on her way out and said, "If I'm not back in forty minutes, call a search party."

Lettie might be scared of Brandy's wrath, but I wasn't. She was a force to be reckoned with, that much was certain, but I wasn't afraid of her by any means. I was probably the only person on this planet that wouldn't back down from a fight with her. That was our problem—we could battle it out all damn night if it got that far, but she always walked away before it escalated into something worse. I had the slightest idea of why.

"Where's the Bronco?" Bailey asked as they got out of the car.

"Getting a pedicure," Brandy said.

His brows pulled together. "Is that code for new tires or something?"

Lettie sidled up beside Bailey, smiling up at him as he wrapped a hand around her waist, still holding his gloves. "No, honey. She was joking."

I leaned back against the tailgate of my truck, my arms still crossed, as I watched Brandy approach. My eyes didn't fail to catch the glimpses of bright pink lace shining through the holes in her t-shirt, right where her breasts were. My jaw pulsed with the thought that any guy could see her fucking bra if they looked.

"Got a hole in the radiator. Wyatt is coming by tomorrow to fix it," she said as she continued past us.

The thought of Wyatt being there, possibly seeing her in this shirt, made me blurt out, "I can fix it."

"No, thanks," Brandy called over her shoulder, not bothering to look back.

Bailey and Lettie looked back and forth between the two of us, then braced themselves when I shoved off the truck and followed after Brandy. A mumbled, "Uh oh," came from my sister.

"Wyatt's not fixing it," I grumbled, quickly catching up to her.

She still didn't spare me a glance as she headed into the med room. "Yes, he is."

I filled the doorway, watching as she opened a lower cabinet. "And he'll charge you for it. I won't."

She closed the cupboard door a little too hard, whirling on me.

There are those blazing eyes.

"And *you* will only make it worse."

"I know how to work on a car." I didn't know everything, but I knew the basics, and if Wyatt had already ordered the part, I could pick it up and install it myself.

She snorted, grabbing the clipboard on the wall. My eyes caught on her hand where a long cut had begun to scab over from midway up her thumb to the base of her hand. She approached me to walk out of the room, but before she could slip past me, I grabbed the doorframe, blocking her in.

"What happened to your hand?"

Her nostrils flared slightly as she slowly moved her gaze to mine, her eyes narrowed. "Wouldn't you like to know?"

"I would."

"That's too fucking bad. Last I checked, you didn't have the privilege of knowing jack shit about me. So if you'd get the fuck out of my way so I can get to work, that'd be lovely."

My fingers gripped the doorframe harder. I was half surprised the wood didn't break under my hand. "Last I checked, I'm the one who knows the most about you."

Hurt flashed across her face before she covered it up with the shield she donned the best—masking her emotions with anger. She raised a hand, shoving my arm away. I dropped it to my side as she shoulder-checked me on the way out. I stood there, not bothering to follow after her.

Not giving a shit where she went, I stormed back out of the barn, barely slowing as I said, "Nova's done for the day. He can go back to the pasture."

"Got it," Bailey replied where he still stood with Lettie. No doubt they were trying to eavesdrop.

Instead of sticking around, I headed up to my parents' house to let my mom know I was leaving for the day. Some days were busier than others, but all I had on my list were the personal horses here at the ranch. The rest of the chores could be taken care of by my family or the volunteers.

After entering the house and rounding the corner, I tapped a knuckle on the office door. "I'm heading out."

My mom set her reading glasses on the desk, closing her laptop. "Do you have a minute?"

"Sure." I walked farther into the room, taking a seat in the chair across from her.

"Have you talked to your brother since he's been back in town?" she asked.

"Which one?"

She frowned. "Only one of your brothers leaves Bell Buckle on the regular."

"I know, Mom. I'm just giving you a hard time. Yes, I've talked to him a couple times. Nothing serious, though. Why?"

Beckham was younger than me by three years. He'd been into rodeo for ages, him and his best friend getting into bronc riding as kids. They traveled a lot to different events, something about getting more points or some shit I didn't care to follow, and in between the weekends, he'd stay at friends' houses. He had essentially been a couch hopper for the last nine years, but as of a few weeks ago, he was back in town.

"He's moving into that house he bought, and I'd like it if you helped him. You *and* your brothers."

"Okay." I had no problem showing up for anyone in my family, so I wasn't sure why she was asking like I might say no. "Is everything okay?"

She sighed, leaning back in her chair. "You tell me after you go see him tomorrow."

That didn't sound very good. "Have you tried talking to him?"

"I have. He insists everything is fine, but I'm a mother, Reed. I know when things aren't fine."

I offered the barest smile, standing from the chair. "I'll let you know how it goes. Don't worry yourself sick, Mom. I'm sure everything is fine. He's probably just moody being away from the rodeo and his friends."

"I hope so. Your brothers should be there, too, and Bailey already said he would help."

I dipped my chin. "Sounds good."

I headed for the door, but paused before walking out, looking back at her. "I love you, Mom. We all do."

The corner of her mouth ticked up, but it didn't reach her eyes. "I know, sweetie. I love you, too."

Whatever this was, with Beckham and everything else, it would pass.

Though, I wondered if the same would ever be true for me and Brandy.

A big part of me was convinced the feud between us would never end, especially if Brandy had anything to say about it.

But for now, I'd shove all of that aside and focus on my family.

6

REED

The next day, after finishing my morning chores, I decided there was no way in hell Wyatt was going to go help Brandy with her car.

"Yello," Wyatt answered.

"Seems old habits don't, in fact, die hard," I said.

"I knew it was you calling, Reed. I had to do it to piss you off."

My brothers and I used to give him shit for the greeting back in high school, but with answering phones as a part of his job, the habit stuck.

"It's cute you think I believe you."

"What do you want, Bronson? I know your shiny ass truck ain't broke," he said.

I leaned a hip against my truck, my elbow resting on the side of the bed. "You're just mad I replaced the old beater with something new since you lost my business."

"Unfortunately, I didn't lose your friendship along with it," he mumbled.

My lips ticked up at the corners before the hint of a smile fell. "You know about Brandy's car, from what I've been told."

"Yep. Hole in the radiator. Why?"

"Is the new one in your shop?"

"Yep. Sitting right next to me. Why?"

"Do you ever not ask questions?"

"Do you ever answer them?" I sighed as he chuckled into the phone. "I'm just giving you shit, Bronson, but not nearly as much as Brandy will be giving you if you show up to her place with this radiator."

"I can handle her." I'd been handling her attitude my whole damn life. I had no choice.

"Mhmm. You let me know how well you handle it when she breaks your damn nose."

"She wouldn't punch me, Wyatt. Get over yourself."

"How are you so sure? Have you seen that woman bite?"

Because I knew. Brandy wouldn't raise a hand to the people she cared about. And that included me, even if she pretended not to by covering her true feelings with hate.

"Far too often. I can be there in twenty to pick it up on my way to Beck's."

"Beck's back in town?" he asked, surprise evident in his tone.

"Yep."

"For good?"

"Who's the one with the questions now?" I asked with a smirk.

"Actually, if you'd look at the time... I can get over to Brandy's in about ten minutes if I leave now."

"Wyatt," I warned.

He chuckled again. "Don't get your panties in a bunch. But seriously, though. Beckham's home?"

"He is," I replied. "Bought a house and everything."

"Sounds serious," Wyatt said, the sarcasm no longer in his voice.

"He may be willing to settle down, too, if you're open to it."

"Alright, dipshit. I'm hanging up now. Her radiator is by my desk if I'm busy when you get here."

"Thanks, Wyatt."

"Yeah, yeah."

I hung up the phone, pocketing it before getting in my truck and starting the engine. Heading out of the pasture, being sure to close the gate behind me, I pulled onto the main road.

On my way to Beckham's new house, I picked up the radiator. Wyatt was talking to an elderly lady about her tire alignment when I got there, clearly stuck in conversation with her as he sent me pleading eyes, so I'd given him a quick wave and was on my way. I was sure he'd give me shit for that later.

Beck had purchased a double-wide off the highway on a twenty-acre parcel. From the looks of it on the outside, it seemed pretty new. He'd never purchased a home before now, not seeing the reason for it.

Buying a house meant he was staying. Was he truly done with rodeo for good?

It didn't seem like the Beckham I knew, but a lot changes as you grow up. We'd been trying to get him to quit bronc riding for a while now. Maybe he'd finally come to his senses.

I was only thankful he wasn't hurt in order to realize he wanted to leave.

Bailey and my brothers, Callan and Lennon, were already here, their trucks lined up out front.

I parked and got out, approaching them where they stood next to Beckham's small moving van.

"There's honestly not much," Beck said, moving to open the rolling door of the van after I stopped next to the others. "It's all just stuff I've accumulated over the years that I liked or saw on sale."

Lennon had his arms crossed where he stood to the left of Callan, his dark blonde hair hidden under his ball cap. "That'll change as you get settled."

"No shit," Beck muttered before pulling the door up.

Bailey gave me a nod in greeting before I looked inside the van.

"There's three boxes and a table, Beck," Bailey said.

"There's more than that," Beckham defended.

"A couch and a mattress," Lennon added, eyeing the bare van.

Beckham frowned. "Okay, not a *ton* more, but it's enough to get started."

"That's okay. We all start somewhere." Callan landed a pat on Beckham's back. "We'll get it inside." He hefted himself up into the back of the van.

"You sure we can handle all this? We might need more guys," Bailey joked.

I pressed my lips together to keep from chuckling.

"Listen, Cooper, you want to be a dick—" Beck started.

Bailey clapped him on the shoulder before getting in behind Callan. "I'm only kidding. With me here, we've got it handled. I'd be worried if it was just those other guys."

Lennon shook his head despite the smile on his face.

I grabbed the box closest to the edge to bring it inside as Bailey and Callan got to work lifting the couch.

When I was halfway to the door, Lennon asked, "What the fuck is this, Beck?"

I turned, looking to where Lennon was deep in the van, holding up a longhorn skull with horns that stretched farther than my arm span.

"An antique," Beckham said, grabbing it from him and hopping down from the back.

Lennon raised his brows, looking down at him from where he'd moved to the edge of the van. "*That's* what you accumulated over the years?"

"No," he defended, but offered no further explanation.

He picked up another box from the back of the van, walking past me with a slight brush of the shoulder. Lennon raised his brows at me and I shrugged in response.

I didn't know what the fuck was up with Beckham, and I wasn't going to get in the middle of it. Our mother had every right to be worried about him. His closed-off behavior only solidified it.

With the light amount of Beckham's belongings, we got everything moved inside in less than thirty minutes. I left the door to his house open behind me, letting the cool, early fall air breeze through the house.

"Pretty full place," Bailey said, surveying the living room. "Might get crowded in here."

Callan surveyed the scribbled writing on the boxes. "Do you need plates or anything? Sage and I have an extra set since she and Avery moved into my place." Avery was Sage's daughter, who Callan loved like his own.

Beck waved him off, taking a sip of his whiskey he'd grabbed from the kitchen counter. I glanced at the clock on the oven from where I was standing with a shoulder against the wall, my arms crossed. One p.m. and he was drinking. I couldn't judge, though. If I had just gotten done moving into my first house, I'd want a beer or two to celebrate, too.

After he swallowed his first sip, Beck said, "All good, Cal. I'm covered. I actually have someone coming over in about"—he glanced at the clock on the oven—"twenty minutes, if you guys could skedaddle."

"Oh, so we're just your pack mules now," Bailey said.

Lennon grabbed his truck keys off the counter. "I have to go anyway. We'll have to all get together for a beer once you're settled, Beck."

Callan snorted. "Not much settling he has to do. It'll take him an hour tops."

"Real funny, Cal." Beckham set his glass next to the bottle of whiskey on the counter, heading toward us.

That was our cue.

We filed out the door, saying our goodbyes and heading to our trucks. Beck had barely stuck around long enough for us to close our driver's side doors, already heading back inside to presumably pour another glass of whiskey.

With a subtle shake of my head, I started my truck and was on my way. Brandy had no idea I was coming in place of Wyatt, and I planned to keep it that way.

I drove up her driveway, parking my truck next to the patch of lawn that led up to her porch. As I got out, I noticed only some of her rose bushes were pruned, some perfectly shaped, the others a mess of branches sticking up in every direction. Was that how she'd cut her hand, cleaning up her rose bushes without gloves?

"Please, enlighten me on why the fuck you're standing in my driveway right now," Brandy said, emerging from her house and immediately crossing her arms as she stopped at the edge of the porch.

My gaze moved from the roses to her. *Just as dangerously beautiful.*

She was wearing an oversized crewneck and shorts that disappeared under the hem of the sweater. Likely having not been expecting anyone this early, she was barefoot, and her hair was loose, waves of it rolling down around her shoulders, nearly touching her hips.

"Wyatt couldn't make it," I replied, moving to get the radiator box out of my truck bed.

"Bullshit. He said he'd be here."

"He had something come up," I said as I walked over to the Bronco, setting the box in the dirt.

She glared at me. "Again, bullshit. Get off my property, Reed."

"If I leave, the radiator goes with me."

She shrugged. "I'll just have Wyatt order another."

"Horse training has you loaded, huh?" I said, finding the clasp and lifting the hood.

"Maybe I'm making money another way."

My nostrils flared, but I refused to give in. She was baiting me, wanting a reaction. I wouldn't give it to her.

She heaved a dramatically heavy sigh, and then her front door slammed as I assumed she went back inside.

I had no desire to be around her. Her radiator needed to be fixed, and I didn't want her wearing some revealing clothes around Wyatt. Not that he gave a shit, but Brandy would do it just to piss me off.

I rolled the sleeves of my button-up up my arms, revealing the tattoos that covered my skin. Ink decorated my arms in different large pieces, but that wasn't the only place I had them. A few years ago, I'd decided to get one on my thigh, and just recently, I got a piece done on my chest.

Setting my black cowboy hat on the hood of my truck, I got to work taking the old radiator out of Brandy's Bronco. I knew how to work on trucks because Bailey always suckered me into helping fix his old Chevy, not to mention I had my old shit box years ago, so I assumed installing a radiator on a Bronco wasn't all that different. To be safe, I looked up a video to be sure I was doing it properly. After about two hours, the work was done.

Brandy didn't come back outside once.

7

BRANDY

It took all my willpower not to peek out the blinds to see if Reed was fucking my Bronco up like I thought he would. Just because he'd worked on old trucks a time or two didn't mean he was certified, let alone *allowed*, to work on my car. But instead of going out there and trying to make him leave again, knowing that it was no use—Reed did whatever the fuck he wanted anyway—I stayed inside.

No matter how many times I told him, he never got the sense to leave me the fuck alone.

A light knock sounded, but before I could get the pleasure of telling him to go the fuck away, my front door creaked open, announcing he was coming inside. I didn't give him the respect of getting out of my seat.

"Radiator's installed and the car is running fine. No leaks," Reed said, rounding the corner into my kitchen to find me seated at the small dining table. He was wiping his hands on a rag, the movement causing my eyes to stray to his tattooed arms and the way his tan skin flexed over the tendons. He had the sleeves of his button-up rolled to his elbows, stains of grease smudged across parts of his forearms.

He cleared his throat and I darted my gaze away, not wanting to see the damn satisfaction on his face over me studying him. If Reed Bronson could even show such an uplifting look.

"I'll believe it when I see it," I muttered.

In my peripheral, he gestured to the door. "Go right ahead."

I sent him a glare. "Not with you here. Last thing I need is to give you another excuse to stay. Plus, I have somewhere to be."

He fisted the rag, keeping his stone exterior in place when he said, "You know, Brandy, one day, you're going to have to drop it."

I pasted on the fakest smile I could and raised my brows. "Drop what?"

He gave the barest shake of his head, dropping his arms to his sides. "Try not to end up stranded again." Then he disappeared. The only indication that he left the house was the door clicking shut and his truck starting up outside.

I sat there for a good five minutes to be sure he was gone before I stood and grabbed my bag off the kitchen counter. Digging in the fridge, I grabbed two ready-to-eat salad kits and headed out, making sure to lock the door behind me.

After tossing the salads and my bag on the passenger seat, I opened the hood to make sure everything was in the right spot. To my surprise, it looked as it had before, but with a brand new radiator.

I wouldn't give him the mental praise yet, though. I wasn't sure if it'd even run.

Hopping behind the wheel, I started up the engine, then got back out to make sure there were no leaks. I let it run about ten minutes before calling it good and closing the hood.

I supposed I should thank him for fixing it, but we both knew that wouldn't happen. I hadn't thanked him for that night seven years ago, and while I probably should have after much thought, I couldn't get past what he did.

Getting back in the car, I dialed my mom and set the phone on speaker next to me while I pulled out of my driveway.

"Hey, honey," Mom answered.

"Hey. I'm coming over with lunch," I said, turning onto the main road.

"I thought your car was down?"

"It was, but it's fixed now. Running like new."

Mom's tone raised a pitch. *"Oh.* Was your blind date a mechanic?"

"Mom," I chastised.

"What?" she asked innocently.

"I know what you're doing," I said as I clicked on my blinker to turn toward town.

"I want to know how it went! Is it so wrong for a mother to be curious?"

When it was my mom, yes. We were close, sometimes probably a little too close, which meant we knew everything about each other. Well, aside from my dad hitting her well before I'd first witnessed it.

She'd learned to keep that hidden from me well.

"No, he wasn't a mechanic, and it went terrible," I answered.

"Terrible? What happened?"

Just the question I didn't want her to ask.

"This is why I didn't want to tell you," I said.

"Come on, I'm begging," she pleaded. Someone's muffled voice sounded in the background, but I couldn't make out who it was.

"Who's that?" I asked.

"Oh, about that. I'm not home. I meant to tell you, I'm out with some friends."

I adjusted my grip on the steering wheel, trying to hear who it was. Whoever she was with stopped talking as soon as she mentioned them.

"No lunch, then?"

"Rain check?" she asked.

I glanced at the salads on my passenger seat, letting out a small sigh. "Sure."

"Sorry, honey. Promise I'll make it up to you."

"That's okay, Mom. Have fun. I'll call you later."

"Love you," she said.

"Love you, too," I replied, then reached over to press the end button on my phone. As I looked back up, a truck was coming straight toward me on the road, and I quickly swerved as they blasted their horn, getting back in my lane and pulling off the road before slamming to a stop.

"Shit," I muttered, heaving a breath as my heart pounded out of my chest.

I needed to get my shit under control. Between the blind date and my Bronco being out of commission, I was losing myself. Just because things weren't going as planned didn't mean the world was falling apart.

Once I got my bearings, I made a U-turn and headed toward Bottom of the Buckle Ranch. I figured if seeing my mom was out of the question, I could at least work some horses for the Bronsons. I'd just give Lettie the extra salad. Bailey would love that, given Lettie had a bad habit of forgetting to eat and take her iron supplements for her anemia.

About twenty minutes later, I pulled up the dirt driveway to the Bronsons' property. I parked in my usual spot outside the rescue barn. For safe measure, before turning off the engine, I got out to double check that the radiator still wasn't leaking.

Satisfied with the way it looked, I closed the hood and came around the driver's side to turn off the car. With being on the Bronsons' property, I didn't bother locking it after grabbing the two salads.

"What are those?" Lettie asked, coming out of the barn.

I turned to her, holding them up. "Salads. Want one?"

"Did Bailey put you up to this?" she questioned with a skeptical raised brow.

"If you want to be suspicious of anyone, let it be my mom," I said.

She stepped forward, taking one of the bags from me. "I take it she canceled?"

I nodded, tossing my bag back on the seat. I wasn't in the mood to eat. "Says she's with friends or something."

The hint of a smile played on Lettie's lips. "Are you jealous?"

"Of my mom's friends?" I scoffed. "Please."

She shrugged. "She did choose them over you."

I frowned. "I highly doubt it's really friends she's with." I walked past her, heading into the barn.

She followed right behind. "Who do you think it is?"

"Probably some new boyfriend." I grabbed a halter from the hook and a bag of apple-flavored horse treats off the wood counter by the tack room.

"Not one of the others she's seen in the past few months?"

I shook my head. "Definitely not."

Lettie set the bag of salad down where I'd grabbed the treats, then followed me out to the round pen. My mom didn't stick with one boyfriend very long, and it was never a mystery as to why. At least to me, it wasn't. Deep down, even after my father left for good, she was afraid a man could do what he did, so she never let it get too serious. A few dates, and she'd break up with them. I wish she didn't think she had to do that, but if I brought it up, she'd tell me she was fine, that she was getting old and wanted to have fun.

The way she put it, it sounded more like a midlife crisis than anything else.

I opened the gate, stepping into the round pen and latching the chain behind me. Lettie had rescued a gray quarter horse from an auction about a year ago, and the progress with the gelding had been slow. I was determined to get him to at least trust me, though. I didn't want him to go through life afraid of any hand offering to help him.

"Well, I hope this one works out," Lettie said, her tone sympathetic.

"It won't," I deadpanned, grabbing a fistful of treats and setting the bag in the dirt by the gate. I looped the halter around my shoulder, and all the while, the gray stared at me. He had a fire in him, and I didn't want to put it out. I just wanted him to let us burn together.

"You know, naming him might help," Lettie said.

"It's your horse," I reminded her without looking away from the gelding.

"I don't think he's mine anymore."

"Why's that?"

"You two seem to get along just fine."

I rolled my eyes, though I knew she couldn't see it from where she was standing against the fence behind me. "I think you need your eyes checked."

"Oh, I can see just fine."

I held the handful of treats out toward the horse, then took a slow step forward. He didn't move as he kept his wide eyes trained on me, though I could tell he was nervous with the way his nostrils flared slightly.

"It's alright, buddy," I murmured.

"Buddy would be a good name," Lettie said behind me.

"Not helping, Lettie."

"I'm just saying. Name him and see how far you get."

"Who's the horse trainer here?" I asked, not looking back.

"I had to ask myself the same question," she joked, then her footsteps sounded as she walked away from the round pen.

"Good riddance, huh?" I said to the horse. "She never stops talking sometimes."

His ear twitched as a fly landed on it, his tail swishing on impulse to bat the insects away.

"Unless you like the talking?" I asked him. "You know, I could get some fly spray on you and take care of that problem real quick."

Every few seconds, I'd take another slow step toward him. It wasn't much, but it was progress that he hadn't tried to move away from me yet. Typically, he'd stay as far away as he could, always trying to point his ass toward me.

Horse 101? Don't let them disrespect you with their body, whether it's on the ground or in the saddle.

This guy, however, could be named Disrespect with the way he'd been acting for the last year. I'd given him a few months off in the pasture, hoping he'd get it out of his system, but when I took him out, he was just as hateful toward me as the day I put him in there.

"Maybe you don't like apple-flavored treats," I said.

"Are you talking to that horse?"

In a flash, the gray spooked, darting away from me. He kicked up dust in his wake, doing a few laps for good measure.

My nostrils flared as I inhaled deeply, trying to calm myself before I acted.

I spun on the person who ruined the little progress I had been making. The man who ruined *everything*.

"What the fuck, Reed?"

He kicked a boot up on the bottom of the fence, crossing his arms over the top. He was wearing a black t-shirt that hugged his biceps just fucking right, and his typical black cowboy hat cast a shadow over his face. "You're dancing with the devil, you know."

I give up.

Today was not my fucking day.

I grabbed the bag of treats from the ground, tossing the ones in my hand to the dirt, then hopped over the fence, not bothering to go through the gate. As I jumped to the ground, dust kicked up around my boots.

I barely glanced at Reed as I headed toward the barn. "Only one that close to the devil is you," I said over my shoulder at him.

I'd never get anywhere with this damn horse if he kept popping up like this. He was already pissed I was attempting to gentle the gelding, so he was doing everything he could to sabotage it.

Well, newsflash: you don't get everything you want.

The world was cutthroat, and you had to work for it, no matter the obstacles.

I'd just have to figure out how to get past the one in front of me.

8

REED

The gray finally calmed down after a few minutes, huffing on the far side of the round pen. I hadn't bothered looking back to watch Brandy leave, despite some deep part of me wanting to. I was half convinced she would've carved my eyes out with a rusty spoon if I tried.

For months now, I'd been telling her to quit working with this horse. He was dangerous, unpredictable, and anyone with half a brain could see it, but Brandy kept at it. I wasn't sure if it was because she truly was determined or if she did it to spite me. It was probably a mix of both, with a heavy hand of the latter.

I wasn't about to pick a bigger fight with her, so I shoved off the fence and headed for my parents' house. I could tell Brandy had something on her mind with the set of her jaw and the stiffness in her body. I hated to admit I noticed the little shifts in her demeanor, but I did. The woman was a firecracker, but she was always relaxed in her sass. Today, it was different.

It truly wasn't my business to ask, and I was sure if I did, she'd just tell me to fuck off. Those were her favorite words. Had to be.

Dirt fell off the soles of my boots as I walked up the porch steps. I gave them a good dusting on the boot brush nailed to the porch, then walked inside, finding my mom seated in the kitchen on her laptop.

"Busy day?" I asked as I grabbed a water from the fridge.

She finished typing, then took her glasses off, setting them beside the computer. "Just dealing with finances."

After downing half the bottle, I leaned back against the counter, facing her. "Sounds like fun."

"If your idea of fun is keeping track of all your transactions for the rescue, then have at it." She gestured to the laptop.

I sucked air in through my teeth. "See, my hands are meant for tools, not a keyboard."

She rolled her eyes as she shut the laptop. "I should probably get off of here anyway. My eyes are starting to hurt."

"I heard some fresh air can cure that real quick, and you're in luck. There's an entire ranch right outside."

"Very funny, Reed."

I didn't hear that very often.

I set the water bottle on the counter beside me. "Seriously, Mom. You need to go outside more."

"A rescue doesn't run itself, honey."

"No, but a tired woman who balances the world on her shoulders can't do her best job if she's burnt out." I didn't miss the bags under her eyes from late nights staying up dealing with the paperwork for the ranch we ran, along with all the tasks for the rescue. Balancing both was no easy feat, and yet Mom did it flawlessly. How she raised five kids and put up with Dad was beyond me, but that's what you did when you raised cattle, grew hay for your own livestock—and then some—and ran a horse rescue. You got up, you did the damn thing, and you didn't complain. Ain't nothing getting done if you're whining about it.

"You could take one thing off my plate," she said.

I crossed my arms. "What's that?"

"You can help Beck settle in."

I scoffed. "Mom, he's twenty-seven years old."

"And he needs his family more than ever right now. Especially his brothers."

I silently stared at her for a few seconds before saying, "He's got two other brothers that I'm sure would love to give him a hand."

She cocked a brow. "And you don't?"

"I'm a busy guy."

"You're standing in my kitchen talking to me, aren't you? That's ten minutes you could spend with Beckham."

I frowned. "You do know he had all of five things when we moved him in, right?"

She stood from her seat, using the counter for support before scooting the stool in. "So he's a minimalist."

My frown deepened.

Her face fell slightly. I wasn't trying to fight her on helping him, but I wanted to know why she was so concerned. Of course, she cared about her kids, but this felt different.

"What aren't you telling me?" I asked.

Her heavy eyes met mine. "I just don't want him to feel alone while he's here."

I inhaled deeply. She wanted me to convince him to stay. "Mom, I don't think he's going to leave again."

She blinked a few times, presumably clearing away building tears. She loved her children, and we appreciated the fuck out of her for it. But the woman would worry herself to death if she kept up like this.

"He's going to be fine, okay? I'll check on him, stop in every now and then."

She gave a closed-lip smile, some brightness coming back to her eyes. "That's all I want."

Grabbing my water, I pushed off the counter, coming around to give her a kiss on the temple. "I'll head over there soon."

"Thank you." She gave my arm a quick squeeze. "Now get out of here. I have work to do."

"Yes, ma'am."

***

Though Beckham's porch was small, he'd already managed to litter nearly the entire space with trash. A half-empty bottle of whiskey laid by the stairs, three red Solo cups rolled in the wind, and a paper plate sat dirty on the plastic chair. By the looks of it, he was settling in just fine only days later. Or terribly, and the result of the mess wasn't due to some party.

Maneuvering around the trash, my knuckles rapped on the door. A minute ticked by, and no movement sounded from inside, so I knocked again. And again. After five minutes, I was done waiting.

"Alright, Beck, I'm comin' in. Don't shoot," I announced, trying the handle. It opened right up, and I hesitantly stepped inside. I didn't bother closing the door behind me as when I entered, the stench of dirty dishes filled my nose. The breeze would help clear out some of the mustiness.

Walking around the wall of the kitchen, my focus landed on Beckham passed out on the couch. His shirt was stained with what seemed to be drops of whiskey and...was that pizza sauce? His five o'clock shadow was quickly turning into a short beard, and he wasn't wearing pants. I silently sent up a thanks for the boxers he wore.

I crossed the living room and nudged him on the shoulder. "Beck."

He groaned, but ultimately ignored me.

"Beckham, wake the fuck up."

"Go away," he mumbled, burying his face deeper into the pillow.

I didn't have fucking time for this.

I grabbed the pillow and yanked it out from under his head. His eyes shot open as he shoved up on his elbows. "What the fuck, man? I was sleeping."

"For how many days?" He looked like shit.

"Sleep is important," he defended.

I threw the pillow at his chest and he grabbed it, shoving himself up to a sitting position. I took the seat across from the couch, a weird crinkling sound coming from the cushion. I reached under my ass and pulled out a breakfast bar wrapper. With a slight shake of my head, I tossed it on the end table.

"You have a coming home party we weren't invited to?" I grumbled, surveying his house. It looked like he'd been trashing it for weeks, and yet it'd only been days.

"No," he answered groggily as he rubbed the back of his head.

"Got a headache?"

His hand moved to his now-shaggy hair, running his fingers through the messy strands. He usually kept it short, but even when he'd arrived back in Bell Buckle, it was longer than it typically was.

"Kind of," he replied.

"Great. Stop fucking drinking and go to the ranch."

He narrowed his eyes at me. "Why would I do that?"

I sat back, crossing my arms. "Oh, I don't know, dipshit. Because your family lives there?"

He shook his head before leaning it back against the couch. "No shit."

"Mom's worried about you."

"Tell her not to be. I'm fine."

I scoffed. Like it was that easy. Charlotte Bronson trusted her boys, but she was a worrier. And if she saw the state of his house, hell, even just the front porch, she'd know something was up.

"Don't look real fine, Beck. Your place is a mess." I gestured to the clothes littering the living room floor before crossing my arms again.

"It's laundry day," he muttered.

"When? A week ago? Cleaning all the clothes from years of being on the road?"

He glared at me before shoving off the couch and heading for the kitchen. Rather than grabbing a cup from the cabinet—because I was sure they were all dirty or still packed—he stuck his damn head under the faucet to drink.

I stood, quickly coming up behind him and turning the water on harder so it overflowed from his mouth. He coughed, shoving me back as he turned the sink off. "What the *fuck*, Reed?"

"What the fuck is wrong with you? Did the rodeo make you a fucking animal, too?"

"Don't make some fucking joke about me being stupid because I fell off a horse one too many times," he said, wiping his face with the top of his shirt.

I leaned back against the counter, crossing my arms again. "At least you already know it."

"Because you guys always make it! You want to say I'm stupid, Reed? Go right the fuck ahead, but don't repeat it every fucking time you see me."

"Beck, it's a joke," I said, my voice losing a bit of its hardness. Having so many brothers, you got used to picking on each other. It was in our DNA at this point, and Beckham was never this worked up about it. Hell, he did most of the joking around.

He opened a few cabinets, the doors slamming shut when he found each was mostly empty, before finding a bottle of pain pills and popping two. "Whatever, Reed. Is that all you came here to say?"

I dropped my arms. What the fuck was up with him?

He was in a bad mood, and I didn't want to be the victim of his piss poor attitude.

I shoved away from the counter, heading for the front door. "Clean this mess and light a fucking candle or some shit. It stinks."

I hated to be that guy, but if our mom showed up here to check in like she did on all her kids, she'd call an emergency family meeting and lose her shit.

Beckham was the craziest of all our siblings, always doing the most outlandish shit to get a rush, which was probably where Lettie got her love for Brandy. Because of that, Beckham and I clashed. I was more reserved, kept to myself, rarely took risks, and Beckham did it all. Rodeo unfortunately aided in egging his personality on, which was why it was such a shock when Mom told us he was coming home for the foreseeable future. He went through so much to get where he was, years and years of training on broncs, just to drop it all? It couldn't be for no reason.

But with Beck and I having the relationship that we did, I doubted he'd open up to me about it. Callan was too busy with the baby on the way, and his girlfriend and her daughter, that he wouldn't be of use here. Though he'd drop anything for family, my mom would have my ass if I involved him. Lennon, on the other hand, had his hands full managing Tumbleweed Feed and being with his girlfriend, Oakley, which left me with Lettie, but she was no use because she was currently knee-deep in wedding planning and, again, Mom would have my ass if I interrupted that.

Which left me to figure out what the fuck was wrong with Beckham. I didn't do well with emotions, and if I had to guess, Beck was fucking full of them at the moment. I could clean up messes of all kinds, be a shoulder to cry on, but to try to dig deep into that brain of his, find the problem and fix it? That wasn't in my wheelhouse.

9

BRANDY

I'd thankfully been successful in avoiding Reed the following week. There was no telling what I'd do if he interrupted another session with the gray. Or just approached me in general.

I'd been staring at this horse for an hour. I had all the intention to work with him when I got here, but instead, I found myself sitting on the bottom rung of the fence, watching him. He studied me right back, and we were content.

Lettie's idea to name him bounced around in my head, but I doubted it'd fix our problems. Although, horses could feel your emotions, so maybe if I felt a connection with him, he'd come around. Life wasn't like the movies, though, and that wouldn't be the solution to our issues. He'd been hurt in his past, clearly abused at some point. He had no reason to trust me, and I related to him for keeping his guard up. You let it down? You open yourself up for hurt.

"How about Billy? You like Billy?" I asked the gelding.

He just stared, swishing his tail at a fly.

"Maybe Cumin?"

Yeah, like he wanted to be named after a fucking spice.

Hell, Lettie wasn't all that creative with names anyway. She named both her pets after the color red. Her dog was just the color in French, and her horse was straight up Red.

How unique.

"Gray?" I shot out. "Maybe you'd rather be White?"

He turned his head.

"Sorry to tell ya, bud, but you didn't get that rare gene. You're just a gray."

"Are you talking to him finally?" Lettie asked, coming up beside me. Much unlike how he reacted to Reed, the horse stayed in place, keeping an eye on the two of us.

"Trying to take your advice for once and give him a name," I told her.

"Hm, maybe Snow?" she offered.

I snorted.

She climbed through the fence, sitting beside me. "What?"

"Please let Bailey name your baby if you ever have one," I said.

She braced her hands on the metal, looking at me. "What's wrong with the names I pick?"

"You'd end up naming it Human or something."

She tried to hide her smile with a frown, elbowing me in the arm. "I'd pick a better name than that."

"What? Person?" I teased.

She snorted. "No. More like Miracle."

"Lettie, come on."

Her gaze fell to her boots. "No, I'm serious. What if my anemia somehow makes it hard for us to have kids?"

I set my hand on hers. "That's a battle we'll cross when the time comes."

"We?"

"You and I are in it together. Tell Bailey to get ready," I joked to lighten the mood. "Auntie Brandy is hands-on." I didn't like seeing her beat down on herself about things she wasn't sure about. There was no telling what'd happen when they were ready for kids, and while I knew she'd worry about it regardless, it was a hurdle to cross if the problem presented itself. My best friend needed to enjoy this time in her life, not worry about obstacles that didn't exist in this moment.

She smiled, and my job was done. "Yeah, I'm sure he'll love to hear that. So speaking of me and Bailey," she started.

"Oh, no," I muttered.

She bumped her shoulder into mine. "His tux is ready to be picked up, and I was wondering if you could take that off my plate? I have so many other things to do already, and the wedding is in a few days."

That'd be easy enough.

"Alright. Where at?"

"Salt Lake City," she answered.

I turned to her with wide eyes. *"Utah?"*

"It's only a little over a four-hour car ride, and you'll have a buddy, so it'll go by fast," she added.

"Who's this supposed 'buddy'?" I held air quotes up around the word.

"Reed," she chirped. "*If* he says yes."

I stood abruptly, perching my hands on my hips as I faced her. "No fucking way."

"Brandy, please. Everyone else is busy, and I don't want you having to go all that way alone."

"I don't need a babysitter, thank you very much." How many times was she going to try to set me and Reed up together? Did she hope this would be like her and Bailey's little road trip up to the horse auction in Montana where they fell madly in love? Because that would *not* be happening.

"I wouldn't be asking if I wasn't desperate."

"You don't even have to be desperate to ask me a favor, but with Reed? No." I was putting my foot down and never picking it the fuck up again. They tried with their little blind date stunt, and we all knew how that went.

She stood up right as the goddamn devil himself marched his way out of the barn.

"Could you two keep it down?" Reed asked.

"It's a fucking ranch, dipshit, not a goddamn library," I spit back.

"Guys, please," Lettie begged. Her eyes were getting glassy, and that was not fucking good.

I rolled my eyes and muttered, "Now big ol' protective brother is going to swoop in and save the fucking day."

Reed sidled up to the fence, leaning over it with his stupid tattooed arms. His hands were dirty from working all day, and I was tempted to dump a bucket of water over him just because. Maybe he'd take his shirt off. Maybe I'd hate it.

"What am I saving the day for?" he asked, aiming the question at Lettie.

She turned to him, and his face instantly went soft when he saw her glassy eyes.

Fuck my fucking life.

"I need you to go to Salt Lake City with Brandy to pick up Bailey's tux," she said.

"Alright," he replied at the same time I said, "Not happening."

They both looked at me, and the gray pawed at the ground behind me. Maybe he liked the bickering.

"For me?" she pleaded, puffing out that bottom lip of hers. This was how she always got her way. Lettie and I grew up together. I knew her damn tactics.

"Do you not realize that if Reed and I spend more than five minutes in a car together, it will quite literally explode? We'd die, Lettie. We wouldn't make it to the wedding. You'd lose your maid of honor, and Bailey would lose his best man, and instead of a wedding, you'd be attending a funeral. It'd be tragic. You don't want that."

"Ever the drama queen," Reed mumbled.

"What was that, Satan?" I snapped.

He shoved off the fence. "Put your grudge aside and do your best friend a fucking favor. She only gets one wedding."

"And you only get one dick, and I can't guarantee I won't chop it the fuck off," I snided.

He snorted. "You'd never dream of getting that close to it."

"I can set my disgust aside for a minute while I get the job done," I shot back.

"You guys!" Lettie shouted, and we both snapped our attention to her. "It's an eight-hour round trip. Surely you could both grow up a little and get along for that short amount of time."

"Did you not hear my tidbit about the funeral?" I asked.

She rolled her eyes. "Tragic, I know. But then maybe I wouldn't have to hear you two bickering constantly."

I chewed on the inside of my cheek, glancing back at the horse. I needed a break from him anyway, and it'd be one day. I'd give Lettie the world if she wanted it. She was my best friend, the closest thing I ever had to a sibling, and this was her big day. I could put my differences with Reed aside for eight hours. I couldn't tell her how the day of the wedding might go, as I wanted to actually vomit thinking about walking down that aisle next to Reed, but the road trip was doable. At least, I hoped. The real verdict would come when we had to be alone.

"If you don't mind your brother possibly losing his dick, I'll go," I said.

She shrugged. "Doesn't affect me."

"Great. We'll leave first thing tomorrow," Reed said before turning to head back to the barn.

"We'll leave when I decide to wake up," I shouted after him. I'd need my beauty sleep if I had to sit in a truck with him for that long.

"Pick you up at six," he said over his shoulder, not looking back.

My hands fisted at my sides as I yelled, "I'm not getting in your damn truck."

But instead of replying, he ignored me as he disappeared into the barn. The fucker knew my Bronco wouldn't make it all the way to Utah, so he didn't even try to argue, which only pissed me off more.

I pinned vengeful eyes on Lettie. "I hate you," I whispered.

She smiled. "I know."

10

REED

Brandy had been in the passenger seat of my truck for all of an hour, the ice in her massive water bottle clinking around with each bump, and I was sure the cab would explode at any time now. I'd been outside her house right at six a.m., and to my utter surprise, she was waiting in the driveway for me all dressed and ready to go. I didn't get a good morning, but I also didn't have to go inside, drag her out of bed, and fight over which vehicle we were taking, so I called it a win.

If there was one thing Brandy was good at, it was holding a grudge, so I was surprised she'd somewhat set our feud aside for Lettie's wedding errand. Even I wouldn't let her ruin my little sister's wedding. Not that she would—they were best friends—but Brandy would do anything to piss me off. I guessed that was another thing she was good at: getting under my skin. But for our little road trip to Salt Lake City, she could let our past go.

Hopefully.

In my peripheral, Brandy reached over to the knob on the stereo, turning up the song that just came on shuffle. "Austin" by Dasha blasted through the speakers, the seats vibrating with the bass.

Okay, maybe Brandy couldn't put our shit under the rug for a day.

I used the button on my steering wheel to turn it down a few, and naturally, Brandy turned it right back up. Immediately, my finger punched the minus button on the wheel, but she kept those fingers on the knob, twisting and twisting.

I shook my head, letting out an exaggerated sigh, even though Brandy couldn't hear it over the female voice blasting through the damn speakers. Without thinking, I cranked the wheel, turning off the next exit to park at a gas station.

Leaving the music blasting for her enjoyment, I opened my door.

"The tank is full," she called over the guitar.

"Well fucking aware, Brandy. I need a goddamn minute out of this truck." I slammed the door a little too hard, but fuck, I didn't give a shit.

I shoved the door to the gas station open, the little bell aggressively clinking with the force. I didn't even want anything, but sitting next to Brandy for even just a meager hour made me restless. Not only with the way she purposely tried to irritate me, between smacking her gum and kicking her feet up on the dash, but with her presence alone. She hated me. Loathed me like I was the bane of her existence, all because of some fucking night seven years ago, and there was no way in hell she'd ever let it go.

I was staring at the chip aisle when the bell dinged again, and over the top of the rack, Brandy's brunette head appeared. Her hair was wavier today, which meant she'd taken a shower before I'd picked her up and let it air dry. I knew that because of all those days she and Lettie spent at the pond growing up. She'd come back to the ranch in a bikini and half-dry hair, always letting it air dry throughout the rest of the day.

She was wearing jean shorts and an oversized t-shirt that hung off her shoulder just enough to show the neon pink strap of her bra. She did that shit on purpose, making sure to pull it just enough to where it'd peek through. She was a goddamn tease, and it pissed me off because she didn't understand the kind of trouble it could get her in. Not with other men, but with me. She should be thankful she never let me near her.

She was well aware I was standing in the aisle as she slid past me, her shoulder brushing my back. I watched her walk up to the fridge and pull out a water, and as she headed to the front to pay, my eyes caught on an older man staring directly at her ass. Instantly, my jaw clenched, my teeth grinding, and I wanted to stab his eyes out with a fork.

I made sure Brandy had her back to me as she waited second in line at the register and then strode over to the guy. I pretended like I was looking at the hats, and though I was right the fuck next to him, his eyes never strayed from her.

If I could get away with murder, he'd already be six feet under the concrete subfloor.

"Nice day today, isn't it?" I asked him, trying my best to sound casual, despite the utter rage that flowed through every inch of me. No one got to eye fuck Brandy Rose on my watch. I didn't give a fuck how revealing her clothes were. She was a stranger to this asshole, and I was sure his thoughts were anything but innocent.

"Yep," he replied as he practically drooled.

"Some great views 'round this part of Idaho," I said, baiting him.

"Amazing ones," he replied.

Brandy paid, and I waited until that little bell dinged before I shoved his shoulder, grabbed the front of his shirt, and slammed him back against the wall.

"You ever look at another woman like that without her permission, you'll wish you were blind," I seethed, my voice quiet but holding all the threat it needed.

He'd eye fucked my Brandy Rose in a fucking gas station. He was lucky I didn't take his eyes out now.

"I was just looking," the guy whined, panic lacing his tone. He was a heavier man, his chin wobbling with his tremor. "I didn't mean no harm."

I shoved him into the wall again before letting go and stepping back. "'Round here, perverts don't get the benefit of the doubt. They get dealt with."

It took all the self-control I could muster to walk away from him. My fist wanted to land straight into his cheek, but I wouldn't do that. Fighting ruined something for me long ago, and I wouldn't repeat it. This guy wasn't worth it.

On my way out, I gave a small salute to the cashier, who gladly returned it. People stuck together around here, backed each other up if they needed it, which was what I thought I was doing for Brandy all those years ago, but I guess I was wrong.

After exiting the gas station, I hopped back into the truck to find Brandy sitting in the passenger seat on her phone. The music was off, so I connected my phone to the bluetooth and queued a random playlist. Old country filled the speakers, though the sound was turned down to an acceptable volume now.

"Took you that long in there and you didn't even buy anything?" Brandy asked, not bothering to look up from her phone.

"Why'd you get a water if you tote that giant ass cup around?"

She set her phone on the center console, then unscrewed the lid on her tumbler. "It doesn't fill itself." She balanced it between her thighs as she uncapped the plastic bottle, pouring it into the other one.

I stared ahead through the windshield as the bottle emptied. "Why don't you just drink it out of the plastic ones, then?"

"Because I like this cup," she explained.

I ran a hand over my chin, losing my patience to even try to understand her, then kicked the truck into reverse once the top was back on her metal cup.

This was going to be the longest trip of my life.

11

REED

SEVEN YEARS AGO

The image of Brandy sitting in my passenger seat this morning looking so fucking defeated filtered through my mind. I would've covered my thoughts with the burn of whiskey, but thought better of it tonight. Who knew what the fuck I would do if I mixed a few drinks with the impulse to go teach her father a lesson.

I'd pound his fucking face in if given the chance, just to see how he liked it.

But Brandy had told me to stay out of it, and what Brandy wanted, she got.

An aluminum can being crushed blurred all thoughts from my mind, sending them away like dust on the wind.

"Damn fucking right I did," Beckham hollered, tossing his flattened can at the trash bin and making a clean shot. "Green ones ain't got nothing on me."

"Do you ever not brag about sitting out a horse's little bunny hops?" Lettie asked, that typical sisterly annoyance clear in her tone.

Beck raised a brow at her. "Bunny hops?" He scoffed. "Please. Those were full-on ass-bruising bucks."

Bailey tipped his beer in Beck's direction, a finger pointing in agreement. "I saw it, Huckleberry. He's right. That horse tried its best, but Beck wasn't having none of it."

Lettie rolled her eyes, sitting back in the chair on our parents' porch. My dad, Travis, had spent the whole day out on the ranch making sure shit was prepped and ready for the early winter this year. We typically had a few more weeks, but the forecast had predicted snow in a few days. With the long hours he had been working, he'd turned in early, so we were trying to be somewhat quiet to respect his rest. Though, after a few beers in each of my brothers, that was proving difficult as time passed.

"Even my students can ride that out, Beck. It's not anything special," Callan said before taking a swig of his longneck.

Lennon pursed his lips to hide his grin while I just fucking sat there listening like I always did. Bailey and I got along great one-on-one, but put him in a room with my other siblings? We were practically polar opposites. But Bailey and I understood each other on a level my brothers didn't, and that's what drew us closer. He didn't try to pry shit out of me. Instead, he had some way about him that made me an open book. To everyone else? I dared them to try to flip to page fucking one.

Beck stood from his chair, the legs scraping across the deck. "Then let's go see how well you can do it, smart-ass."

Callan shook his head, not bothering to look up at Beck as he swayed on his feet. "I'm not riding after this many drinks."

Beckham shrugged. "Suit yourself."

Lennon leaned forward to grab the beer out of Beck's hand. "And you shouldn't either. You can compare how long your rides are tomorrow when you're sober."

The corner of my mouth tilted up slightly at the insinuation.

My phone buzzed in my front pocket, so I set my water bottle on the table and shifted to slide it out. Wyatt Pearson's name lit up the bottom of the screen with a text. He was a good friend of ours, but a text from him this late at night couldn't mean anything good.

I swiped up to unlock my phone, clicking his text.

> **Wyatt**
> Party at Jefferson's place is a little wild

I debated not even replying because I couldn't give two shits less about some party, but thought fuck it. Wyatt was a nice guy, and leaving him on read was probably a dick move. Anyone else, and I probably wouldn't have cared, but he'd done more favors for my family than I could count on one hand. Never gave me a reason to ignore him.

> Little?

> **Wyatt**
> Code for *it's getting out of hand*

> What do you mean?

The three dots appeared that he was typing, then disappeared. Wyatt wasn't one for crowds as far as I was aware, which was why I was the slightest bit surprised he was at a party to begin with.

After about two minutes of waiting for his response, I locked my phone. Right as I was pivoting to slide it back in my jeans, his name lit up my screen again. I swiped up on it, doing a double take when I saw the name in his text.

> **Wyatt**
> Brandy's here. She looks pretty tipsy

> Did she come with anyone?

My only concern was that she had a ride home if she was drinking.

> **Wyatt**
> Not that I saw, but she's hanging with some older guys now. Keeping an eye on her

> You are, or they are?

If there were some pervy fucking drunk guys copping a feel of her, I wouldn't hesitate to break their fucking noses.

> **Wyatt**
> Both?

A sigh passed my lips as I stared at his text.

"Something wrong?" Lennon asked.

I shook my head, staring at the screen like Wyatt would reassure me everything was fine in a moment. Or better yet, he'd tell me it was a joke. What if she was acting out because of what happened this morning? If she wasn't thinking, or in the right frame of mind, who knew what the fuck she might do at that party. And if she was drinking, was anyone making sure she didn't overdo it? Wyatt being there to make sure no one tried anything with her did little to ease my growing worry, despite my trust in him.

But she wasn't my fucking responsibility to worry about.

"Nothing," I replied.

"That crease between your brows is deeper than usual, so I'm going to have to call bullshit." Lennon was too fucking observant.

The rest of them were in some heated debate about who'd been thrown off a horse more times, but I wasn't paying attention.

No. My mind was only running rapid with concern for Brandy while it had no fucking reason to.

If I had to blame it on anything, it'd be this morning. She'd had a bad start to the day and was clearly taking it out by going to a simple party. That was it. There was nothing to worry about.

But what if something else happened with her dad after she left our ranch earlier? Had he hit her, upset her? What if he hurt her when she inevitably came home drunk? She wouldn't be able to fight him off—not some fifty-year-old who had no respect for women to begin with.

Better yet, how was she going to get home in the fucking first place? Lettie was seated at this table with me, which meant unless Brandy had someone else drive her, she'd be walking.

And that didn't fucking sit right with me. Not with the sun having just disappeared behind the horizon now.

"I'm fine." I stood from the chair, about to abandon my water, but then thought she might need it if she was drunk, so I swiped it in a fist. "I have to head out."

Lennon's mouth was a thin line as he dipped his head in a nod. "See you tomorrow?"

"Yep."

I left the rest of them bickering at the table, heading for my truck in the driveway. As I walked, I glanced at my screen three more times before tossing it on the passenger seat and sliding in behind the wheel. No more texts from Wyatt. That was a good thing.

Regardless of trying to convince myself of that, I started the engine and headed down to the main road. If Brandy wouldn't let anyone else know what happened—if shutting everyone out was that damn important to her—then she could make that decision.

But no way in hell would I let her keep me out, too.

12

BRANDY

"Welcome in! Shopping for your wedding today?" the lady asked as we walked through the crystal-clear glass sliding doors. A cheery smile spread her bright pink lips, showing off glistening, straight teeth. Her eyes snagged on Reed's arms for just a second too long, and all it did was piss me off when it shouldn't.

I sent a scowl her way—for insinuating we were together, and for checking him out. Though it wasn't her fault for the former. The two of us were in a bridal store. But even a stranger from halfway around the world could see that Reed and I would rather cut our tongues off than admit we held any feelings for each other aside from detestation and annoyance.

"Not ours," I grumbled. "We're here to pick up a tux for our friend."

The blonde clasped her fingers together in front of her. "If you're just picking up and not needing measurements, you can head over to the front desk and they'll take care of you."

"Thanks." I turned to head for the beige desk pancaked between two creepy mannequins wearing massive gowns.

Reed matched my pace. "Surprised you used your manners."

"If we weren't in a bridal salon right now, I'd stab you with my keys," I muttered, quickening my stride.

"Always so violent," he shot back. "You ever stop to think that maybe that turns me on?"

I nearly tripped over my feet as my head swiveled his way. "I didn't think it was big enough to get hard. I'll be sure to let the girl at the front know." *Yeah, Brandy, resort to diminishing the size of his cock. Great fucking tactic.*

We stopped in front of the desk before Reed could respond, and I pasted a smile on my face for none other than the fact that what he'd said fazed me. He did it on purpose, and that just pissed me off more.

A woman with short brunette hair popped her head up from the calendar she was jotting notes down on, her eyes widening slightly in Reed's direction. If I had to watch one more fucking person check him out—

"Typically, we don't want the groom being here if you're trying on dresses—"

"No one's trying on anything," I snapped, and quickly reeled myself in with a deep inhale. To my right, Reed glanced my way, clearly taken aback by my outburst. I hated being in public with this man. I was a ticking time bomb waiting to go off.

The brunette's eyes widened slightly as she dropped her pen to the desk.

"We're picking up a tux for a friend," I explained, my tone a bit lighter this time.

She swallowed, moving her hand to the mouse. "Alright. Name?"

"Should be under Bailey Cooper," Reed said.

My lips pressed together with my slight annoyance at him answering for me.

Her perfectly manicured nails clacked on the keyboard before she slid her chair back. "Ah. Cooper. Is he able to try it on before you take it home?"

I slid my arms onto the counter. "No"—my eyes dropped to her name tag—"Mary. Unfortunately, it's just his best man and me."

She stood, facing Reed. Her eyes traveled down his biceps, and I knew she was taking in his tattoos. I wanted to spoon her goddamn eyes out for it. "Is Mr. Cooper about the same size as you?"

Speaking of fucking dick jokes.

"About the same," Reed answered at the same time I said, "No."

I wanted to get in and out quickly, not stick around and play fucking dress-up.

"Would you like to try it on for him?" she asked Reed, clearly ignoring me.

This wasn't fucking protocol, and we all fucking knew it. She just wanted to see him in a goddamn suit.

Reed must've sensed my complete and utter indignation at the entire thing, because he turned to her with the sweetest fucking expression I'd ever seen Reed Bronson make, and said, "I'd love to."

I swore my lips were going to lose all blood flow with how tight they were pressed together as I slowly faced him and the goddamn smirk he wore on his face.

"I'll go grab it and meet you by the dressing rooms," she said before turning on her high heel to head for the back.

"Something wrong?" he asked, knowing exactly what he was doing.

I forced the corners of my mouth to tilt upward slightly as I shoved off the desk. "Everything's fucking dandy."

I walked past him toward the dressing rooms in the back corner, and of course, he was right beside me the whole time.

"Why do they even have tuxes here?" I mumbled under my breath. This was a fucking bridal salon.

"Lettie did say they sent it to the wrong place," he reminded me.

"Might as well have sent it to a strip club," I muttered.

"I wouldn't be complaining."

I rolled my eyes as we stopped by the row of doors. Reed wasn't that kind of guy and he was well aware I knew that. He was just trying to get under my skin, and I needed to keep that in mind before easily giving him the reactions he was trying to pull from me.

Mary emerged from the back with a plastic cover hanging off a hanger to protect the suit underneath. "Any one of the dressing rooms is fine." She handed him the tux, making sure their fingers grazed. My eyes did another roll, and this time, they nearly disappeared into the back of my head. "We just ask that only one of you occupy a room at a time."

She glanced my way, finding my bored stare. If she was insinuating we'd have a quickie in one of the changing rooms, she clearly hadn't sensed the imaginary daggers being shot back and forth between us.

If only they were real.

"That won't be a problem," Reed said.

Mary gave a quick nod. "If you need me for anything, I'll be up at the front. I can check you out there when you're ready."

Every fucking word out of her mouth could be taken a hundred different ways, and I wasn't in the mood to dissect what she meant by any of it. Typically, I wouldn't be so irritated with some stranger, but the way they all ogled over Reed like he was a piece of candy irritated me to no end. Had they never seen a man before?

Mary retreated back to her spot behind her desk while Reed crossed to one of the rooms. Before he closed the door, he pinned me with his gaze. "Remember, Brandy. Don't get any ideas. Only one at a time."

I glared at him, taking a seat in one of the cushioned chairs. As I waited, I let my eyes wander to the rack of wedding dresses sitting off to the side of a floor-to-ceiling mirror. Crossing a leg over the other, I wondered if my mom knew what her marriage was going to look like when she found the right dress. Was she aware my dad was abusive back then? That he'd cheat on her for years, and leave her with their only child?

The day I wore my own wedding dress—if that day ever came—would I know? Would my marriage end like theirs did, leaving me a single mom hopping boyfriend to boyfriend just to fill the void?

Or would I even be strong enough to risk going through that after seeing how it tore my mother apart, day in and day out?

The amount of times I'd come home from school to find her crying on the living room floor with an old photo book sprawled out in front of her, or when he finally left her and she didn't leave the couch for a week... I saw every emotion she battled because of him, and it made me never want to subject myself to that kind of pain.

Maybe I wasn't meant for a grand wedding or some pretty white dress. Perhaps the life I was dealt was just warning me to never go down the same road she did—to not make the same mistakes by falling in love and becoming blind.

But seven years ago, I almost did make a mistake, and while I liked to blame my father for it, there were a lot of hands at play that night. I just didn't expect Reed to be one of them.

The hinges on the door squeaked as Reed opened it, and as I turned to face him, I froze.

He looked...handsome.

Cleaned-up, with his black cowboy hat and Bailey's tux. I nearly had to make sure my jaw wasn't on the floor.

Like he didn't sense my reaction at all, he turned to face the tall mirror, adjusting the lapel before moving to fix the cuff on his right wrist.

"How's it look?" he asked, finding my eyes in the reflection of the mirror.

I stood as I cleared my throat.

"You? Not so great. But the suit looks perfect. Bailey will love it."

He stepped back to get a better look, but as he did, a woman appeared in the reflection, standing by the front doors. My eyes widened at the girl I hadn't seen in almost seven years.

My heart pounded as I forced myself to think fast before she could see me. With no other options, I grabbed Reed's arm and yanked him into the dressing room, then quickly shut the door and twisted the lock.

"What the fuck are you doing?" he demanded, his voice anything but quiet.

With my back to the door, I held a finger to my lips. "Shh!"

Clearly, he didn't get the message, because he simply glared. "Let me out of the room, Brandy."

I shook my head. "We can't go out there," I whisper-shouted.

He set his hands on his hips, staring up at the ceiling like it may give him the strength to deal with me. Newsflash: nothing would. But a man could dream.

And apparently, I could, too, because with the way he had his arms spread, the button-down was stretched across his chest, showcasing every taut muscle underneath.

I coughed and swallowed at the same time, nearly choking over the fact that I was gawking at the asshole. His gaze shot back to me. "Who's out there?"

With watery eyes, I regained my composure. "What makes you think someone is out there?"

He gave me a bored look. "Why else would you willingly drag me into a dressing room?"

He had a point, but I didn't answer.

He dropped his arms, his hands slapping his well-defined thighs through the slacks. With a shrug, he moved his fingers to the button on them.

My eyes widened to the size of saucers. "What are you doing?"

He got the button undone, then moved to the zipper. "I can't just stay in Bailey's suit forever."

"But I'm in here," I said hurriedly.

Hazel eyes met mine. "Then step out."

"I can't," I bit out in a hiss.

With the zipper now pulled down, he moved his fingers to the waistline, ready to pull the pants down. "Not my fault, then."

He cocked a brow in my direction. "You can watch, though, if you want."

Fuck, no, I didn't *want* to. But my eyes couldn't tear away from him in that suit. He was always Reed, the dirty, asshole farrier who was unfortunately my best friend's older brother. Now he was some cleaned up, somehow hotter version of himself, and I couldn't even believe I was mentally admitting that.

Fuck, fuck, fuck.

What was he *doing* to me?

I hated Reed Bronson with every fiber in my body. He ruined my life, and now I was standing here practically drooling over him. What the fuck was wrong with me?

He began to pull them down, giving me no time to think before I threw myself at him and slammed his back up against the wall.

He had a good seven or eight inches on me, though I wasn't very short myself. Still, I had to tilt my chin to look up at him. The brim of his hat cast a shadow over both our faces from the overhead light, and my skin practically burned with having to touch him. My hands were on his chest, his pants were way too fucking low on his waist, and this was so wrong.

"Do I need to call for help?" he asked, his voice still not fucking quiet.

I pressed my lips together, grinding my jaw. If he so much as dared—

His mouth opened, and I slapped a hand over it to keep him quiet. Both his brows rose a good inch up his forehead. I was frozen to the spot, one hand on his hard chest, the other pressed up against lips I never wanted to touch in a million years, even with a ten-foot pole.

I couldn't help it as my eyes drifted down his body, just to see how low his pants really were. Right when my gaze stopped below his belt-line, my body froze as my stomach somersaulted.

Tell me Reed Bronson did *not* have a boner while he was alone in a dressing room with me.

I shot my focus back up to him to find the asshole had one brow cocked. I pulled my hand away from his mouth and took a step back. I needed distance. Less than three minutes alone in this room with him, and it was too much. Being close to Reed was never a good idea. His and my presence mixing together only led to catastrophic fallout, and I did not want to be on the hook for disrupting the peace in this bridal salon.

I went to turn around to give him the privacy to change—because I wasn't about to go sit out there with that woman in the same building as me—but stopped mid-spin as he said, "Who are you hiding from?"

"Get changed, Reed." This was not a conversation I wanted to have with him.

"Who, Brandy?"

I inhaled, only to maintain my composure, and faced him. "It doesn't matter."

"If whoever it was made you come in here with me, then it must matter."

My eyes narrowed. Did the Bronsons ever let anything go?

"It's just some girl from high school," I explained.

He waited for me to continue, but I didn't. I'd already said too much.

He shoved off the wall, moving to walk past me. "Then let's go say hi."

I grabbed his wrist before his hand could touch the knob and yanked it away. "No," I hissed. The asshole fucking baited me just to make me explain. I let go of him. "Would you just drop it?"

He crossed his arms, indicating that no, he wouldn't.

I sighed, debating just keeping my mouth shut, but instead said, "She used to make fun of me."

Every inch of him went rigid as he dropped his arms. "About what?"

"What do you think?"

It was partially why I still hated him for that night. For him, it was a few hours where he got to act like a fucking hero. But for me, it ruined what was left of my high school years, and followed me for long after.

Realization hit him as he stiffened, like this was the first time he had ever thought that night haunted me. I didn't want his fucking pity.

Not now.

"Get dressed," I muttered, turning around to face the wall. Unfortunately, there were mirrors on every wall in this room, so even averting my gaze, I could still see him. I squeezed my eyes shut.

The room was quiet aside from the rustling of clothes as he stripped himself of the suit. My back hummed with the thought of him possibly naked behind me, but I didn't dare peek.

"Done," he announced.

I opened my eyes just in time to see him pulling his black t-shirt over his stomach. The little bit of skin I glimpsed told me all I needed to know—Reed was dangerous. If I never found myself alone in another dressing room with him, it'd be too soon.

With a deep breath, I unlocked the handle, twisting it slowly to open the door. I peeked out through the crack to be sure the woman was gone. I checked left, then right, but before I could be sure the coast was clear, a large hand grabbed the side of the door right above my head and pulled it wide open.

"Reed!" I hissed.

He walked around me with the hanger in hand, heading for the front counter. I took one step out of the dressing room, double checking she wasn't around, and followed him.

"Everything fit?" Mary asked.

Reed nodded, setting an elbow on the counter. "All good."

She leaned forward in her swivel chair, twirling a pen in her fingers. "I'm surprised your friend is the same size as you. It's almost perfect that you came in his place."

I wanted to vomit.

I sidled up next to him, too close for my liking, but I needed to send a message loud and clear. Besides, I'd already been too close to him too many times today, so what was one more?

"Thanks so much for your help, Mary. The suit looked amazing on him." I pasted on a gleaming smile to send it home. "Have a lovely day."

I didn't bother to glance at Reed as I turned to head toward the front doors. I wanted out of this air-conditioned, pristine place.

I got to the truck and pulled on the handle, but of course, it was fucking locked. Crossing my arms, I tapped a foot, waiting for Reed to emerge. Two minutes later, he did. I had no doubt he stayed behind a moment longer to apologize for my behavior.

He took his sweet time getting the keys out of his pocket. "What do you feel like eating?"

"Aren't we going home?"

He beeped the locks. "Gotta eat."

He opened the rear driver's side door and hooked the hanger on the plastic piece hanging from the ceiling, then closed the door.

"I'm not hungry," I snipped.

"Still gotta eat," he replied before getting in behind the wheel.

I stood there a few seconds longer, attempting—and failing—to calm the smoke practically billowing from my ears. With a frown, I yanked on the passenger door handle, getting in myself.

Today would be the death of me. I just knew it.

13

REED

"You gonna tell me who that was in the store?" I asked after finishing my bite of burger. I'd found some hole-in-the-wall diner off one of the main roads in downtown Salt Lake after Brandy refused to say what she was in the mood for—and by the looks of it, it wasn't this.

I stared at Brandy across from me, waiting for a reply as she stabbed multiple fries with her fork. She'd already told me it was someone from high school, but I wanted a name. To know what they made fun of her for, for how long, and why. Though I had a feeling I already knew the answer to one of those questions.

I dropped the burger on my plate, leaning back in the booth as I wiped my hands on the napkin in my lap. "You choose to finally stop talking right when I want an answer."

She used the edge of the plate to slide the fries off the utensil, then began stabbing them again.

"Just fucking eat the damn food, Brandy."

"I'm pretending they're you."

I frowned, watching as the metal spokes tore into the soft potato.

"Such a violent thing," I muttered.

"Only when it comes to you," she mumbled.

I darted a hand out to grab the utensil before she could pull it away, yanking it out of her hand. I tossed it on the table, the metal clanging against the ivory surface as it bounced. She kept her hand positioned how it was for a moment, then proceeded to pick up a knife. Before she could slice into the mutilated pile of fries, I plucked it from her grasp and set it on my side of the table in case she got any ideas and wanted her fantasies to come to life.

"How did she make fun of you?" I asked, trying a different approach.

Brandy lifted a hand in the air, and a moment later, our waitress was sidling up next to the table. "Anything I can get you?"

"Just the check," Brandy said.

The woman eyed our plates full of food. She'd brought them out merely minutes ago. "Need boxes?"

"We're not done," I interrupted.

"No, thanks," Brandy answered.

I rolled my lips together, staring directly at her with a narrowed gaze. Ever since the dressing room, she'd avoided eye contact, and now it was starting to piss me the fuck off.

"Be right back," the waitress said, deciding not to interrupt the feud going on between us, and disappeared.

I gritted my teeth together. "Brandy."

"Learn how to take a fucking hint and drop it." Still, those hazel eyes didn't find mine.

There was no doubt in my mind why she'd been made fun of in high school, but the fact that I didn't know about it prior to right now pissed me off. I didn't need to know everything that went on in Brandy's life. In fact, I didn't *want* to know. But if people had been making fun of her for that night when none of it was her fault, Lettie had to have known, right? She would've let it slip at some point. My little sister was terrible at keeping secrets.

And if Lettie didn't know, that meant Brandy battled it all on her own. The taunting clearly still bothered her because she'd avoided the woman at the bridal salon like she'd burst into a million pieces if she so much as caught a glimpse of her.

Had that night truly stuck with her this long?

As soon as the waitress came back with the check and laid it on the table, Brandy was gone. I watched her retreating back, forcing my eyes not to drift to those tiny shorts, and pulled my wallet out from my back pocket.

I set two twenties on top of the bill. "Can I get two boxes, please?"

The blonde grabbed the check and cash, nodding. "Of course. Is everything okay with your girlfriend?"

That bite of burger nearly came right back up my throat. Could a guy and a girl not hang out without automatically being in a relationship together? Well, I guessed it wasn't really hanging out... More like forced to be in proximity together against our will.

"She's fine."

The waitress raised a brow, her hands idly folding the cash and bill in half. "That what she told you?"

I wanted to say, *No, because she's the most complicated woman on the planet and doesn't talk when spoken to, unless it's to spew insults or start a fight.*

"Something like that," I answered.

"Little tip," she started, folding the items again and stuffing them in her apron. "Women are *never* fine when they say they are."

With a tight-lip smile, I gave her a courteous nod. "I'll keep that in mind."

She disappeared for a few minutes before coming back with my change and two boxes. I set the contents of our respective plates in their own containers, left the extra cash as a tip, and headed for the doors. As soon as I was outside, I found Brandy standing on the sidewalk with her back to me. I could tell her arms were crossed, and if I had to guess, she wore her usual scowl.

I stopped as the door quietly shut behind me, standing there like an idiot holding two to-go boxes as I stared at her. Her hair fell down her back in waves, but even I knew she hated the texture sometimes. Especially when it was windy, and the curls were unruly. I'd overhear her and Lettie talk about the most random things growing up, and that was one that stuck in my mind, among many other things. Like how she hated when Lettie slept with the TV on, and that she was scared of the dark but didn't want people to know she slept with a night light, or how her favorite color was peach because all the other colors were too boring.

I tuned a lot of voices out in my life, but never hers.

A lot of the time, it was because Brandy demanded to be heard with just her presence alone, but other times, it was simply because my focus always snagged on a piece of her when she was around. Whether that be her laugh, or her stubborn side voicing itself, one part of me was always hyper-focused on her—and if I had to guess, it was because of the night I nearly killed a man for her.

"Are you just going to stand there or unlock the damn truck?" Brandy asked, turning to find me staring.

I shook my head to clear her from my thoughts, continuing on my way. Holding the boxes in one hand, I fished my keys out of my pocket and unlocked the doors. "Was just trying to figure out a way to leave you in Utah for good."

I went to the driver's side and opened the door at the same time she did on the passenger side.

"Oh, great. I'm stuck on a road trip with a guy that wants to leave me stranded," she groused.

I got in and set the containers on the center console. "Nah, I wouldn't have the heart to leave you alive. Might decide to go ruin someone else's life besides mine." I shot her a glance as she closed her door a little too hard. "Couldn't have that happen, now could we?"

She rolled her eyes. "Lettie always did like true crime podcasts. I'm sure she'd be over the moon to know her best friend made it on one." She yanked on the seat belt, the strap instantly locking with the force. She pulled on it again, but it was stopped a few inches out. She let out a frustrated groan, trying again and again. "Your truck fucking sucks."

"It doesn't like angry people," I explained.

In between another few hard yanks, she gritted out, "I'm surprised it hasn't tried to get in a wreck with you in it, then."

I watched as she continued to struggle with it for another few tries. She knew that if she let it go back in the compartment and pulled gently, it'd fix itself, but she was Brandy, and if there was an option, she'd always choose a fight.

"Fuck, Brandy, quit it." I pushed the styrofoam containers back a few inches and leaned over the center console. Vanilla and a hint of peppermint wrapped around me as soon as I was in her space, just like in the dressing room.

I pried her hand from the strap, then let it retract into the wall on its own. My eyes caught on the way her chest rose and fell slower, almost like she was holding her breath. My lips were a good two inches from her cheek now, and it was more than obvious she was trying to ignore our proximity.

"Don't forget to breathe, Brandy," I murmured, catching her gaze as her attention shot to me. "Wouldn't want that little, black heart of yours shriveling up any further from lack of oxygen."

Those caramel eyes narrowed as I eased the seat belt over her lap. I didn't scoot back as I clicked it into place between our bodies. Her back was pressed so hard up against the seat, I thought she might become part of it.

Seeing the way she was mad at me, and we were about to be forced in this truck together for the next few hours, I needed her to get her aggression out on something that wasn't me.

And I knew just the place to do it.

***

"This isn't the highway," Brandy pointed out as we pulled into the parking lot.

"I'm glad all the glaring hasn't affected your eyesight," I said, positioning the truck in one of the empty spots directly in front of the establishment.

She let out a frustrated breath and leaned forward in her seat to read the sign on the building. "A fucking rage room?"

I tried to hide my smile, but this was one of those rare times I couldn't. "Yep."

I turned the truck off and unbuckled before getting out. She stayed firmly seated, staring at me through the open door. "No way in hell."

I set a hand on the door. "Well, I've thought about it, and I actually would rather not lose my cock to your wrath on the way home, so this is more for me than it is for you."

She crossed her arms as the corner of her mouth faintly twitched. "Why would I do anything for you?"

I tilted my head in thought. She had a good point.

"Then consider it a half-hour of letting loose." I was sure there were quite a few faces she could imagine pounding in, and it was a no-brainer mine would be on that list. It didn't bother me as much as it should. If I was her outlet for taking her anger out on anyone, I was glad she chose me.

I may verbally give her a hard time, but I'd never fight back.

That was something her father couldn't say for himself.

She sat there for a moment, probably thinking of all the ways she could accidentally hit me with a mallet instead of a plate or TV. She must've figured out some grand plan to injure me, because that frown finally lightened up for the first time since this trip began, and she unbuckled. "Fine."

I shut my door and waited for her to meet me at the front of the truck before we headed for the entrance. I clicked the lock button on my key fob, then pocketed it as I held the glass door open for her.

"Don't start acting like a gentleman again, Satan," she said as she grabbed the other handle on the door next to it.

"Never claimed to be, Little Devil."

She shot me a glare as we went in through our respective sides of the double doors and approached the desk off to the side. There was graffiti littering the walls with not an inch of blank space showing. I didn't like these gimmicky types of places. All they did was suck your wallet dry and you got nothing out of them but a faint memory. A beer on the porch sounded much more enjoyable than breaking random shit, but for one, I'd never share a drink with Brandy, and two, she needed to lighten the fuck up before I sat beside her for a few hours. If she didn't, I was sure the whole truck would blow.

Maybe that was why her Bronco was always breaking down.

"Welcome to Ram's Rage Room," the man behind the counter greeted. He had wildly curly hair sticking up in different directions, but he wore a huge grin all the same. "My name's Ethan. First time?"

I leaned an elbow on the scratched up counter that sat a little below my chest. "First time for me. Brandy here is a pro at breaking stuff."

She shot me a glare, crossing her arms.

"Well, pro or not, I'm gonna have to ask that she wear long pants if you guys want to rage," Ethan said, glancing at Brandy's shorts.

"I don't have any pants," Brandy stated.

Ethan's smile was clearly trying to lighten her attitude. The poor guy didn't know that'd never happen. "No problem, miss. We've got some you can rent for five bucks."

Her mouth was a thin line as she simply stared at the guy, blinking.

I looked at her beside me. "What's wrong, Little Devil? Scared to wear someone else's clothes?"

She turned her nose up at me. "I have no problem wearing other people's clothes. Is it you who has a problem with seeing me in them?" I ground my teeth together as she faced Ethan again. Pulling a five out of her shorts, she slapped it on the counter.

He slid it off, setting the cash beside his keyboard. "I'll grab you a pair. If they don't fit, just let me know and I'll swap them out."

He stood from his stool, disappearing into a room off the side. I stared at the side of Brandy's face as she tapped her foot on the concrete floor. Ethan reemerged less than a minute later and set a pair of folded gray pants on the counter. "Bathroom is down that hall. First door on the right."

Brandy grabbed them off the counter and stomped off.

Once the door clicked shut, Ethan said, "I see why you brought her here."

I simply stared at him. "Why's that?"

"Girl's angry. At you or something else, it's damn clear." He let out a little chuckle, moving his gaze to his computer screen.

My jaw popped as I ground my back molars together. "Surprised you work at a rage room and judge people for their attitudes."

His hand lifted off the mouse for a second, flipping it over to gesture a pathetic shrug. "Lots of women got problems, man. There's a reason it's always their boyfriends bringing them in here."

I leaned forward on the counter slightly, looking down at him on his seat. "Damn lucky I'm not her boyfriend, Ethan, or you'd be up against that wall instead of perched on that little stool."

His clicking froze, and he blinked a few times, processing what I said. I relaxed a bit, getting out of his space. With an audible swallow, he grabbed two papers off the desk and set them directly in front of me with a pen. "Here's your waivers." His words were rushed now, small.

As they fucking should be.

The bathroom door opened, and Brandy approached me from the side. My gaze drifted down to the pants that cinched at her waist and flowed to a more baggy state around her lower thighs and calves. Her curves were almost more attractive under them than with the shorts.

Forcing my attention away before she could catch me gawking, I picked up the pen and signed the form. As she stopped a good foot from me, I held the pen out to her. She took it. "Gotta sign this," I said, sliding the paper toward her.

As her eyes trailed down the tiny print, Ethan cleared his throat and said, "Thirty minutes is standard, but if you do an hour, you get more items to break. Half an hour is thirty dollars per person, a full hour is sixty."

Pulling my wallet out of my back pocket, I tossed a hundred and a twenty in front of him. "We're going to need the hour."

Brandy slapped the pen down on the paper, and I turned to find her glaring at me. I simply smirked.

Once everything was signed and taken care of, Ethan showed us to the room we'd be stuck in together for the next hour. He kept his eyes downcast and didn't make a single comment about Brandy again. Once he left, I tossed my mallet to the ground and crossed my arms, leaning up against the wall.

Brandy held a baseball bat in a fist at her side. "What are you doing?"

"Watching," I answered.

"Oh, no." She took a few steps toward me, then bent over and grabbed my mallet. She held the wooden handle out to me. "I'm not doing this alone."

I lifted a shoulder. "You're the one that needs to get her rage out."

She moved closer, pressing the end to my chest. "Don't give yourself so much credit, Satan. You've got just as many anger issues, if not more."

I grabbed the handle, yanking on it to draw her even closer. Mere inches separated us now. "One would say it's warranted, given the circumstances."

To my surprise, she stepped up on her toes, pressing the mallet into my torso. "It's your fault they were given to you in the first place."

I lowered my head, feeling the tension radiating between us like a live circuit. This whole place was going to go up in flames in a matter of minutes. "What would you rather have happened, Brandy?"

She hesitated for a split second, but it was enough for me to catch.

"Huh? Let him have his way?" I asked, my tone hoarse now.

Her chest rose on a heavy inhale, like she could barely catch her breath over her hatred for me in this moment.

My other hand closed around hers still gripped around the mallet, and I pried her off finger by finger. "We've only got an hour, Little Devil." I nodded my chin behind her. "Get smashing."

As if on cue, the heavy metal music started blasting through the speakers mounted in the corners of the room. She stepped back and spun, landing her bat directly in the center of the TV that sat on the floor. The screen shattered, and she swung back, hitting it again. It split to pieces, littering the ground with shards of glass.

She went feral on the flat-screen, slamming the weapon over and over again into the screen. Then she moved to the glass bottles lining the table a few feet to the left and wiped them out in one swing.

She went full-on crazy, crashing into everything in sight. Within minutes, the floor was full of debris, but she kept on going, finding item after item to smash.

It almost made me fear that once the contents of the room were obliterated to pieces, she'd move on to targeting me, but then I remembered she'd be too bored without having someone to constantly fight with, so she'd spare me. That, and I had the keys to the truck. Though I wouldn't put it past her to pick my pockets and leave my cold body on the floor if it came down to it.

After a while, I tossed my mallet on the floor, the thud drowned out by the music and relentless smashing. When I brought her in here, I truly didn't think she'd take advantage of it, but now the floor was a complete, utter mess, and her psycho side was out to play.

The side of her I ached to get out just to see her light up like a match, her flame licking at anyone close enough to get burnt. Lucky for her, I was used to the heat. Craved it sometimes, actually.

Time passed as she moved around the room, hitting every available object, likely imagining it was me. Finally, she seemed satisfied enough to take a breath and tossed her bat to the ground. My mallet had landed sideways, and as soon as the bat hit the ground, it bounced, and the handle slapped across the head of mine, causing the end of the stick to ricochet up. The piece of plastic from the TV that was lying over the tool flew up, and I moved before I could think. My chest hit hers, and my hand came around the back of her head as I pressed her up against the wall, out of the way of the flying debris.

Her lips parted as her chest heaved with her rapid breathing. Tiny droplets of sweat rolled down the side of her face, down to her well-defined chin. Her cheeks held the slightest tinge of peach against her tan skin, the shade only making her hazel eyes pop more than they typically did.

My fingers moved on their own accord, weaving into the strands of her wavy hair as my other lay flat on the wall beside her. I barely heard it as the plastic piece hit the ground somewhere behind us, or as the bass of the music thrummed between the two of us. Rather, it was her pulsing heart beating against my chest and her panting breaths that my focus was caught on.

In a world of things I tried to avoid focusing on, she was never one of them. Not even when she made it clear day in and day out that she hated the very ground I walked on.

"Gotta be more careful," I grumbled.

"I don't need saving," she hissed, though her tone didn't hold its typical murder-like quality.

I dropped my hand from her hair but kept her boxed in. "As you've reminded me for years," I mumbled.

"Clearly seven hasn't been enough, so maybe another century will get the message through your thick head."

I cocked a brow.

Her jaw moved as she clenched it, and then she was pressing a palm to my chest and shoving me away. There was little effort behind the move, but I stepped back anyway, dropping my hand from the wall. Her shoulder barely brushed my chest as she turned and headed for the door.

"We still have twenty minutes," I called to her.

She didn't look back as she said, "I'm done." She opened the door with a little too much force, and it wasn't until she disappeared, letting it slam behind her, that I finally moved, following in her haste.

As I waited in the hallway for her to change, I could only hope that forty minutes of getting her aggression out on random pieces of trash was enough to save me on the drive home.

Even if it wasn't, though, I'd survive. I'd handled her wrath before—I could do it for one more car ride.

14

BRANDY

I didn't bother with the radio this time around. Instead, I sat with my temple pressed up against the window as some pop country song played in the background. The sun was setting, casting a pink haze over the mountain range that bordered the bustling city. We sat at a stand-still on the highway, having gone barely a mile in the last five minutes. I blamed Reed for us being in rush hour traffic by forcing us to do that little detour to the rage room.

I wasn't sure what came over me, but the second I had the go-ahead to absolutely obliterate whatever I could touch in that room, my body took over. I felt a little psycho afterward, which in turn made me feel ashamed for behaving like that. I shouldn't have resorted to letting myself break things. Letting my feelings rush out like that could be addicting, which was evidenced by my father. His rage room was in the form of my mother, his mallet traded for a hand.

That was why my emotions needed to stay bundled inside me. What if I became the monster he was? One hit of anything, and you could become addicted. It was that easy—that destructive.

The cluster of cars started to lighten up a bit in front of us, so Reed pressed on the gas, but as soon as we picked up speed, the front right side of the truck started wobbling.

I straightened, leaning forward like I could see what might be causing it out the window.

Reed let out a curse and turned on his blinker.

"What?" I asked.

He took the exit, getting us off the highway. "We've got a flat. Can you look up the closest tire shop? It might be able to make it there."

I stared at him, mentally shooting daggers into him because like the traffic, this was his fault, too. All because that stupid fucking rage room we just had to go to. "You don't have a spare?"

"No."

I could feel my jaw starting to tense up. "Why the fuck not?"

"They're aftermarket rims and tires," he replied, pulling to a stop at the light.

"Why the fuck wouldn't you get a spare in that size?"

He ran a hand down his face, letting out a sigh. "I was going to eventually. The tire shop, Brandy."

I pressed my lips together, then grabbed my phone from the cup holder beside me. I searched for the nearest shop and found one less than a half-mile away. "Turn right at the next light."

He did, following my directions until we pulled into the parking lot and both got out. Reed came around to the passenger side, took one glance at the flat, and turned for the doors. I glanced at the hours on the window before heading inside past him, seeing that they closed in one hour. Surely they wouldn't turn us away, and we'd be back on the road in no time.

I was that much closer to being free of him once more.

The man behind the desk looked up as we approached. "How can I help you folks?"

"Got a flat we were hoping you could help us with," Reed said as I crossed my arms.

"What size tire?" Gary, according to his name stitched into his button-up, asked.

"Thirty-three by twelves, on seventeens."

Gary typed loudly on the keyboard, presumably checking their inventory. As he took his sweet time on the computer, I walked over to a tire mounted on a glossy black rim and read the all-weather informational card like it was the most interesting piece of literature on the planet. The tiny lobby smelled like oil and sweat, and the concrete ground was littered with random stains and old pieces of gum, indicating this used to be a portion of the garage, but they'd walled it in to be a separate room.

"Doesn't look like we've got that size in," Gary said.

My head spun his way, nearly giving me whiplash and a neck kink, and I stomped back over. "Maybe your inventory is wrong."

Reed cleared his throat. "I think what she's trying to politely ask is if you could double check in the back."

Gary glanced my way, but I didn't back down as I stared at him impatiently.

"I can do that," Gary said, his words so damn slow and relaxed. My foot tapped the ground with the need for him to hurry the fuck up.

He stood from his metal stool and disappeared through a door into the garage. At my side, Reed's gaze moved down to my shoe as it tapped a quick beat.

"Nervous, Brandy?"

My eyes shot to him, narrowing. "No."

He just stared, not believing it for a second. I was more so antsy to find out if they had the damn tire or not, because if they didn't, we'd have to find another shop, and from the quick glance at my phone in the truck, they all said closed aside from this one. Which meant, if this place didn't have it, we'd have to wait until the others opened, and there was no way in hell I'd spend my night hanging out with Reed fucking Bronson.

The door opened, and Gary rounded the desk, plopping his ass back on the stool. "No luck."

I wasn't sure if I wanted to break down and cry or start walking my ass back to Bell Buckle immediately.

"Are there any other shops that might have that size we could go to?" Reed asked as my tapping became more insistent.

"There's one off Woodruff. They've usually got the odd sizes, but they don't open 'til eight in the morning."

I nearly slammed my head down on the counter, but I thought better of giving myself a head injury before I had to make a two-hundred-and-something mile trek on foot to get back home.

Reed tapped the counter. "Sounds good. Thanks, Gary."

Gary dipped his chin. "Not a problem. Good luck to ya both."

Reed headed for the doors, and I hurried to match his pace.

I stopped at the threshold. "Are we breaking into the other place?" I muttered as he held the door for me.

His eyes turned to slits as he set a hand on my shoulder blade to direct me out the door. "No."

I shrugged him off, spinning on him. "So we're walking home, then?"

"No," he replied again, stopping at the front of his truck on the sidewalk to pull out his phone.

I came up next to him, staring at the side of his face. "Flying?"

"No." His fingers moved, and then he dropped the phone to his side after locking the screen.

I followed his line of sight, only finding a half-dead tree standing by itself in the middle of a grass-filled center divide. I moved my gaze back to him. "Then what the fuck is the plan?"

"Sleep, fix the tire tomorrow, and get back on the road."

My mouth opened and shut like a goddamn fish out of water, because Reed Bronson was *not* suggesting we spend the night in even remotely the same vicinity.

"I ordered an Uber," he added.

My jaw dropped, and I wouldn't have even cared if a fly flew in. Let it cut off my airway and choke me to death. Anything was better than this.

Reed glanced my way, doing a double take before staring at me. "Just say it, Brandy. Say whatever smart fucking remark you want to make."

"Did you order two?" I asked.

"Why the fuck would I order two Ubers?"

"For one to take me to one side of the city, and you to the other."

He sighed, shaking his head. "It's one night."

I froze, remembering those three words all too clearly.

He must've realized it, too, because his usual hard demeanor shifted, and I almost hated the soft look that overcame him even more. "Brandy, I—"

"Let it go," I interrupted, turning back to face the road.

"Brandy."

"I said let it go," I gritted out.

Because those three words were the same excuse I used seven years ago when he ruined everything.

***

By the time I called the fourth hotel, I knew they had to be pranking us. There was no way every single hotel in this massive city was fully booked.

Reed emerged from the lobby doors, pocketing his cell. "She said there's some sporting event this weekend, as well as a concert tonight, so we're not going to have much luck."

The Uber had dropped us at the closest motel, but when they said they only had one queen available, I ran outside. Well, ran was an exaggeration. But I was half tempted to start hitchhiking before I'd tried a couple other places, to which they said they were all booked.

I clicked on the next place on my phone and hit the call button. Pressing it to my ear, I tapped my foot, crossing an arm under the one holding up my cell. It rang and rang, and after four minutes passed, I hung up. I gripped my phone hard, wishing like hell it would shatter, if only to distract me from the inevitable.

"The shop opens in eleven hours. I think you can get over yourself enough to handle being in the same room as me for that long," Reed said, eyeing my white-knuckled grip on the device.

I spun on him, stomping closer so we were chest to chest. "I don't even want to survive ten minutes with you, let alone eleven hours."

"There's no choice here, Brandy."

I stepped back, holding my phone up as I pulled up my contacts. "Maybe Callan will come—"

"And leave his pregnant girlfriend alone with Avery all night?"

I shot a glare at him. "I want to go home."

"So bad that you'd inconvenience my brother instead of being the bigger person and spending one damn night in a motel?"

My nostrils flared as I exhaled. "You're leaving out the fact that it's with you!"

He inched closer. "What are you scared of? Huh, Brandy? You think I'm going to take advantage of you? Have my fucking way with you?"

"No!" I shouted, having to hold my wince at the rise in my voice. I knew he'd never do that.

At this point, we were chest to chest again, and I was doing all I could to make myself taller.

"Then what is it?" He was keeping his cool, giving me all the opportunity to get space from him.

For some fucking reason, I didn't.

"I don't want to be around you, Reed! You're an insufferable asshole who thinks you get to call the shots on fucking everything! Well, news flash, Satan. You don't."

The vein in his cheek pulsed, indicating he was clenching his jaw tight. "You think me coming to your rescue is somehow calling the shots?"

"I don't need you to fucking rescue me! Not then, not now, not ever."

"Stop pretending like things don't affect you," he bit out.

"They don't."

He raised a brow, leaning so close I could smell that faint hint of hay and cinnamon on him. "That's a lie."

I squeezed my arms in between our bodies to cross them over my chest. "It's not."

"If it's true, then why do you still hate me?"

"Why do you care?"

His jaw ticked, and I could practically hear his teeth grinding together. "Because of all the things you may think, Brandy, I still have a fucking heart. Something you can't say for yourself."

My eyes turned to slits as the breeze blew a shorter piece of hair across my face. What he didn't know was I lost my heart the day the world showed me kindness didn't exist. Everything was false acts and pasted smiles until one day, their fake personas snapped, and the world as I knew it crumbled.

"Sleep on the curb if you so fucking please, but I'm going inside. Room twelve. The door will be unlocked until eleven." He didn't give me the chance to respond before striding past me. I didn't bother turning to see which way he went. Rather, my eyes scanned the lot for a discarded mattress or bed of cardboard boxes.

Anything would be better than sleeping next to Reed.

15

REED

I lay in bed staring at the dimly lit wall while I waited for Brandy to come inside. I was giving her thirty more minutes before I went out to drag her ass in here. I understood the need for space and the fact that Brandy needed an abundance of it, but sleeping in a trashy parking lot in the middle of a city was not an ideal way for her to spend the night. Aside from that, the fall temperatures dropped dramatically at night, and with her in those little shorts and loose tee, I knew she had to be getting cold.

The thought didn't sit well with me, but forcing Brandy to do much of anything was like pulling teeth. Once she set her mind on something, that was it. There was no changing it unless you wanted to deal with her wrath.

She wasn't always like this. We used to *actually* get along—that was, until I interrupted her night of poor decision-making. She'd been acting out because of her father, and I couldn't, in good mind, let her make bad choices simply because she was upset and didn't know how to properly get that out.

Everything with Brandy was extreme. My little sister blamed it on her being a Gemini, but I had the biggest feeling it was simply just because she was Brandy Rose. A girl who, despite her mother's love, was taught to bottle things inside and never let anyone see her weak side.

But what she didn't know was emotions didn't make people weak. Being vulnerable wasn't a bad thing. Although I held my walls up stronger than most, I could admit it wasn't the smartest way to live life. Fortunately for me, I didn't give a shit.

The door to the room opened, then snicked shut after Brandy slid inside. In the dim light coming from the crack in the bathroom door, I could see her faint silhouette stiffen, her body reluctant in her movements. I'd kept the light on for her arrival—one, so she could see, and two, because I knew she wouldn't like walking into a pitch black room.

One glance at the red digital clock on the nightstand had me holding back an eye roll. One minute after eleven. It was typical Brandy behavior to push my limits, so much so that I should have expected it.

She flicked on the main light, the brightness blinding me for a second despite the bulb flickering from the ceiling. "What are you doing?" she asked.

"What do you mean, *what am I doing*? I'm lying in bed," I replied.

She raised her brows in a *that's the problem* motion. "Shouldn't you be on the floor?"

I was conflicted on whether the sass in her tone was better than the silence I'd been stuck in before she walked in.

I sat up, the blanket falling to pool around my waist, exposing my bare chest. I didn't miss the way her eyes fought not to steal a glance. "You want me to sleep on the floor." My tone was flat, unamused.

Her lips rolled together before she said, "Better grab a pillow and get comfortable, Satan. It's the gentlemanly thing to do."

I settled back against the scratchy pillows. "Nah. I think I'm good."

Twin flames lit in her gaze, licking at my skin. "*Now* is the time you choose not to be a gentleman?"

My fingers folded around each other in my lap, resting atop the sheet. "Who said I was a gentleman?"

She did. And we both fucking knew it. She wanted to mock me for it when I tried to be nice to her? To set aside our differences and treat each other like human beings rather than punching bags? Then this was what happened.

"So your plan is to what? *Sleep* next to me?" she asked.

I flipped up the corner of the sheet, gesturing to the empty spot. "Are you scared, Brandy Rose?"

Those eyes turned to slits. "Not even the slightest."

I patted the mattress to piss her off a little more. I shouldn't poke the tiger before she was about to sleep beside me, but maybe I wanted those claws out, ready to strike.

With a quick flick of the switch, the room went dark, save for the sliver of light from the bathroom. A shoe was thrown to the ground, then another. Feet padded across the creaky floor and slowed right before the bed dipped beside me.

Brandy slipped under the covers, pulling them up to her chin and, of course, clean off of me. I got comfortable, lying with my back to her back, to which she inched away. When she readjusted for the sixth time with a sigh, I knew what was coming.

"If you weren't such a hard person, this wouldn't be so fucking uncomfortable," she muttered.

I reached behind me, grabbing hold of the edge of the sheet and pulling it over my body.

"I'm not hard, Brandy," I grumbled, my cheek plastered against the pillow. I shifted my head, trying to find a comfortable position with her constant movement.

"You were in the dressing room," she pointed out. I froze—her comment caught me off guard. But two could play at that game.

"Is that how you would prefer me?" I asked.

With an exaggerated groan, Brandy yet again yanked the blanket off of me. I waited for her comeback, but it never came.

Eventually, the sound of her breathing evened out. My body relaxed knowing she was finally resting, that mind of hers quiet for once.

Then I fell asleep beside the woman who never dropped her guard—not even for me.

16

BRANDY

SEVEN YEARS AGO

"Did you hear Bea made the cheerleading squad?" Madison asked before taking another swig of her beer.

We weren't supposed to be drinking—none of us were—we were all underage. But some guy's brother brought alcohol to the party, and it only got out of hand from there. I didn't give a shit, though. I wanted to drown in the buzz, not the thoughts that'd stuck around all day.

My father had been just as mad at my mother as when I left this morning, so the moment I walked through the door after coming back from the ranch, I snuck right back out. For all they knew, I was sleeping in my room like the perfect daughter he wanted me to be. My mother didn't care what I did so long as

I was safe—and I was. Drinking at seventeen wasn't the worst I could do. Kids at school did it all the time, so what was one night for me? Aside from the few times I'd snuck some liquor with Lettie, of course. Those occurrences didn't count.

"Yeah, and did you hear Stacia was trying to make out with Wyatt behind the bleachers while his brother watched Bea make the tryouts?" Lindsey asked.

The two had been gossiping back and forth all fucking night, and I was growing beyond bored. The only reason I was tolerating it was because it beat sitting at home listening to my parents argue.

"*Trying*?" Madison repeated.

Lindsey nodded like it was the sweetest fucking conversation to be had all night. "Yep. Guess Wyatt rejected her."

"Wyatt's been single for, like, ever," Madison commented.

"I know. I wonder what his type is. What do you think, Brandy?" Lindsey asked. The two of them turned their attention on me.

I blinked, trying to remember what she asked as my focus was on everyone around us chanting over keg stands and shouting over beer pong. "What?"

Lindsey paused with her cup at her lips, like she wasn't expecting to repeat it. "What do you think Wyatt's type is?"

My brows pulled together. "Um. I'm not sure?"

Madison laughed. "Well, whoever it is, it's not Stacia."

"He's here, you know," I told them.

Their gazes searched the room, trying to find Wyatt.

"Probably not the brightest idea to talk shit about the two of them while they're in the same room."

Lindsey rolled her eyes, trying to be discreet but failing miserably, as Madison turned back to the two of us.

I downed the rest of my beer as Lindsey pointed Stacia out in the corner with another group of girls. "Takes guts showing up here after *that*."

"Not really," I said blandly.

Both girls snapped their eyes to me.

I set my empty cup on the end table beside me, already wanting another. "It's just a rejected kiss. Not a big deal."

Lindsey pressed her lips into a thin line as Madison cleared her throat, then took a sip of her drink.

"Right," Madison mumbled.

"Well, I'm gonna get another drink," I said, not offering them a refill as I turned for the kitchen. I didn't think I wanted to come back to them anyway.

I grabbed an empty cup off the island and turned the handle on the tap of one of the kegs lying around. Once the plastic cup was filled to the brim, I twisted the knob to stop the flow. Right as the edge hit my lips, someone was calling my name. I took my sip, finding the guy who called for me.

"Come play," the guy shouted, waving his arm in the direction of the group he was sitting with. They sat in a circle on the living room floor, a bottle lying in the center of the six of them.

I guessed playing spin the bottle with a couple of teenagers was better than hearing Lindsey and Madison gossip for the rest of the night. I wanted to let loose and have fun, not sit around listening to petty high school drama.

Crossing the kitchen, I joined them in the living room. The guy made space, scooting closer to Derek on his right. I knew him from school, but not the one who called me over. Lettie and I liked to stick to ourselves, but being in the classes I was in, I knew a lot of the obnoxious, popular people. Lettie never cared to hear their drama, so she kept quiet in the halls, finding me in the library on our breaks. It was quite the opposite compared to her personality outside of school.

The guy held his hand out to me after I sat criss-cross next to him. "I'm Matt. Derek here told me your name."

I slipped my hand in his, shaking it. "Couldn't ask me yourself?"

Matt smiled. "Sassy, huh?"

"Just honest," I replied, dropping his hand.

I took a sip of my beer as Matt gestured to the glass bottle. "Wanna try your hand at luck?"

"Luck in spin the bottle?" I questioned.

He laughed, the others around him smiling. "Nah. Seven minutes in heaven."

"A kiss not do it for you, Matt?" I teased, feeling bold with the alcohol flowing through my system.

"From you? Nah." He leaned closer, looking over my shoulder as he murmured in my ear, "I think I'd like a taste of something else."

I felt my cheeks heat as he turned back to the game, acting as if he hadn't just whispered dirty things to me.

"Who wants to start?" he announced.

"I'll go," Derek said, reaching for the bottle. With a hard spin, it eventually landed on Erin across the circle. With the cock of a brow, Derek was getting up with her and heading up the stairs to one of the rooms.

With five of us remaining, Matt went next. We watched as it spun, but right when it began to slow and it was clear it would land on someone across the circle, he grabbed it, aiming it at me.

"Looks like it's our turn," he said with a smirk.

I rolled my eyes, taking a long sip of my beer before getting to my feet. I wobbled slightly, blinking to clear my spinning vision before following him to the stairs. He held a hand out for me, and I took it, letting him lead me to the second story. I was thankful for his steady presence as the alcohol hindered my balance on the way up.

"You ever play this before?" he asked.

"No," I replied as we turned a corner. He opened the door, letting me go inside first.

"It's fun. I promise."

I turned in time to see him lock the door. He glanced over his shoulder, finding me watching. "For your privacy," he explained.

I nodded, taking a couple steps back. The backs of my thighs hit the bed, and I stopped. "How old are you?"

"How old are you?" he questioned.

"I asked you first."

He approached me, stopping mere inches from where I stood. He set his hands on my cheeks, brushing my hair behind my ears. My tongue felt dry in my mouth, my feet heavy. "I asked you second."

I did my best to roll my eyes, but it only made me spin more. "Seventeen."

"Seventeen," he answered finally.

Okay, so at least he was my age.

His hands felt warm on my cheeks as his chest pressed into mine, and then I was lowering to the bed, my ass hitting the soft mattress.

His touch slid down my sides to the top of my jeans. "I'll make you feel good, okay?"

I managed a nod, but all I could do was watch as his fingers undid the button, then glided the zipper down. His eyes caught on the black lace panties I wore. "Looks like you knew what you wanted coming here tonight."

I didn't tell him I had no intention of hooking up with anyone, but a little bit of alcohol and daddy issues might do that to a girl.

"Are you a virgin?" he asked.

I shook my head, but he didn't bother looking up. I didn't think he cared, really. He pulled my pants off, along with my sneakers and socks, then got on his knees before me.

"You can lay back," he said, and when I didn't, he looked up at me, waiting.

I did as he said, letting my elbows hit the mattress so that I was still propped at an angle and able to see him. Well, what seemed to be two of him now.

He set his hands on my thighs. "Why don't you take that shirt off?"

I swallowed, my throat dry. "I'm okay like this."

A small sigh escaped him, like he was growing annoyed or something, but I brushed it off. His hands slid to my knees, pushing them apart. Downstairs, someone yelled, causing me to jump. Matt gave me a scolding look, pulling my legs apart again. "Just a party, baby. Don't be scared. I'll take care of you."

His smooth hands ran up the insides of my thighs, stopping at the hem of my underwear. Right before he began pulling them down, I sucked in a breath. "Wait."

A burst of air exited his nose. "What?"

Outside the room, something crashed into a wall, causing me to jump again.

"I told you to keep your legs open," he said, pulling them apart again. His fingers dug into my thighs.

I shoved up on my elbows, trying to sit straight but having to work for it through the spinning of my head. "Hold on. I—"

"Brandy!" a voice boomed from somewhere in the hall, and my gaze snapped to the door.

Matt shook his head. "Ignore them."

"Brandy, where the fuck are you?" the same voice shouted. Something crashed again, and then the wall vibrated as a body presumably hit it. "Where is she?"

"In there, man. Calm the fuck down," a guy said, his voice more high-pitched than the other.

Movement sounded on the other side of the door, and then the knob was wiggling. "Brandy, are you in there?"

My vision spun as I tried to focus on the door. "Reed?"

"He your boyfriend?" Matt asked.

I shook my head as I tried to figure out why he was here. "No."

"Open the door," Reed demanded from the other side.

I moved to stand, but Matt held me back with a hand on my stomach. "She'll be out in five minutes," he called out.

"Open this fucking door, Matt," Reed said, his words nearly a growl as the handle jiggled again.

"Five minutes," Matt repeated.

I grabbed his hand, shoving it away as I tried to stand again. "I want out."

Matt moved his hand to my waist, gripping it to keep me in place. "We're just playing a little game, Brandy. Come on. Don't be a baby."

"I'm not a baby. I want out," I repeated.

"Just five minutes," he said again.

But not a second later, the door was being ripped off its hinges as it flew into the room.

17

REED

Brandy had woken up before dawn, despite knowing the tire shop didn't open until eight. She'd barely spoken a word to me this morning, and not an hour after we got on the road, she'd fallen asleep in the passenger seat. I let her rest, preferring it over the bickering. I was tired, her presence all too apparent as we slept beside each other last night, making it nearly impossible to fall into a deep sleep.

All I wanted was to be home and away from her. I'd had enough Brandy to last a lifetime, but unfortunately, I only got a day break before I had to see her again.

A few quiet hours later, I pulled up to her house and put the truck in park. I looked over at her, her chest rising and falling with her even breaths as the side of her forehead rested on the window. Giving myself a minute before I woke her, I turned my focus on her house and the rose bushes lining the yard.

I thought Brandy and I might have been making progress on this trip, but one line, and I ruined everything. So much like that night that clearly still haunted her. How she could blame me for the whole thing was beyond me. I was the only good in her life that day, and this was what I got in return. Seven years of bullshit.

To my right, Brandy stirred, pulling my attention to her. Her eyes fluttered as they opened, and she straightened in the seat when she realized the truck was parked.

"We're here," I said, interrupting the silence.

Without a word, she unbuckled and got out, grabbing her bag from the back. She closed both doors to the truck, and I watched as she walked to her door, unlocked it, and went inside. With a shake of my head, I shifted into drive and headed toward my parents' ranch. Bailey had texted me earlier to let me know he'd be there all day, so I could leave the tux with him and head home.

I pulled up to the ranch, put the truck in park, and pulled the key from the ignition before getting out. Bailey approached the vehicle, a big grin pasted on his smug face.

"How was the trip?" Bailey asked, stopping beside me.

I opened the rear driver door. "How do you think?"

"I know the feeling. I was once forced to go on a trip with someone's little sister who wasn't quite fond of me at the time, too," he said, setting a hand on the door.

I shook my head, pulling the tux out of the back by the hanger. "There's a difference. Lettie didn't want you dead."

Bailey shrugged. "She probably did. Just didn't get around to it after—"

I shoved the garment bag at his chest. "I'm gonna cut you off right there."

His grin only widened, but movement in my peripheral drew my attention away as he grabbed the hanger from me. Beckham crossed the driveway, a thermos in his hand, despite the seventy-degree day.

"Surprised he's out of the house," I muttered.

Bailey turned to find Beckham getting in his truck. "He's just adjusting to home life again, is all. This is good for him."

I shut the rear door, leaning a shoulder up against it. "Shaving that five o'clock shadow would be good for him."

Bailey's brows shot up. "You're grumpier than usual."

"Two days with your fiancé's best friend, and you expect me not to be?"

"Good point."

"You excited for the wedding?" I asked.

His brows raised higher. "Did you just use the word 'excited'?"

I rolled my lips together, giving him a blank stare.

"Hell yeah, I'm fucking excited," he continued, turning to look out at the ranch. "Feels like I've been waiting forever for this."

I crossed my arms, following his line of sight. "Probably because you have."

He looked over at me, leaning back against my truck. "You're gonna be on your best behavior, right?"

I gave him a sidelong glance before turning my attention back to the horses in the pasture. "It's not me you have to worry about."

His silence made me do a double take.

"I wouldn't ruin your wedding, Cooper," I said.

"Mhmm. I'll believe it when I see it."

"Just no more wedding errands, or I'll make it a personal goal to sabotage the ceremony."

He placed a dramatic hand to his heart. "Holy shit. I think Reed Bronson just teased me? Are these butterflies I'm feeling? Are you *flirting* with me?"

I rolled my eyes with a shake of my head. "You're fucking ridiculous."

"Is that a smile I see?" he asked, leaning into my space with his focus glued to my mouth.

I shoved at his shoulder. "Don't you have work to do, asshole?"

He pushed off the truck, grabbing his gloves from the back pocket of his jeans. "Yep." He took a few steps in the direction of the barn before turning around, walking backwards. "Make sure to floss."

"Why?"

"Because I don't want your breath stinkin' when I kiss you at the altar."

At the gate to the pasture, my dad's head popped up. "The fuck did you just say, Cooper?"

Bailey turned his gleaming grin on his soon-to-be father-in-law. "I'm marrying your offspring, Trav."

"Wrong fucking one," my dad grumbled.

Bailey shrugged. "I ain't picky." He shot me a wink before turning and disappearing into the barn.

I found my dad's scowl and couldn't help the twitch of my lips.

Poor guy was always getting the ring around 'round here. I knew exactly how he felt.

18

BRANDY

I had just made it out the door and was about to send my foot through the dash on my Bronco in a fit of rage when my phone started blowing up with texts. It was a cold morning, and the battery was probably having a hard time, but today was not the day I wanted to deal with this.

Plucking my phone from the cupholder, I read through the texts.

> **Lettie**
> Guys I'm so nervous

BITE THE BULLET

Oakley
Why??

Sage
Don't be nervous!! Love is such a rare thing, and I'm so happy you found it with Bailey

Oakley
What she said! You guys are soo cute together

Lettie
not about that. About this aquarium I'm bringing home

Sage
A what?!

Oakley
Oh no

Sage
How are you expecting to sneak a fish tank into the house?

Lettie
Can you guys help?

Can't. Hanging with my mom today

> **Oakley**
> I can be there in ten? Call your brother and say it's an emergency

> **Lettie**
> Bring fish food

> **Sage**
> Avery says she wants to come see the fish

> **Lettie**
> It's a party. bring wine

> **Oakley**
> Lettie she's pregnant

> **Lettie**
> I didn't say it was for her. I'm going to need it once Bailey sees this tank. it's huge

> **Oakley**
> Why'd you buy it then??

> **Lettie**
> It was on sale

I nearly burst out laughing at her response as I set my phone down. I tried one more time to start the car, and finally, it purred to life.

"Oh, thank fuck." I did *not* need to be getting rides from anyone anymore. I wanted to be the one behind the wheel, in control, in my own vehicle.

I headed down the road to visit with my mom for a bit after having been gone for nearly two days. Ranting to her about the trip would do me good, and hopefully cool me down before the wedding tomorrow, where I'd unfortunately have to see Reed again. As if that wasn't bad enough, I'd have to act cordial with him and pretend like I didn't want to rip his head from his body.

Okay, that was a bit dramatic, but after little sleep the past couple nights and all my vehicle problems, all my rage was centered on that man and his asshole-ness.

I pulled up outside my mom's house, the parking spot I usually took in the driveway filled by some fancy red SUV. After turning off the car, I got out and aimed for the door, glancing at the unfamiliar vehicle again to see if I recognized it at all. Nothing came to mind, so I ignored it, settling on waiting for my mom to explain who it belonged to.

I used my key to unlock her door, going inside and closing it behind me. "Mom?"

"In here," she called back from the kitchen.

I headed past the small living room to the kitchen. The dining room was attached to it with a narrow walkway to the back sliding door. As soon as I reached the linoleum floor, I froze.

My dad was sitting in a chair at the table, a leg swung over his knee as if this was just another Tuesday visit.

The corners of his lips lifted at the sight of me, like he knew his presence here grated my every fucking nerve. "Hi, Brandy."

"Mom" was all I said as way of asking what the *fuck* was going on. He hadn't been here in years, and now he showed up out of the blue? Did she even know he was coming? She would've told me if she did.

"Your father stopped by for a visit," she explained, and I turned to find her at the stove, tending to two pots. "Hungry?"

"Your mother and I were about to have lunch. Alone." His voice echoed in my mind like the ghost he was supposed to remain, yet he sat not five feet from me.

"She can stay if she's hungry," my mom said, her voice a bit softer than before.

"It's fine, Mom." I didn't want to sit around the table and play happy fucking family with him anyway. "I was just stopping by."

Her brows pulled together, a concerned look filling her eyes. "Is everything okay?"

"Yep. I'll talk to you later," I said, turning to leave.

"Now, hold on a second," my dad said, setting both feet flat on the ground but keeping his ass planted in the chair. "You see your father after, what, four years, and I don't get a hug?"

He acted like his leaving was some light thing. As if he hadn't abandoned my mom multiple times. Plus, I knew he didn't want a hug from me. He only wanted to get under my skin more than he already was, to press my buttons and see how far he could push me.

My lips rolled together as I stared at a speck of dirt on the ground, trying to keep my composure. "No."

Even without looking, I knew his brows shot up his forehead at the disrespect. "I am your father—"

"Fathers raise their children. They respect their wives." I looked at him now, practically seeing the rage pouring off him in puffs of smoke. "You don't get to touch me. And if I find out you've put a hand on my mom—"

"Brandy." My mom tried to interrupt, but it was my dad standing from his chair that shut me up. He was tall, easily trumping me and my mom by over a foot in height.

"I didn't raise you to be disrespectful and talk back," he snapped, taking a step toward me. But before he could get any closer, I turned on my heel and was storming out the door.

His anger hadn't changed one bit since he'd been gone, and I fucking hated that sometimes, I felt it, too. Maybe not as strong, never enough to hit someone, but the fear was always there. What if those same tendencies passed down to me? Would a relationship ever work if they had? Would I accidentally do the things he did to us one day and not be able to control it?

Questions and fear spun together like a tornado in my mind as I let the front door slam behind me. In seconds, I was pulling away from the curb in my Bronco and speeding down the road toward my house.

My hands were slick on the steering wheel, but I chalked it up to the gray clouds covering the sky. Rain was in the forecast today, but thankfully not for Lettie's wedding tomorrow. It was fitting, actually. A brewing storm on the day I found out my dad was back in town, and sunshine for the day I got to celebrate my best friend. The one who deserved anything and everything. To be happy for the rest of her life, with the love of her life.

Would I ever get the same?

But as I passed my house, driving just to fucking drive with no destination in mind, I got the feeling I never would.

Sometimes good things simply didn't happen to people like me.

I had come to accept that.

19

BRANDY

As soon as I pulled up to the ranch the next day, emotion clogged my throat. Oakley and Charlotte had done so well decorating the red barn to make it everything Lettie had dreamed of. She wanted to recite their vows in the barn she and Bailey refurbished shortly after Lettie returned from Boise last year.

White streamers hung from the rafters, and the large double doors were open wide to showcase the setup. Strings of lights weaved with the streamers, hanging low above the chairs lining the aisle. They had moved the family horses into the stalls for tonight specifically. Avery, who was also the flower girl for the wedding, had brought up that they should be able to watch, too, and Lettie agreed, so Bailey followed through on the request.

"You gonna keep gawking or come inside to get ready?" Lettie called from the porch as Rouge, her and Bailey's Australian Shepherd, came darting out to greet me. After a quick pet, he ran off toward the barn, disappearing from sight.

I adjusted the bag in my hand so I could turn away and wipe underneath my eyes just in case a tear had slipped free.

"Are you crying?" she asked in disbelief.

"No," I said with a sniffle, crossing the driveway to meet her on the porch. She was already wearing her white "bride" robe, and by the looks of it, she had mine in her hands. "Just got some dust in my eyes."

Lettie walked beside me as we headed inside her parents' house. "My mom spent all night cleaning that barn top to bottom, so I know that's a lie."

"There's still dirt on the ground, you know." I looked around at the setup they'd put together in the living room—a giant mirror with little stations to do our makeup at. There was water, champagne, whiskey, and a delicious looking charcuterie board on the coffee table.

Lettie led me down the hall rather than to the living room. "You make a valid point."

The way her words dropped off indicated she wished I'd continue. Tell her I was crying over my best friend getting married tonight. To her brother's best friend, of all people.

But I wasn't sure if I was emotional over today in general, or everything all at once. I still hadn't recovered from the trip to Utah, given my one day to do so involved finding out my father was back after disappearing for years. Now my mind was just a complicated mess of thoughts, the pressure getting to be too much, like a soda being shaken up with the cap still on.

But I wouldn't blow. *Especially* not today.

Today was for Lettie and Bailey, for love and happiness and big feelings.

"What's wrong?" Lettie asked, stopping me in the hallway outside her old room.

I tried my best to look confused. "Why would something be wrong?"

She frowned. "You're my best friend. I can tell when something is up."

I shrugged. "Where's Sage and Oakley?"

"In the backyard spraying glitter in Avery's hair." She pinned me with her eyes. "Now talk."

"It's your wedding day—"

"And you're my best friend. *Nothing* comes before us."

I chewed on my bottom lip, hating that she used the best friend card on me. "Lettie—"

Her glare only intensified. "If I have to pry it out of you, I'm going to be real upset."

"My dad is in town."

Instantly, her face softened, then contorted in confusion. "I'm sorry. What?"

I nodded.

"For how long?" she asked.

I glanced down the hallway to be sure no one was coming. "I'm not sure. I didn't really say much to him."

"You *saw* him?"

I nodded again, pasting on a smile this time, though it was clearly fake. "In the flesh."

"Did he say anything to you?" Her underlying question of *if he touched me* hung in the air, not needing to be spoken aloud. I hadn't told her when it first started happening as a kid, but over the years, I confided in her. We didn't talk about it much, but her knowing brought a small comfort.

I shook my head in silent response, then said, "Just the same old bullshit I'm used to." I set my hands on her shoulders, gripping her gently. "I'm fine, Lettie. I promise. But seriously, the last thing I want to do on your wedding day is talk about my dad. Let's get fucking wasted and have the best day."

The corners of her mouth inched up the slightest, proving I did my job of deflecting well. "We can get wasted after the vows. I want to remember that, at least."

"Oh, I'm sure after tonight, you'll remember all of it, regardless of how drunk we get."

"Brandy will forget after one glass of champagne. We all know it," Oakley teased, coming around the corner at the end of the hallway.

My smile lit up as Sage popped up behind her, Avery with her glittering hair on her heels. They each wore their own "bridesmaid" robes, while Avery wore one that said "flower girl" in the top right.

Avery ran in my direction, throwing herself at me. I caught her under the armpits, lifting her above my head before plopping her back on the ground. After Callan and Sage got pregnant and started hanging around the house more, Avery had become my mini best friend, always wanting to help with the horses I was working with. She never failed to come up with the best ideas for desensitizing the more skittish ones.

"I'm the flower girl!" Avery reminded me for the hundredth time.

"I see that. I like the added touch of sparkles, too. Never seen another flower girl with that," I said, looking down at her.

"Really?" she asked.

I nodded. "Make sure to take lots of pictures today so all of this goes down in history, alright?"

"History?" she questioned. "Like, old stuff?"

Behind her, Sage laughed with a hand on her belly.

Oakley pressed her lips together to hide her smile as Lettie said, "Great. Me getting married means I'm old."

I gave her the side eye. "Please don't get all emotional now."

"Better now than after her makeup is done," Sage said. She had a point.

"I won't," Lettie declared a little too confidently.

Oakley cocked a brow at her. "Oh, really? No, *am I making a mistake* sob sessions?"

Lettie shrugged. "I avoided him for so long and he never gave up. I don't think me saying yes to him could ever be considered a mistake."

"True," I agreed. "He really is a lost puppy around you."

"A puppy?" Avery piped in.

"Oh, no," Oakley muttered. "You did it now."

"Not an actual puppy," Sage told her.

"Speaking of, how'd that fish tank fiasco go?" I asked.

"A little love goes a long way, if you know what I mean," Lettie answered with a wink.

Oakley let out a snort, shaking her head.

Bailey was down bad for my best friend. So much so that he'd let her keep her horse inside if she really wanted to.

"Are there going to be puppies today?" Avery asked, jumping back to the puppy situation with so much hope in her tiny voice.

Sage gave me a *did you have to say that word* look. I nearly laughed. The last thing she needed with a baby on the way was another pet. Callan had already gotten Avery her dream animal, and while that was going well in itself, they certainly didn't need more on their plate at the moment.

I set a hand on Lettie's arm. "Come on, ladies. Let's go get ready to watch Lettie and Bailey kiss."

"As if we don't see that every day," Oakley muttered as we headed down the hall toward the living room.

"They're going to kiss?" Avery questioned.

Sage sent another glance in my direction. I really needed to stop bringing shit up in front of the kid. Soon, she'd know all about the birds and the bees. Then Callan would have a real problem on his hands.

Charlotte joined us to get ready in the living room as we all shared stories about Lettie's years-long avoidance of Bailey, and for those couple hours of laughing, snacking, and drinking, I almost forgot about all the bad things.

Almost.

20

REED

The chairs were full, and I guessed someone had counted wrong, because a few stood at the back, watching as Lettie and Bailey recited their vows in front of family and friends. It wasn't a Bronson event unless at least one thing wasn't going to plan—even our family's horse rescue had had its ups and downs over the years. But tonight, everything was perfect for the two of them, and I was sure Lettie wouldn't want things any other way.

I stood off to the side as Bailey held Lettie's hands while he spoke, but I wasn't really listening to what he was saying. Not when Brandy was standing on the other side of Lettie, biting the inside of her cheek like it'd wronged her somehow.

My eyes narrowed on her, ignoring the awes and sniffles from the crowd as my gaze fell to her finger tapping an uneven beat on the inside of her wrist where her arms were draped in front of her. As if she felt me staring, she turned her attention to me. I raised my brow in question, but all she did was scowl in response.

She kept the look discreet enough that the guests wouldn't realize. I rolled my lips together, rubbing the inside of my wrist to pull her attention there. Her eyes fell, watching as I did it, her own fingers stopping their incessant tapping. She glared, but the look didn't hold its usual murderous affect with her hair curled in loose spirals, falling down the open back of her dress with the two front strands of hair held together at the base of her skull. Even I couldn't deny she looked beautiful tonight. The soft pink dress she wore complimented her suntanned skin, and the satin fabric hugged every curve on her body.

I shifted my stance, my hands held together in front of me. I blinked, shaking my head to pull my focus away from her. Then, the crowd was clapping, and I turned to find Bailey and Lettie kissing. Brandy was clapping, too, tears pooled in her eyes as she watched them become husband and wife.

I wondered if Brandy dreamt of a life like that. With a husband, some kids, and a few pets. She didn't seem like the type of girl, but I didn't really *know* Brandy aside from what I'd gleaned over the years of overhearing Lettie and her talk. Other than that, I knew her in the now. Not what she wanted ten years from now, but in this present moment. Like how, when my eyes fell to the flowers gripped in her hand, they caught on the raised fabric at her breasts, right where her nipples were.

I blinked a few times, surely seeing things. My hand came up to rub my eye, but no. There was something there.

Then I nearly choked.

Did she have *nipple piercings*?

I quickly turned away, finding Beckham on my other side. He was already buzzed, his words slurring as he said something to Lennon while Lettie and Bailey headed down the aisle. But I couldn't make out any of what anyone was saying. Not with what I just fucking saw.

Brandy's form shuffled down the aisle as others crowded around her, everyone heading outside to the reception. I had no choice but to follow, trying my best to think of every nasty thing on this planet to keep my mind off—

No, Reed.

You're not thinking of her fucking breasts.

***

"About how long until you think he causes a scene?" Wyatt asked where he stood beside me, nursing his one and only beer for the night. He lifted the top in Beckham's direction, where he was attempting to make small talk with some girl our cousin brought. From where we watched, it was clear he was miserably failing, not seeming like he was into the conversation at all. She, on the other hand, was yapping his ear off.

"You think he will?" I asked, my shoulder pressed against the bark of the tree I'd been leaning on for the last thirty minutes. Rouge was passed out at Wyatt's feet. The poor dog had stolen one too many pieces of cake off various plates, effectively putting him into a food coma.

The sun had disappeared completely, the only light coming from the fairy lights hung from the branches above the field. People danced and laughed, most of them feeling the effects of the alcohol from the open bar. I'd grabbed a whiskey, only in an attempt to numb the thoughts I couldn't fucking keep at bay. Images of Brandy flashed in my mind—images I should most definitely not be thinking of when it came to her.

Like how her mouth might pop open as I played with those piercings. Or if she was pierced anywhere else. How she might look above me, tugging on the jewelry as she rode me.

I wanted to fucking throw up.

Brandy Rose was the only person on this planet I'd likely never sleep with, but knowing what was under that dress?

I needed to snap the fuck out of whatever stupor this was. She wasn't a drug—she was fucking poison. I wouldn't simply get lost in her if that ever were to happen, I'd likely be ruined for the remainder of my life.

"You don't?" Wyatt asked, taking a small sip from his longneck.

I watched as Brandy left Oakley to get a refill of her champagne, which was likely a mistake. She'd already had three, and it was no secret she was a lightweight.

I shrugged. "I don't know what he'll do recently, if I'm being honest."

The champagne splashed over the side of Brandy's glass as she attempted to pour it, laughing to herself as it got on her fingers clutching the glass.

Wyatt loosed a breath. "You just gonna gawk all night or actually talk to her?"

"She doesn't want to talk."

"How do you know that?"

I lowered my brows, glancing at him. "Do you know her?"

"Maybe she'll be different with a few drinks in her," he said, as if that was really possible.

I shook my head before taking a long swig of my whiskey. "Only gets worse when she's drinking."

"It's all in the approach," Wyatt added.

"What are you, the fucking love doctor?"

"Do I need to be?"

"Wyatt, respectfully, if I'm going to take advice from anyone, it'd probably be the guy that just got married, not the single mechanic that hasn't been on a date in years."

"I've been on dates," he defended.

"My statement still stands."

Brandy grabbed a napkin off the table, attempting to wipe the side of her champagne flute, but all she succeeded in doing was spilling more as the glass tipped sideways.

"Fucking hell," I muttered before shoving off the tree, abandoning Wyatt to storm over to her. I grabbed the glass from her, setting it on the table. "You're a mess, Brandy."

"Wow, you're so charming," she slurred, shoving the napkin in between her fingers to wipe the lingering alcohol away.

Her words fell...flat. There was no death threat, no insinuation of plotting my murder. That wouldn't do. "What's wrong with you?"

Her eyes found mine, an ocean of muddled thoughts swimming in her hazel depths. "You really have a way with words. Has a girl ever told you that?"

My jaw clenched. "Why are you upset?"

Something akin to fear flashed across her face, but it was gone in a blink. "I'm not upset."

"You wanna quit trying to lie while you're drunk?"

"I'm not drunk either." But the way her words stumbled into each other told me otherwise. She tossed the napkin in the trash bin beside the table, sending me a closed-lip smile. "I'm gonna go back to dancing now."

She turned to leave.

"What about your drink?" I asked.

She stopped to spin on her high heel, but the act sent her stumbling sideways. I quickly stepped forward and shot a hand out, grabbing her upper arm to steady her. She blinked a few times, her forehead creasing as she stared at my chest. She snapped out of whatever stupor she was caught in, pulling her arm from my grasp easily—not that I'd been holding tight to begin with. Plucking the champagne glass from the table, she raised it in my direction, then headed back to the group she'd been with before.

I stood there, watching like a fucking idiot as she gulped her champagne. All the while, her eyes held mine, heat blazing in them. My hands flexed at my sides as her throat moved, my focus caught on the movement, forcing myself not to let my gaze travel further south.

Once she'd taken her sip, she lowered the glass to her side, holding it by the top. Like an idea struck her, a smirk lifted the side of her lips. She took one quick glance at the man standing in front of her, who was lost in conversation with another one of my cousins.

Her hand rested on his shoulder, causing him to look down at her. With his attention now on her, she reached up to pluck his hat from his head, then proceeded to set it on her own.

My teeth practically shattered as they ground together at the sight of her in his cowboy hat. She was trying to rile me up, doing her best to get a reaction out of me because she was drunk, and she was fucking succeeding.

Before I could stop myself, I beelined for her, tunnel vision taking over as every fucking sense in my body homed in on her in that thin bridesmaid dress wearing another man's hat.

Her smirk only grew as I approached, and the moment I reached her, I was grabbing the hat and shoving it at the guy's chest. I didn't give a fuck who he was—Brandy didn't get to wear his hat.

Not giving a shit if he grabbed it from me, I let go, taking her wrist in my hand. I pulled her away from the mass of people, hoping we didn't make a scene but also not caring if we did.

Brandy's laugh echoed behind me as she hurried to match my pace.

"What's wrong, Reed? Are you jealous?"

As soon as the word passed her lips, I spun on her, yanking her wrist with barely any effort so that her chest collided with mine. "I don't get jealous, Brandy."

The effects of the alcohol made her eyes glossy, which in turn made the lights reflect right off them like the stars in the night sky. *Fuck*, seeing her like this wasn't good. Not when I knew for a damn fact she was nothing but repulsed by me—only using me as her fucking play toy because she was bored.

"Tell me what the fuck is wrong," I demanded.

She pouted out her bottom lip. "I'm having fun."

I drew her closer, so close that her breath coasted off my cheeks. "You think wearing some random guy's hat is fun, Brandy?"

She nodded.

"You think him sleeping with you would be fun?"

She shrugged. "Probably."

"No. It wouldn't be. Because you'd lie there bored like you always are while he got off on you, and then you'd leave unsatisfied."

Her lips pressed into a thin line, all traces of her smirk now gone.

"You want to know how I know that?"

Somehow, those lips pursed tighter as she gave no response.

"Because you like when a guy handles you like a fucking slut. Not like some precious little gem he found and wants to cherish."

Her cheeks tinged pink as her eyes darted between mine.

"Because I bet, if I felt under this dress of yours right now, you'd be fucking soaked. All because of your little act, trying to get a rise out of me." My nose nearly brushed hers as I lowered my voice. "That's what you like, isn't it? When I react to the shit you do?"

"Shut up," she muttered, but her words were soft. *I* wanted her fucking mad. I wanted to see her react, and maybe that was fucking toxic, but I didn't give a shit.

"Tell me what's wrong," I demanded, each word clipped.

"Wouldn't you like to know?" she questioned, her tone taking on that playful lilt I liked to hear.

"You're drunk."

A gasp escaped her bee-stung lips, dramatically so. "You're so smart."

My fingers flexed on her wrist. "Tell me what's upsetting you."

Her eyes narrowed the slightest. "You've never cared before, Reed, so don't start caring now." She pulled back an inch. "It'll ruin your reputation of being an incurable asshole."

She yanked free of my grasp, then headed back toward the party, leaving me standing there like a fucking possessive idiot.

21

REED

SEVEN YEARS AGO

The door splintered off its hinges as I kicked it in, not wasting a single second after Brandy's muffled voice carried through the door. Her words had ignited a wrath in me I'd never felt before, my vision tunneling as only one goal roared in my head: get her out.

As soon as the door hit the floor, my eyes flew to Brandy, where she sat curled up in a ball on the bed. Her pants were off, her legs shaking with her arms wrapped tightly around herself. I wanted to relight the match she kept lit deep inside her, hating how scared she looked in this moment. Like all she wanted to do was fold in on herself because of him.

My eyes snapped to Matt. "You think taking advantage of underage girls is fun, now?"

I knew the guy from high school. He was always such a fucking prick, and even more so now by the looks of it. It hadn't taken long for one of the other idiots downstairs to fess up where Brandy was and who was with her.

"We're just having fun, man," Matt defended.

My fingers flexed as they curled into fists, my boots stomping across the plush carpet. Matt backed himself into a corner as I approached with every intent to crush the fucking life out of him. "You have fun with someone who fucking consents, not a drunk seventeen-year-old girl."

One look at Brandy, and I knew she'd had too much to drink, which only pissed me off more because if I could see it in one glance, I damn well knew Matt was well the fuck aware.

Matt's back hit the wall with a thud. "She wanted to."

I swung a hand in Brandy's direction, keeping my eyes on him. "That look like she fucking wants to?"

"She didn't say no," Matt said.

All I saw was fucking red. Her asking to be let out was her saying no. Her shaking on the bed was her saying no. Her having more than two drinks in her system was her saying *no*. Her being underage was her *fucking saying no*.

My fist connected with his jaw, and his head snapped to the side as a crunch filled the room. The force of it sent a flurry of pain through my fingers, and I shook my hand out, not satisfied with just one hit. "She said she wanted out."

Matt's hand lifted to touch the blood pooling on his lower lip as he turned his head. "Fuck, man. Not out of the room. Out of her shirt, finally."

I rolled my lips together a moment before sending another punch to his nose. Another crack rent the air, and he groaned. Another hit. Another crunch. More and more until I couldn't fucking stop. He wasn't going to stop with her, so why should I? Why give him the benefit of the fucking doubt when what he wanted to do to her was ten times worse than what a punch could do? The physical healed, but not the fucking mental. If he had gone one step further, it would've stuck with her for life, yet he thought it was simply a moment in time. One opportunity to get off, while she lived with the memories forever.

He deserved to fucking die. To bleed out and succumb to his injuries.

I kept going. Even when he slumped against the wall, even when his eyes became so swollen he wouldn't be able to open them. I. Kept. Going.

As soon as I'd come upstairs, everyone had fled the hall, retreating to empty rooms or down the stairs, so when I finally stopped throwing fist after fist, when Matt slid down the wall, groaning from the pain, I knelt before him and made my next words real fucking clear.

"You say a word of this to anyone or even *think* about touching Brandy again, and you'll fucking regret it."

Behind me, Brandy's whispered words pulled me from my tunnel vision. "Please. Please, stop."

I looked over my shoulder to find her rocking back and forth, her hands covering her ears as tears streamed down her cheeks. I didn't give Matt another glance as I stood and crossed the room to her.

I wrapped my fingers around her wrists, causing a yelp to escape her lips.

"Brandy, look at me." I lowered myself so we were eye level. She had hers squeezed shut, tears slipping from her eyelids. "You're safe. I'm here."

Slowly, she opened them, finding me immediately. Her hands shook as she removed them from either side of her head.

"We need to go," I said, regaining my composure and doing my best to lighten my tone.

"Go?" she questioned.

I nodded, turning to search the ground for her pants. I let go of her wrists, bending over to retrieve them from the ground as well as her shoes and socks.

"I'm taking you home."

I twisted, finding her staring directly at Matt's slumped form in the corner. Instantly, her breathing quickened, and I moved, blocking her sight of him. "Don't look at him. Look at me."

She blinked, angling her head back to look up at me.

"Now, Brandy."

She immediately began moving, nearly tipping over as she stood. My hand shot out, grabbing her upper arm to steady her. Her eyes fell to my skin, finding my knuckles bruised and covered in blood.

"I-is he dead?" she asked, her words barely a whisper.

"No," I answered, hoping it was the truth, despite a small part of me wishing it wasn't.

I led her out of the room, but once we made it down the hall to the top of the stairs, I stopped her. I didn't want her going down there in her shirt and underwear and to have them all see, guessing what happened up here.

"Lift your leg," I commanded, dropping her shoes and socks to the ground before fumbling with her jeans until I had the top opened wide.

She attempted to listen, but then she careened sideways. I dropped her pants before she could fall down the stairs, righting her. An impatient sigh escaped me, but I immediately felt bad as shame filled her features. This wasn't her fault, as much as she might believe it was.

"Arms up," I ordered instead, forgetting the jeans on the ground and lifting my shirt over my head.

Once it was off, I found Brandy standing there with her arms elevated. I situated the shirt over her, the hem falling to her mid-thigh, covering her far more than her own top. Quickly grabbing her clothes, I wrapped an arm around her waist to help her down the stairs.

"Anyone says anything to you, you ignore them," I muttered to her as we reached the bottom.

"Please don't kill anyone else tonight," she whispered, keeping her eyes downcast as we walked through the living room.

I ignored the watchful eyes, keeping my focus trained on the front door.

"I didn't kill him," I whispered back.

She didn't say anything else as we exited the house, but as soon as we were outside and the cold air hit our warm skin, she was bending over, heaving.

I tried to straighten her with my arm around her waist. "Don't you dare vomit, Brandy Rose."

She let me guide her to my truck, reaching it without any stomach remnants making an appearance. She had a hand on her belly, taking slow, even breaths to likely calm the bile that threatened to rise.

"How much did you drink?" I asked as we approached the passenger side.

"A few."

I opened the door, dropping my arm from around her. "How much is a few?"

"I think there's two of you," she slurred.

I frowned in response.

Once she caught sight of it, she said, "I lost track, okay? A lot, probably."

My frown only deepened as I gestured to the seat for her to get in.

As she climbed into the truck, she kept a hand on the bottom of my shirt she wore, making sure it kept her covered. Once she was seated, she reached for the seat belt, but her fingers fumbled with the fabric as she couldn't quite get a grasp. On the third try, I finally grabbed it, tugging it across her to secure it.

I closed the passenger door, then rounded the truck to get in on the driver's side. I set her clothes on the center console and buckled myself before starting the engine.

"Why'd you go out tonight?" I asked, keeping my eyes trained ahead as I pulled onto the road.

"Because I wanted to," she clipped, her words tired.

My hands twisted the steering wheel. "Because of your dad?"

"Shut up," she snapped, the warning clear that if I continued, she'd likely get mad. I almost wanted to push my luck. Anything was better than seeing this beat down version of Brandy, hopeless and scared.

"Because of what happened this morning?"

Silence, save for the exhaust rumbling beneath us, was the only response.

"You don't go out and get fucking drunk to deal with your problems, Brandy," I scolded.

"I said shut up," she snapped again.

"He's twenty-four!" I yelled back. "What, did he lie and tell you he was your age?"

She remained quiet once again.

I scoffed. "I knew it."

"Knew what?" That usual sass was back in her tone.

"You're resorting to acting out, to *ruining* yourself, instead of facing your problems."

"What do you want me to do, hit my dad right back?" she shouted.

I shook my head, my grip on the wheel tightening. "Not fucking act out like some child."

"I'm *not* acting out," she retorted.

"No? That why you're at some stupid high school party, getting drunk and letting a guy take advantage of you?"

"Stop."

My tongue darted out to wet my lips at the memory of her voice. *I want out.* I wanted nothing more than to turn around and make sure the fucker was dead.

"That's not how you handle having an abusive dad," I said, which was probably the wrong thing to say right now, but I was so fucking *mad*.

She twisted, pulling on the seat belt to face me. "Oh, yeah? Do fucking tell me how I should handle that. With your perfect, happy family and all, tell me. How should I react to my father hitting my mom in front of me? Should I beat him like you just did to Matt? Handle my problems like an *adult*?"

My jaw ticked. "Not like this. Not with acting like a fucking teenager."

"I *am* a fucking teenager!" she yelled. "Stop treating me like I'm some fucking child!"

"Then stop acting like one and maybe people wouldn't have to fucking save you!"

All this was becoming was a fucking yelling match, but *fuck*. I didn't know what else to do. What if I hadn't shown up? Why was I so fucking concerned for her? I was mad at myself for not showing up earlier, mad at her for being at this damn party in the first place, and mad at Matt for having the *fucking audacity* to touch her.

She didn't reply, and when I glanced her way, I found her eyes filled to the brim with tears she tried to hold at bay. I struck a chord I hadn't meant to, and she was hurting.

God, I'm not fucking good at this.

I pulled up to the curb outside her parents' house, not knowing where else to take her. If I brought her to the ranch, her dad might just end up more mad. We were all fucking stuck with no solution to *any* of this.

I shifted into park as she ripped my shirt off over her head in one swift motion.

"Brandy."

She tossed it at my lap and didn't stop as she unbuckled and grabbed her belongings off the center console and shoved open the door.

I couldn't let her go thinking I was mad I got her out of there. Fuck, if anything, I was grateful I did. She didn't deserve that.

I quickly pressed the button on my seatbelt, letting it whip back against the frame as I opened my door and jumped out.

"Brandy."

She didn't turn around as she crossed the sidewalk to the path leading up to the house.

"Brandy, stop."

She did, but she didn't look my way. She stood there, in the dim light of the moon, her bare legs shivering in the cold, and all I wanted was to tell her everything was okay because it was.

It's a bad day, Brandy Rose, not a bad life.

But something told me she thought it couldn't get worse than this.

That rock bottom was a familiar face to her.

"This isn't like you," I said, forcing my tone softer, quieter, in case her dad woke up. Last thing I needed was him seeing me out here with his daughter in her fucking underwear.

"It's one night, Reed." She shook her head, still refusing to look at me. "Get over it."

Then she disappeared inside, and I feared I wouldn't be the one having trouble letting go of this night.

It'd be her.

22

REED

Mornings were my favorite. Not because I liked getting up early, but for the sole reason that the world was still quiet. No expectation of small talk or a forced smile. Add in the lowing of the cattle while you doled out their breakfast, and it was nearly perfect.

Feeding the herd in the mornings was typically my job. I'd drive my truck from my house on the other side of the property over to the barn, load up the hay, and head back out to drop flakes in their usual spot. The cows knew what to do, never putting up a fight.

Felt nice to have that.

It was after breakfast that war was likely to happen. When my siblings would show up, or Brandy would arrive to start working on some horses. My mom paid her a good bit to socialize the rescues, and an even better cut for breaking the younger horses. Putting those first few rides on a green horse was no easy feat, and I could never stand to watch Brandy do it.

We'd both had our shares of being bucked off, but the risk was higher with the young ones. The groundwork before that first ride helped tremendously, and if there was one thing I'd willingly compliment Brandy on, it'd be her ability to do that shit well. Not everyone had the patience. Hell, it was a miracle even she did—with her short temper and all. It made me wonder if that was the key to getting on her good side. Being a fucking horse.

I parked my truck by the barn after getting done with feeding, my attention snagging on something out in the field after I hopped out. It'd been a few days since the wedding, and all traces of the festivities were now cleared. My mind jumped back to Brandy wearing some other man's hat, and my jaw clenched. I shook my head. *Forget about it.*

Leaving the keys on the driver's seat, I shut the door and walked toward the fence to the pasture. Kicking a boot up on the bottom, I squinted against the morning sun to find Beckham sitting in the middle of the field with that old bronc he had Bailey and Lettie rescue from a kill pen last year.

I debated ignoring the fact that he was out there and heading inside my parents' house for a cup of coffee, but Beck being alone in the middle of a field didn't sit right with me. Something was going on with him, and I didn't get why he wasn't fucking telling anyone.

Not that I was the most open book either, but Beckham was a hell of a lot better with handling his feelings than I was.

Unlatching the gate, I stepped inside, securing it behind me before walking in his direction. The old bronc's ears perked up, but Beckham didn't look my way as my boots rustled in the grass.

"No need to check on me, Reed," Beck muttered as I stopped behind him.

"How'd you know it was me?" I asked.

"You and Dad are the only two out here this early, and Dad doesn't walk that fast."

I set a hand on the bay's neck, looking out at whatever Beckham's gaze was trained on, like it might be the most interesting sight in the world. "There a reason you're out here so early?"

"Just wanted to sit with Bucky for a minute before the day started," he replied.

I stared down at him sitting there with his knees pulled to his chest like a fucking kid. "Does the day even start for you?"

He held a hand up against the sun as he turned to look at me. "There somethin' you want to say?"

"You haven't got a job since you moved home," I pointed out.

He faced forward again, pulling on a few blades of grass to twist them between his fingers. "I've got some money saved."

"Can't imagine it's a ton."

His fingers froze, and from this angle, I could see his lips flatten. "If all you're gonna do out here is pick on me, fuck off."

"Why'd you come home?" I asked instead, trying to reel in what I really wanted to say. That he needed to get his shit together and stop worrying the fuck out of our mom. Hell, out of all of us.

"Already told you. Wanted to see my family."

I grunted. "Mom believe that?"

"Doesn't matter if she does."

I flexed my fingers, trying to contain the frustration that flowed through me at his comment. He was being fucking selfish. "Yeah. It does matter, because she's fucking worried about you."

His fingers went back to pulling on the blades of grass. "What about you, Reed? You worried 'bout me?"

"That your goal with this little act? To get people to feel bad for you?"

"No," he answered, honesty clear in his tone. "Would just surprise me, is all. You don't worry about anyone but yourself anyway."

"'Scuse me? I didn't fucking hear you over the bullshit coming from your mouth."

Bucky moved at my side, bending his neck to graze.

"You never called," Beckham said quietly.

Remorse hit me in the gut like a fucking punch.

"Never checked in. Never sent a quick text. Nothing. You were quiet when I'd come home, and that was it."

"I'm always quiet." As if that was excuse enough for how I'd treated him. Truth was, he'd left home, choosing to spend more time with friends in between events than with his family. Couldn't fault him for it, though. He had a life to live. But that didn't mean I didn't see the worry etched into Callan's brow every time he watched Beck ride, or how Dad was extra closed-off those days, or that Mom would busy herself, drinking half a dozen cups of coffee to keep on her feet so she didn't have a moment to sit down and overthink.

Beckham shrugged his response, not buying my poor excuse for a second.

"That your reason for moping around, not getting a job? That one of your four siblings didn't call?"

Another shrug.

"Need I remind you that you're the one who chose to leave. Chose to stay at your friends' houses in between events rather than coming home."

"We all make decisions, Reed. Doesn't mean they're the right ones." His voice was softer now, like the little fight he had in him left.

"What the fuck are you getting on about? Whatever it is, spit it out. I've got shit to do."

"You and Brandy, and this constant back and forth battle. Making a scene at our little sister's wedding."

"I didn't make a scene," I retorted.

He was silent, giving it a moment to sink in that maybe I did. I'd had no right grabbing Brandy at the wedding over a fucking hat.

That woman was making me go insane.

I took a step away from Bucky, dragging a hand across my jaw. "You want a job, I can teach you to shoe horses, or Lennon can hire you at the feed store. You've got options, Beck. Don't be an idiot and refuse all of them."

I didn't give him the chance to respond as I turned and headed back for the gate. I wasn't going to stand there and try to pry things out of him all day. I had a job to do.

But as I slipped through the gate and latched it behind me, I instantly knew I wouldn't be getting to that anytime soon. Not as Brandy and Lettie pulled up the driveway in Lettie's car.

Last thing I needed right now was a fucking distraction, and that's all Brandy was.

I kept walking, heading into the barn to grab the wheelbarrow and rake. I'd offered to take care of some of Bailey's chores since he'd just gotten married, which was why Lettie's being here didn't make sense to me. They were supposed to be enjoying their time together.

As I got to work on the first stall, the two of them entered the barn, talking about some plans for Sage's gender reveal. I tried to tune them out, but Brandy's laugh kept filtering my way, making my palms damp against the wood handle of the rake. Every time I heard it, my muscles tensed, wanting to know what the fuck was so damn funny.

After the sixth outburst, I tossed the rake in the wheelbarrow, the sound echoing through the barn. I shoved it out, closing the stall door behind me. Grabbing the two handles, I looked up to find Lettie and Brandy peeking their heads out of the tack room door, eyes wide.

"You good out here?" Lettie asked, her blonde ponytail slung over her shoulder.

"Fine," I grumbled, pushing the wheelbarrow past them with the intent to go to the other side of the barn, far the fuck away from the two of them. Beckham had put me in a shit mood, and all I wanted was some fucking quiet.

"I should get going anyway. Wouldn't want to provoke Satan into burning the place down," Brandy said, my back to her.

"You visiting your mom today?" Lettie asked, their voices carrying through the long hall as I continued walking.

Brandy let out a short sigh. "I don't know. I might. Depends if he's there."

I dropped the wheelbarrow, the feet hitting the ground with a thud. My muscles tensed as I turned to face them. "Who the fuck is 'he'?"

Brandy's gaze found mine, her arms crossed defensively. "Don't know who you're talking about."

My lips rolled together in an attempt to rein in the irritation at her poor attempt to dodge the question. "Don't play dumb."

She shrugged. "I'm not." She faced Lettie again. "Thanks for dropping me off. See you tomorrow?"

Lettie smiled, giving her a quick hug. "Yep. I'll bring the bouquet so we can work on drying the flowers."

With a nod, Brandy started walking, striding right past me like I didn't fucking exist. In her universe, I probably didn't. Too bad I didn't give a shit.

"Brandy." My voice boomed through the hall as I took off after her, my boots pounding on the mats.

She ignored me, as I expected, aiming for her Bronco.

"Brandy, stop."

Not a muscle in her body indicated she heard me.

I started to jog, catching up to her quickly. My hand wrapped around her wrist, pulling her to a stop. "Who the fuck would be at your mom's house?"

She whirled on me, a slight sheen to her narrowed eyes. "She's allowed to have friends, you know."

Fuck, she was stubborn. "Friends you wouldn't want to see?"

She yanked her wrist from my grasp, anger turning her cheeks a light shade of pink. "Leave it alone, Reed."

I took a step closer so she had to lift her chin to keep her eyes on me. "Is it your dad?"

The slight flare of her nostrils told me I was correct.

"Why didn't you tell me?" I gritted out. My hands balled into tight fists, my knuckles aching from the strain.

"It's none of your business," she spit back.

"Is that why you were upset at the wedding?"

Her jaw moved as she ground her teeth together. "I don't have to tell you anything."

"Like hell you don't."

"Why? So you can come save me again? Be my big, broody protector?" Her voice wavered on the last word.

Pure frustration pulsed through me, causing me to get in her face. "Yes, Brandy! That's exactly why you fucking tell me, because no one's going to come into your life and put you at risk and get away with it."

She crossed her arms, brushing my chest with the act. "Too bad! He's the fucking reason I'm alive, so I have to live with it."

"No, you don't."

"You think I haven't tried to get her away from him? She gives in every single time he comes back. He's my *dad*."

My voice dropped lethally low, barely contained rage vibrating off me. "He lost that title the day he hurt his family."

Pain flashed in her eyes at the reminder of it. Though I was sure she never forgot. Brandy was good at holding things inside, especially grudges.

"Let me make this clear, Reed Bronson," she gritted out, our noses nearly touching as she spoke quietly, enunciating each word. "My problems are not your problems. You don't get to come in, guns blazing, and pretend they are. You lost the privilege to that a long fucking time ago."

Her eyes darted between mine, a lock of hair falling in her face before she turned, yanking open the door to her car.

"You know, that's the thing about being Satan," I said, playing into her little nickname. "He doesn't follow the rules."

With pursed lips, she slammed the door in my face, started her engine, and took off down the driveway, spewing dirt in her wake.

And I stood there watching, making sure she knew I wasn't going to back down. The last time she had a shit day because of that man, she nearly ruined herself.

I wouldn't let it happen again.

23

BRANDY

Two days after my outburst with Reed, I shoved the sleeve of my sweatshirt up my arm before reaching over to the passenger seat to grab my phone.

> Is he there?

I hadn't gone to my mom's house the last couple days because when I'd texted the same thing, I'd received a simple *yes*. I'd ask every damn day until the asshole disappeared again, but something told me he wasn't leaving anytime soon.

I couldn't bear the thought of him sticking around, intimidating my mother and keeping us apart. But what the fuck was I supposed to do? Show up there and act like he didn't exist? He'd only prove that he did, that I couldn't avoid him forever.

He'd make it his damn life's mission if he had to.

Controlling women was his favorite activity.

My hands twisted on the steering wheel, the early morning fog making visibility shitty, but it was nothing compared to the rage that filled me at the thought of him hurting her.

The buzz of an incoming text pulled my attention, and I positioned one hand on the middle of the steering wheel to keep it steady while I read it.

> **Mom**
> He's going to be here for a while, honey

My eyes narrowed on the words, as if the text would shift at any moment and turn into something that actually made fucking sense. Why was she so okay with him treating her this way? To leave for years and come back as if nothing ever happened? Had he instantly resorted back to his old ways or was he claiming he'd changed?

A blaring horn yanked me from my phone, and I threw the device in time to pull the wheel, swerving me back into my lane. I overcorrected, my tires catching on the dirt. My foot slammed on the brake, jerking my car to a stop on the side of the road.

I let out a frustrated groan, dropping my hands from the wheel as I tipped my head back against the headrest, my foot still planted on the pedal. I pulled in deep breaths, calming the racing of my heart and the pounding of my head. I was getting careless, letting my anger take over. This was the second time I'd been lost in my phone, stupid enough to lose focus while driving.

But I wouldn't let my outrage take over. Not like he did.

Forcing my neck straight, I stared out at the fog-covered field beside me, my teeth digging into my bottom lip. I didn't want to do shit today, put effort into anything, and most of all, deal with stubborn horses. I needed to do something for me, alone.

And I had the perfect idea of what that'd be.

***

By the time I made it to the Bronsons' ranch, the fog had lifted, but an overcast sky remained in its wake. The property was as empty as it'd ever been, every one of them gone helping the neighbors move their cattle. Lettie had texted me this morning to ask if I wanted to join, but I'd declined with the hope I'd see my mom today. That, and she was supposed to be enjoying her time with her husband. The girl couldn't sit still for long, that much was certain. And as seeing my mom wasn't happening today, I had all the time to do whatever the fuck I wanted. And this was on the top of my list.

Leaving my Bronco parked in the driveway, I headed for the barn to tack up the only horse I knew wouldn't give a shit to stand still for hours—Dessie. She was a palomino paint, my go-to if I wanted to lead a yearling around or do much of anything with the green horses. She was calmer than calm, never fighting me on anything, which meant she'd be perfectly fine with this idea.

I opted for a bosal rather than a bridle, leaving the rest of her bare. Leading her out to my car, I slipped off my boots to pull off my leggings and sweatshirt, leaving me in a bright pink lingerie set. After tugging my boots back on and grabbing my phone, I led Dessie over to the pasture fence. With one hand on the reins, I climbed the metal rungs and swung a leg over her back, situating myself on her bareback.

Once I was comfortable, I reached down to open the gate, slipping through and closing it behind us. Then we took off at a trot, aiming for the patch of tree sitting off to the side. I had Lettie's location, so I'd know if she was on her way back, but the trees would offer enough cover if I needed them.

We made it to the foliage in a few minutes, slowing to a walk as we neared. I led her over to one of the low-hanging branches, then situated my phone against a cluster of twigs and turned on the camera, setting it on the burst feature.

Then, I lay along Dessie's back, staring up at the leaves as they blew in the breeze, and smiled.

24

REED

The morning air held the promise of an early winter, the last few days of somewhat warm weather quickly turning into a brisk chill. The fog that clung to the fields had slowly dissipated as we tacked up the horses at Al's ranch, getting ready to push his family's cattle to another field for the winter.

They'd called my dad last night, asking for our help with the task, and as us Bronsons do, we couldn't turn them down. We'd shoved aside our own tasks for the day, all of us showing up in the early hours of the morning to get ready to head out.

Callan had brought Avery along for the day, letting Sage get some much-needed alone time at the house. Since she was pregnant, riding wasn't the best option for her right now, but in typical Sage fashion, she'd loaded Callan up with a truckload of food to bring out for everyone to enjoy.

Lennon passed out sandwiches to the group, making sure everyone had hot coffee or water along with their breakfast. Everyone was socializing, except for Beckham. He stood off to the side, pretending something was wrong with the cinch on his saddle.

I set my wrapped sandwich on the tailgate of my truck, about ready to walk over to him and ask what the fuck was wrong, when a hand rested on my arm, stopping me.

"That look on your face is never a good sign," Mom said, pulling my focus away from Beckham.

"What look?" I grumbled.

She dropped her hand. "The one you wear all the time."

I shot her a frown before cooling my expression. "I don't want you to worry yourself to death over whatever he's going through."

She set a hand on her hip, that typical *really think about what you said* look taking shape on her face. "Is it me doing that? Or you?"

I heaved a sigh, shifting my boot in the dirt. "I just don't get why he won't tell us what's bothering him."

Her eyes softened. "The same reason you don't."

"Nothing's bothering me," I clipped.

She crossed her arms. "You think I don't know when something's upsetting my kids?"

I moved my gaze out to the field, wishing this conversation was over. "You know, you don't have to have heart-to-hearts with all of us."

She set a callused hand on my cheek, turning me to face her again. Those rough patches only reflected a fraction of the hard work she'd done in her life. "Yes, I do. That's a mother's job."

"Have you talked to him since he moved into that double-wide?"

She dropped her arm, leveling my gaze despite her being inches shorter. "Briefly. But I'm not pushing him. He'll open up when he's ready."

"Yeah, you keep saying that," I mumbled, glancing over at where he was still fucking with the cinch.

"No one will say words worth speaking if you force them, Reed. They have to want to open up on their own. All you can do is be there for them in the meantime."

Her words nearly made my breath hitch. Was she talking about Beck? Or Brandy? It was no secret Brandy had a rough relationship with her father, but no one really knew the extent of it like I did. But maybe my mom sensed that. When we had big dinners, it was no question she was invited. A family event, she'd be there. But the one thing my mom never did was pressure Brandy to talk. She never mentioned her attitude or her inability to open up. She accepted her as she was, welcoming her into the family with open arms. If someone needed a place to stay, my mom gave that to them, no questions asked.

I had a feeling that's what she was doing with Beck now. We lost him for years before, and she was just glad he'd come home.

Maybe I should be, too.

We could all worry about him, sure. But all it really did was put a weight on his shoulders when he already had a boulder of thoughts pulling him down to begin with.

I just didn't know if I was capable of letting it go.

I was a closed-off asshole sometimes, I wouldn't deny that. I kept my feelings bottled inside like the rest of them, but that was me. Call it a double standard, but none of this behavior was like Beckham.

What the fuck happened while he was gone?

"Why don't you go on home. Take the day for yourself," Mom said, interrupting my thoughts.

I looked at her. "I'm fine."

She gave me a pointed glare. "I'm not asking, Reed. We can do this without you. Go relax, have a beer."

"Only after five," I said, reciting her rule. "But why? You don't want me around?"

She dipped her chin in a nod, picking up my sandwich and placing it in my palm. "I don't want you killing your brother out in that field."

"I wouldn't—"

"You're wastin' your breath. Go on."

She patted me on the chest twice before turning to head back to Dad, where he was lost in conversation with Al.

With no other choice but to listen, I shut the tailgate and rounded the truck to the driver's side door. Leaving my Carhartt jacket on, I got in, starting up the engine and heading back to the ranch.

Since Al owned the property about ten miles away, it only took a few minutes before I was pulling up the driveway. I planned to go straight to my house on the far end, but a particular Bronco sitting in the driveway had me continuing toward the barn. I pulled to a stop, letting the engine idle for a second to see if Brandy would appear. When I saw no movement aside from the horses in their paddocks, I turned off the truck and slid out.

I pivoted to close my door, but as soon as I did, something bright pink in the distance caught my eye. Shoving it shut behind me, I narrowed my gaze, trying to focus on whatever it was shining through the cluster of trees.

Once the distraction came into focus, my heart skipped a beat, followed by the blood in my veins turning to ice.

What the fuck was she doing?

I crossed to the pasture, not bothering with the gate, instead jumping clear over the metal fence. My boots stamped down the grass as my pace quickened, beelining it for the trees.

As I got closer, more of Brandy became even more exposed—as if that was even possible when all she was wearing was fucking *lingerie and boots.*

She must've not heard me coming as she set her hands behind her on the horse's rear, arching her back to show off her tiny, perky tits. The image had my cock hardening in my jeans, but I shoved the jaw-dropping sight away, focusing more on her being out here in the fucking cold, wearing *nothing*.

When I was less than ten feet away, she finally turned her eyes on me, those bold brows pulling together. I didn't give her a chance to speak as I closed the distance, only stopping when her knee-high boot hit my stomach and my hands grabbed her waist.

She let out a shriek as I lifted her off Dessie. "Reed!"

I ignored her, pulling her clean off the horse and hefting her over my shoulder.

Fists pounded on my back, but the thickness of my jacket lessened their blow. "Reed fucking Bronson, put me down right now!"

My lips rolled together before I landed a hard smack to Dessie's ass. The horse took off at a gallop, racing toward the barn. Only once the horse was out of sight did I set Brandy down in front of me.

"I was in the middle of something!" Brandy said, her cheeks blazing a deep cherry red. From the cold or her anger, I didn't know. I shouldn't have to fucking guess between the two.

"It's fifty fucking degrees," I muttered, shucking off my coat.

She watched the movement, sensing what I was about to do, and took a step back. I stormed her, whipping the jacket around her shoulders and pulling it tight in the front. I yanked her to my chest, the zipper digging into my palm as I stared down into twin flames of fury.

"I'm not cold," she spit out.

"What the fuck are you doing?" I demanded.

Her eyes turned to saucers. "What am *I* doing?"

"You're out here in fucking *lingerie*, Brandy. I can see your piercings clear as day."

Her hard gaze melted, a smirk pulling at her mouth in turn. "You looked."

I drew her even closer, so close she had to stand on the tips of her toes. "Is that what you want? For me to stare at your body? You want to tease me with it? Flaunt it around, knowing I won't touch you?"

Her nostrils flared, and she twitched like she wanted to move her hands, but she kept them stiff at her sides. "I'm not out here like this for you," she seethed.

"Then who? Huh? Some fucking guy who wants your body and nothing else?"

Those cheeks darkened a shade, and I knew I'd set her off.

Her hand flew to the side, drawing my attention to the phone sitting perched on a branch. Instantly, I dropped the coat. She took a few steps back, keeping herself from falling without my grip on the jacket. She kept it tight around her, though, telling me she *was* fucking cold.

Stubborn woman.

I stormed over to the phone, grabbing it in a tight fist. I glanced down to see the camera was on, and fury ripped through me like a fucking riptide. I stomped back over to her, shoving it at her chest.

"Who's it for?" I asked, my voice louder than I'd like it to be.

"Not for you," she remarked.

"I didn't ask if it was for me." I crowded her space, causing her to step back again. "Who the fuck is it for?"

"For me."

I searched her eyes for the truth. "Bullshit."

"What? You never take pictures of yourself to feel good?"

"Fuck no."

Her gaze flicked over me from head to toe. "Well, that's disappointing."

I shook my head, her words settling in. "You don't feel good about yourself?" My voice was quieter now, losing its bite.

She shrugged, the act almost nonexistent under the size of my jacket on her. "I do."

I took another step closer, and her neck arched to keep those eyes on me. "So let me get this straight. You came out here in the fucking cold wearing nothing but lingerie and boots, sat on a fucking horse, and posed in front of a camera to *feel good about yourself*?"

She nodded, confident as ever. But when I didn't let up on my expression—which I was sure was anything but comforting—her gaze fell. "You think I'm some kind of slut."

Pure fucking feral rage hit me in the chest. I grabbed her chin, forcing her to look up at me. "Never fucking say that again."

A sheen took over her eyes. "Why? You wouldn't be the first."

My jaw clenched so hard I thought it might break. "The only one you will *ever* be a slut for is me, Brandy Rose. Anyone else wants to see you that way, and I'll break their fucking neck."

Some of the sadness left her eyes, that typical lilt lifting the side of her lips. "That's kind of violent, Satan."

"That's how the thought of anyone seeing you like this makes me feel," I admitted, dropping her chin and stepping back. "Besides, you're beautiful whether you take photos of yourself or not," I added on a mutter.

"Was that a compliment?" she asked, humor lacing her tone as she lifted a hand to her ear, as if she didn't hear me properly.

"Take it however you want," I mumbled, my eyes catching on her bare legs above her boots.

She dropped her hand. "Do you want the photos?"

I snapped out of her intoxicating trance, glaring at her. With a scoff, I turned, heading back for the ranch. I could only take so much Brandy for a day, and I'd already reached my limit. It wasn't even nine a.m. yet.

"Is that a no?" she called after me.

I ignored her, not able to say out loud that secretly, I did want those photos. But the next time I saw Brandy in that way wouldn't be through some phone screen.

It'd be on her fucking knees before me.

25

BRANDY

It'd been days since I last talked to my mom, and I was giving in. We saw each other every weekend, and now it'd been too long. I was going over there, whether he was at the house or not. I could pretend he didn't exist—I was good at that. Someone left your life long enough, it was almost like they weren't there to begin with.

Unfortunately for me, though, my mental scars didn't heal. He could erase himself physically, but in the end, he'd always have some kind of hold on me.

I just chose to ignore it.

I pulled up to the curb in front of my mom's house, letting the engine idle as I stared at the front door. There was no movement behind any of the curtained windows, and I wondered if she had them drawn for the sole reason of keeping things private between the two of them.

After he left, she'd open the curtains every morning, staring out of them with her steaming cup of coffee and a book on her lap. Now none of those happy moments permeated through the double-panes. Instead, hollowing silence sat in its wake.

Shutting off the car, I got out and closed the door behind me before walking up the path to the door. The overcast sky clung to my shoulders like the clouds were there solely for me today, reflecting my mood with a sprinkle or two on my sweatshirt. The forecast hadn't called for rain, but it was often that thunderstorms would appear out of nowhere, drenching the ground and spreading its gloom.

Before I could try the handle or knock, the door opened. Standing on the other side of the threshold stood my dad, staring down at me with his typical disapproving look.

"It's not polite to show up unannounced," he chastised, like I was some child again, and not an adult coming to visit my mother.

"Well, if you'd been here the last few years, you'd know that today is girl's day," I responded, the smell of rain filling my nostrils.

He gave nothing but a blank stare, like he was waiting for me to get to the point.

"Where is she?" I asked, not bothering to look around his large frame. He'd block my view if I tried.

"In the shower. If you'd have called first, she could have planned around your visit."

"She has to plan her weekly visits with her daughter, the ones we've been having for years?" I asked innocently.

He went to take a step back. "Don't try to be smart with me, girl."

"Just pointing out the obvious, as it seems I have to do frequently when speaking to you," I said, not letting my eyes fall. That's what he wanted, for me to cower. To back off and leave. But that only worried me, not for my sake, but hers. "Where's my mom?" I asked again.

"Already told you," he clipped, his tone growing irritated.

"She wouldn't be showering when she knows I always come today at this time." Other days, sure, she had plans or chores to do, and the schedules just didn't work out. But today? I wasn't buying it.

He lowered his chin, narrowing his eyes. "Maybe she just doesn't care to see her brat of a daughter anymore."

My lips pressed together in an attempt to hold my tongue from what I really wanted to say.

"Don't worry, though. I'm taking care of her." His mouth spread into a callous grin.

The look set me off, making me take two steps forward. But before my hand hit the door to shove it open, he grabbed my forearm, his grip crushing.

I gritted my teeth together, not moving to yank my arm from his hold. My gaze went vacant as I stared at the door. He wanted my eyes on him so he could see the fear he inflicted. Too bad for him, my demons didn't lurk in the present.

"Be respectful and look at your father, girl," he said, trying to lace sugar over venomous words.

My eyes moved to his, his grip tightening in return.

"If I don't invite you in, you don't come in. Is that clear?"

I didn't trust myself to speak, so I kept quiet, but in doing so, it only pissed him off more. He yanked me forward, causing me to stumble on the doormat. His hold on my arm kept me up as I righted myself, but now we were inches apart. He smelled like pungent beer and my mom's laundry detergent.

"I said, is that clear?" he gritted out, barely contained rage hidden behind his words.

"Yes," I whispered.

His hand moved, and I flinched, squeezing my eyes shut in anticipation of the sting. But when none came, and instead a chuckle rumbled on the cool air, I peeled them open to find his hand on the doorjamb.

He wasn't going to hit me.

I was such a fucking idiot.

He dropped my arm, giving me a little shove. I stepped back, moving my eyes to the ground. I couldn't bear to look at him.

"I'll tell her you stopped by," he said, but I knew he wouldn't.

Without another word, I turned, walking through the now pouring rain back to my Bronco. I rounded the hood, wrenching open my door and sliding in. Slamming it shut, I set my hands on the wheel, staring at the dash. I wanted nothing more than to storm back up that path and take my frustration out on him, but if I did that, I'd be no better than the man who put that feeling inside me.

Grabbing my keys from my sweatshirt pocket, I glanced at the house one last time. My father still stood in the open doorway, watching me through the downpour. With a wicked smile, he raised his hand in a slow wave.

Pressing my lips together so hard I thought they might fall off, I shoved the key in the ignition and started the engine.

Then I drove, rain pounding on the windshield so hard, my wipers could barely keep up.

I didn't know where the fuck I was going, but I didn't care.

I just needed to get the fuck away from here.

26

REED

Water flooded along the side of the barn from the torrential downpour that'd started barely thirty minutes ago. We'd have to dig another drainage ditch so water runoff wouldn't flood the stalls this winter. I tacked it on to my mental to-do list so my dad wouldn't have to. It wasn't hard work, but it'd take a few hours, and the last thing he needed was more on his plate.

Flicking the light off in the barn, I grabbed my bag of supplies and headed for the side door. Pulling it closed behind me, I aimed for my truck parked a dozen feet away. Muddy puddles splashed with every step, the rain drenching me head to toe in seconds. My cowboy hat did its best to shield my face, but it was futile.

Making it to my truck, I opened the door and tossed the bag on the passenger seat as I slid in behind the wheel. As my hand wrapped around the handle, I paused, hearing the familiar hum of an old Bronco trudging up the driveway.

Rain soaked the arm and shoulder of my denim jacket as I kept my grip on the door loose. The Bronco's wipers ceased their movement, and a moment later, the purr of the engine cut off.

I waited. Waited for what felt like minutes to see if she'd step out. Speak to me. Yell at me. Anything. I couldn't see her through the flood on her windshield, but fuck, I wanted to.

Why the fuck was she here in a storm?

Rain or shine, we all had shit to do, but Brandy couldn't break a colt in this weather. Couldn't put a few rides on a green horse. Her being here right now didn't make sense. If she wanted to see Lettie, she'd have gone over to her and Bailey's place.

Not here.

Finally, the driver's door opened, and out stepped the girl who kept invading my goddamn mind. A part of me wanted to tell her to get the fuck out of here so I wouldn't have to know she was out in the cold rain, but another part of me wanted to pull her in. Tell her to stay. To talk.

What the fuck was wrong with me?

The woman hated the very ground I walked on, and I was sitting here thinking it might be nice for her to be around for a change.

With a shake of my head, I pulled on the door, but then she shut her own, and I froze at the sight of her standing there.

That stiff posture she always held, the high arch of her brows, the confidence of her shoulders set back—it was all gone. Like a flame dropped in a rapidly moving river, Brandy looked defeated.

I shoved the door back open, mud spraying up around me as my boots hit the ground.

She lifted her head, those eyes I knew so well—holding so much in their gaze alone—found mine, and there was no hesitation. No question as my legs started moving toward her.

Rain pounded into me relentlessly, but nothing else mattered in this world right now besides her.

She took a few steps, but I was already there, my arms coming around her shoulders at the same time hers slipped under my jacket and around me. She squeezed me so tight, I wanted her to break a rib. To make me feel anything other than this deafening concern for her, because I didn't know what the fuck was happening or how I ended up with Brandy Rose in my arms, but I never wanted to let go now that I had her here.

"I didn't know where else to go," she mumbled into my chest, and I barely heard her over the rain, but her words were loud enough to know the last one broke off.

My hand moved to cup the back of her head, holding her closer, doing my best to shield some of the rain from her. "You can always come to me. You know that."

She shook her head, a sob shaking her body.

Fuck, she was breaking me.

"I don't want to be alone in this anymore. I can't—" Her sentence cut off, but she didn't need to tell me.

My hands slid past her ears to her cheeks, and I angled her head up at me. My hat kept most of the water from hitting her in the face as I stared into her bloodshot eyes. "You've never been alone, Brandy. Not with me around."

Her bottom lip popped out as another sob fell from her, a tear escaping past her eyelashes to mix with the raindrops. I brushed it away, running both my thumbs along her cheekbones. Her hands fisted in my shirt at my back, like she needed to keep her hold tight to know I was here. That she really wasn't alone.

I wanted to ask her what happened to bring her here, but I held my tongue as a shiver rolled through her. Her sweatshirt was soaked, her jeans in the same state.

Like it was second nature, I grabbed one of her hands from my back, intertwining my fingers with hers. "Come on."

I turned, leading her toward my truck.

"What about my car?" she asked, following me.

"I'm not letting you get behind the wheel like this, and you're freezing."

She jogged a little to keep up with me as we rounded the hood. I opened the passenger door for her, keeping my hand in hers until she was seated. Closing it, I went around to get in on the driver's side. After shutting my door, I turned the key in the ignition and cranked the heater.

I peeled out of my wet jacket, tossing it in the back, then looked at her.

"What happened?" I asked, my voice low, grating.

She blinked at me, her hands folding together in her lap as her fingers couldn't figure out what to do with themselves.

Eyeing her sweatshirt, I said, "You won't get warm if you stay in that wet hoodie."

Her gaze fell to her clothes as if she hadn't even realized it was raining, then unclasped her hands to grab the hem. Lifting it over her head, she set it on her lap, leaving her in a thin white tank top. I grabbed the hoodie, tossing it in the back along with mine.

"What happened?" I repeated.

Her gaze moved to her jeans, like she was quickly regretting showing up here. "Reed—"

"What. Happened?"

Hazel galaxies of war found me, contemplating. "You have to promise me—"

"No," I clipped, already knowing what she was going to ask.

"Reed—"

Her hands moved again, pulling my attention to them. But it wasn't her fragile fingers that stopped my heart. It was the faint hue of blue staining dots around her forearm.

My jaw popped, and she followed my line of sight to her bruised skin. Instantly, she covered them up with her other hand.

The hurt I found in her eyes nearly killed me on the spot, so I averted my gaze to the rain rolling down the windshield.

"I'm sorry," she murmured.

I grabbed the wheel, needing something to hold on to. "You have nothing to be sorry for."

She kept quiet. The only sound filling the cab the constant pounding from the storm as it battered the truck.

My hands twisted on the leather, my knuckles white. Every instinct in my body screamed to protect her, to gut whoever put their hands on her.

But I already knew who did it, and that was the fucking sad part.

She didn't even need to say his name, and I knew exactly what demon from her past had the audacity to hurt her.

And I didn't even want to hesitate before killing the fucker.

But I couldn't. She wouldn't want that.

"I'll take you home," I said, instead of all the other things I wanted to go on about. Like how she could go near him, knowing what he was capable of? Or not telling me she was having a problem with him?

But I wouldn't say any of that because today, she changed. *We* changed. She came to me, and that's all that mattered.

For seven years, I thought I'd lost that civil spark between the two of us, but now it might be back, and I didn't want to ruin it again.

"What about the Bronco?" she asked.

I shifted into drive, the cab warm now with the heater blasting. "I'll have one of my brothers bring it by your place."

Driving past her car, I headed down the driveway toward the main road, my windshield wipers doing their best to combat the downpour, my heart doing the same as it tried to shove away my mind's urge to drive over to her mother's house and beat her father senseless.

It might be fucking brutal, or sick, or whatever humanity wanted to call it, but in no right fucking world should another put their hand on anyone and get away with it.

I took care of a similar problem for her before, and I wouldn't hesitate to do it again.

My only fear would be to risk losing Brandy again—for good.

***

By the time I pulled up to Brandy's house, she was dead asleep in the passenger seat. Her head lolled to the side, her long, brown hair curling as it air-dried, those plump lips parted as her chest rose and fell with each deep, slow breath.

I let the truck idle as I peeled my hands off the wheel, watching her rest. I wondered if sleep was the only time her impenetrable walls fell and her mind eased from its constant defensive mode. Was she as tired of this back and forth between the two of us as I was?

I wished I could apologize for the night I nearly beat Matt to death, but I'd do it again in a heartbeat. Fuck, I wanted to right now, and all her father had done was grab her arm. At least, I hoped that was all. I'd get her to tell me everything that happened in the morning, but for now, I'd let her sleep.

Pulling my phone out of the cupholder, I pulled up Lennon's contact. I would've asked Bailey, but he'd tell Lettie, and I wasn't sure if Brandy wanted her to know anything.

> You think you can pick up Brandy's Bronco at the ranch and bring it to her place?

I glanced over at Brandy's sleeping form, wishing I could bring that sort of peace to her even when she was awake.

My phone buzzed in my hands, and I reluctantly looked away, reading the text.

> **Lennon**
> Once the storm lets up, sure. Key in the car?

> Should be on the front seat

My shoulders eased a fraction at his willingness to jump in and help, no questions asked. Our parents raised us to always be there for each other, and I was thankful as fuck for it.

> **Lennon**
> You'll text if she tries to kill you?

My lips pulled down in a frown.

> I think the murderous stage has passed

> **Lennon**
> Really? Never thought I'd see the day

I leaned back in the seat, my cheeks aching with the smile that threatened to form.

> **Lennon**
> Rainbow after the storm?

> I wouldn't say it's a rainbow yet, but the clouds parted at least

> **Lennon**
> Baby steps are still steps. Just be glad you're taking them

My eyes moved to Brandy once more, and I guessed he was right.

This was progress, no matter how small.

Then I got out of the truck after killing the engine and carried her inside, her warmth and tranquility a relief from how distraught she'd been not even an hour ago.

27

BRANDY

The bright morning light shone through the sheer curtains, my eyelids fluttering to adjust. I turned over, facing away from the window, then realized I wasn't wearing any pants and shot up. Scanning the room, I froze, my hands propped behind me to keep me upright. How had I gotten in bed? The last thing I remembered was—

Flinging the comforter off of me, my bare feet hit the cold ground. I reached for the door but pulled my hand back, remembering my state of undress. I couldn't go out there with no pants on. What if Reed was here? But why would he be? Maybe he'd only driven me home and brought me inside, and I didn't remember taking my pants off myself and crawling under the covers.

I shook my head. No, I would've remembered. No matter how upset I was, I wasn't drunk or anything. My brain still functioned.

Grabbing a pair of gray sweatpants from the chair in the corner, I tugged them on and returned to the door. I stood there, hand posed above the handle, not sure what to expect on the other side.

Thinking back on yesterday, regret hit me flat in the stomach. I shouldn't have gone to Reed while I was reeling from my father. It was a mistake, and now it would only cause problems. Keeping things quiet and to myself was the easiest option—it prevented explanations and feelings I didn't want to come to light. But now that Reed had seen my bruise, he'd want an explanation.

A glance down at the skin told me it wasn't as bad as I'd thought it was going to be. Three dots lined the inside of my arm, already fading.

See? Not so bad.

Nothing I should have gone to Reed about.

I'd just go out there, tell him it was a mistake, and we'd go back to whatever it was that we were before all...this. If he even was out there. For all I knew, I was overreacting and he wasn't even under the same roof as me.

Closing my fingers around the handle, I turned it with confidence, but the feeling quickly faded as I cracked the door and found the unexpected.

Reed Bronson was sitting in my hallway, guarding my door like some kind of dog.

He looked up, his eyes gliding over my body like a caress, and I realized then that I didn't mind him looking at me.

Maybe I actually wanted him to.

If not just for today.

No, that was too much.

Just in this moment would I enjoy his attention on me.

"Good morning." I crossed my arms in a futile attempt to show I was irritated with his presence.

But if I was, why would I tell him good morning?

Okay, this wasn't right. I was usually so good at being pissed at him. A pro at getting under his skin. Him holding me in the rain couldn't have changed *that* much of my brain makeup. I was still me.

But maybe just a little less...guarded.

That wouldn't do.

"What are you doing here?" I added, forcing irritation into my words.

His casual perusal of my body finally ended, his eyes focusing on my face. His hat was resting on his knee, to which he plucked it off, set it on his head, and pushed to a stand. Without shoes on, I was much, much shorter than him in his cowboy boots. He tilted his chin down, farther than he usually did, and took a step forward to set a hand on the doorframe above me.

"You fell asleep in my truck," he stated.

I popped my hip, leaning into the frame. "And?"

"And I brought you inside."

I angled the upper half of my body forward, enunciating each word. "Yeah. Last night."

His free hand came up to the back of his neck, rubbing the skin as he looked down the hall. "Didn't realize the sun was up."

"The front window is open." Was the man fucking blind?

Tired eyes found mine. "What happened yesterday?"

My brows shot up. "Is that what you were sitting there thinking about?"

His hand fell from his neck, a little light coming back into him. "Yeah. That's exactly what I was thinking about all fucking night."

When he didn't go on, I scoffed, moving to head past him down the hall. He caught my arm, pulling me back to him. He held the limb up between us, his grip soft but his eyes rock fucking hard. "Because when you come to me crying with a fucking bruise on your arm, I'm going to fucking worry."

I pulled my arm from his hand, dropping it to my side. "I'm *so* sorry I made you lose sleep. You can go home now."

Continuing on my way down the hall, the stomp of boots on hardwood did nothing to hide him following me. "That's not what I'm mad about."

Heading into the kitchen, I opened the fridge to pull out a carton of milk. "I'm assuming you want me to ask what you're so angry about."

I set the jug down at the same time his hands slammed onto the counter. He hung his head, his shoulders hunched as he took a steadying breath.

"Do you need to make everything so difficult?" he asked quietly.

I shrugged, opening the cabinet to pull out a mug. "If it makes you leave me alone."

"You came to me," he reminded me.

I lifted the carton, uncapping it. "That was a mistake."

He grabbed the milk from me, setting it down on the counter and moving in front of me. "That wasn't a mistake. You did that because you were scared."

I froze, unmoving as I blinked at his chest.

Scared.

I'd driven with no destination in mind and ended up at that ranch. I hadn't expected Reed to be there—

Oh, who was I kidding? Yes, I did. I knew he'd be there, and I knew he'd make me feel better because that's what he did. Every time we argued, bickered, picked on each other, aggravated one another, we did it because we craved something from one another, and if that's all we got, that was enough. But yesterday, I hadn't gone to him to fight or to use him as my punching bag. I'd gone because I needed to feel safe, and fuck, if that's not what Reed made me feel.

And I should *hate* that. I should hate that because he beat a man black and blue to protect me. He ruined my high school years to keep me safe. He unknowingly isolated me from everyone but Lettie because he didn't want to see me hurt. Violated. Raped.

And I hated him because that's how my dad should've made me feel. Safe. But instead, I was at that party that night because of the man I was supposed to be protected by. I was in a situation where I was helpless *because* of the man that was always supposed to be there for me.

And instead of him, Reed showed up, barging into that room and making me feel safe when I wanted to feel anything but in that moment. I wanted my dad to save me from the bad men, the monster under my bed, the nightmares that kept me up at night. But instead, *he* was all of that to me. All the bad things in my life, my father was the root of them.

But Reed wasn't.

"Brandy," Reed whispered, pulling me back into the here and now. A thumb ghosted my cheek, and I flinched.

I fucking *flinched*.

But Reed didn't move away. He didn't pull his hand back. No, Reed would never hurt me, and in turn, he knew I didn't react that way because of him.

He set his hand on my cheek, brushing a tear away with callused skin. The touch shouldn't have made me want to lean into him, but fuck, I did. I leaned into his touch so hard that I ended up pressed against his chest, his arm snaking around my waist, pulling me closer.

What was wrong with me? Finding comfort in the man I pushed away for years, like I had a right to his bubble of safety?

The net shouldn't extend to me, and yet, it did. He wrapped it all the way around me, and I never wanted to be let go.

I just wanted someone to *hold me*.

His hand on my cheek threaded into my hair, cupping the back of my head as more tears fell. I was so tired of keeping everything inside.

"He wouldn't let me see my mom," I mumbled into his shirt.

He didn't let go, didn't loosen his grip. He just held me, like he knew I needed it, too.

"I tried to go inside, and that's when he grabbed me." My hand fisted in his shirt, resting against his hard stomach. "He told me I can't go inside my mom's house unless he says I can."

Reed stood firm, his heart a steady beat under my cheek. He was the rock when all I felt was crumbling.

"I don't want her to get hurt," I whispered.

His hand gripped my waist. "She won't."

I shook my head, burying my face deeper into his shirt. I hated crying in front of people, never wanting them to see my walls break, but here I was, laid bare in front of Reed.

"She'll never be the one to leave. It has to be him, but even if he does disappear again, he'll come back. He always does, even if it's years that go by."

He was quiet, his thumb gliding back and forth over the sliver of exposed skin from where my tank top had risen a few inches. I welcomed the feeling of his skin on mine, the sensation the only thing keeping me grounded in this moment.

"You're not going over there alone again," he said, the words so low, I barely heard them.

"She's my mom. I have to see her."

"And you will."

I pulled my face away from his chest, looking up at him. "But if I can't go over there, how will I see her?"

"I said alone, Brandy. I'll go with, and I'll make sure that asshole never puts a hand on either of you again."

28

REED

The bar was far busier than I typically liked, and on nights like these, I'd call it early and head home. That was, if Brandy wasn't around. She was a lightweight and had a bad habit of overindulging, so naturally, I stayed close. But right now, she was across the room, leaning over the bar on her stool, nursing her beer.

On any normal night, she'd be on her third and chanting for shots with my little sister, but tonight, she was confused. Unsure of what these feelings were that were surfacing between the two of us like an endless cloudy sky letting the rays of the sun finally shine through, showing what warmth could really feel like.

She isolated herself in one of the most lonely of ways—mentally.

Physically, she was all there. Surrounding herself with people she loved and work she was passionate about. But inside that head of hers, there was a quiet hurricane, thoughts collapsing in on her at the end of the day, memories flooding the streets of her mind.

It was a tragedy she thought that would work.

I saw it all these years, letting her use me as the punching bag she needed because without me, who would light that spark in her eyes? Who would make her sigh, make her take some of that anger out that she kept so tightly bottled inside?

But I think that was the most devastating of all—that she thought if she let any of that anger out, she'd end up just like her father. The truth was, anyone could end up like that. Taking their anger out on others because they didn't have the right mind to know when enough was enough. Brandy just made it her personal mission to never let it show, unless it was to me.

And I fucking loved it.

She hated being mad and the way it made her feel, and in turn, I reveled in it. The wrath she unleashed on me sometimes—it almost made me hard. She wasn't like that with anyone else. Was I special? Probably not. But Brandy wasn't actually living if she was constantly thinking in the back of her mind, *don't be like my father*. With just those thoughts alone, she was already better than him.

She just needed to realize she'd never be on his level, no matter the emotions she felt. Brandy was hurt by him in the past, and already, that was proof enough she'd never be anything like him.

"You must've really pissed her off this time," Lennon said, watching her from under the brim of his ball cap. It was just me, him, and Beckham here tonight. Brandy had tagged along after Beckham texted her what we were doing.

I didn't want to get into that right now.

Beckham was at the pool table behind where Lennon and I stood, playing a game with some middle-aged man I'd never seen before.

"This time?" I asked.

I'd left Brandy's house shortly after she'd stopped crying, leaving her to do whatever it was she did to fill her days off. I'd gone straight to the ranch, checking on the herd with my dad. Afterward, Lennon had shown up, and naturally, that turned into the few of us ending up at Outlaw's Watering Hole—our favorite bar in town.

Lennon shrugged, lifting his longneck to take a swig of beer. "As opposed to any other time."

"You act like I make her mad on purpose," I said, shifting my elbows on the high-top table.

He shot me a look. "Poking the bear is your favorite pastime."

I sipped my beer, watching as Brandy ran her finger along the condensation on the bar. She was about thirty feet away, with people dancing between us, groups chatting and drinking, but I saw every movement she made.

"Like a hawk to a mouse," Lennon muttered, shoving off his elbows and straightening.

I glanced at him. "Sorry?"

He crossed his arms. "I didn't come out with you two tonight to play babysitter."

I moved my focus back to Brandy, holding the neck of my beer between three fingers. "The only one needing that is our brother."

In my peripheral, Lennon glanced at Beckham, then heaved a sigh, moving back to his earlier position standing at the table. "I don't want to deal with that right now."

Tou-fucking-ché.

Brandy's finger traced the rim of her glass, her shoulders slumped with one elbow on the counter, her palm on her cheek.

"That's it," I muttered, shoving off the table, abandoning my beer. I turned to Lennon. "You get him home."

Lennon's brows shot up. "Oh, he's my responsibility now?"

I shrugged. "You can tell Mom you left him and see how she reacts."

"You're the one leaving me," he pointed out.

I shrugged. "I've got shit to do."

Leaving him standing there, I kept my eyes trained on Brandy's sweater-clad back as I crossed the bar, bumping into shoulders and squeezing through bodies to get to her. As soon as I reached her, I grabbed her hand, pulling her off the stool.

Her eyes, wide and round with surprise, shot to me. "What are you doing?"

A spark, but not enough. I wanted fucking fireworks.

Successfully getting her off the stool, I led her through the crowded bar, aiming for the back hallway. I didn't offer a response as we weaved through drunk, laughing people. Through the thick of it, I kept my hand clasped around hers.

"Reed." Her voice didn't hold its usual bite.

That wouldn't do.

Breaking free from the throng, I pulled her into the hallway, past the bathrooms and around the corner that led to the back exit.

"Reed, what the fuck are you doing?"

At the curse, I finally turned around, but I wasn't finished. My hands left her for a split second before they found her shoulders and pushed her back against the wall. I invaded her space the way she invaded my senses, and then my palms met the cool brick behind her, framing her face.

I was out of breath, probably out of my mind, but I didn't give a shit.

"Riling you up." The last word barely passed my lips before I was on her, my lips melting into her like they'd been frozen in an iceberg for centuries, waiting to find that one flame to melt away their impenetrable exterior.

The earth shook, or maybe that was my heart threatening to beat out of my chest at the way her head fell back against the wall, then shoved forward to meet my every move. Even in this, we fought, but only because we were desperate for more.

I couldn't keep my hands off her any longer as they moved on their own accord, framing her face, then sliding into her hair, gripping the strands with barely restrained fingers, tugging her closer, closer, closer.

She angled left, I angled right. She perched on tiptoes, I shoved her down. I gripped her hair, she tugged my shirt.

Rip it, I don't care, I wanted to say, but I couldn't bear to part from her long enough to mutter the words. It was like a craze came over the both of us, and there was no stopping it. Years and years of war turned into a truce worth going down in history, and fuck, I was glad this was ours.

"I hate you for this," she managed to get out between kisses, her voice raspy, so unlike I'd ever heard it before.

My hands fisted harder in her hair, my body pressing her into the wall. "Good," I muttered, the one word so full of breath.

Her hands moved from my chest to my neck at the same time mine released her, gliding down her body to squeeze her thighs before wrapping around them and lifting her. Her legs wrapped around my waist perfectly, and I could feel the bar of her nipple piercings against my chest, through our clothes. I wondered what they'd feel like with nothing in between us.

Just simply us, in a world where we didn't hate each other, where this wouldn't be the first and last time.

Fuck, I didn't want this to end.

My hands squeezed her ass through her jeans, and she only rocked into me in response.

Fuck, the things I would do to her if we weren't in this damn bar right now.

"You're always so fucking selfish," she murmured into my lips, trying like hell to keep up the ruse, but I felt it slipping from her as much as it was from me.

Nothing would be the same after this.

One hand left her ass. The only thing keeping her up was my other hand and the wall. Reaching up between us, I grabbed her neck, forcing her head back. Her chest rose and fell with rapid breaths, her lips parted and swollen and beautiful. Our eyes met, an eruption simmering between our gazes. Hate, lust, it was all the same for us. I realized that now.

"If this is me being selfish..." I said, leaning forward to kiss her jaw, shoving her head back with my mouth. Her eyes fluttered closed as my tongue tasted her skin, trailing down that slope to her neck, right above where my thumb rested against her pulse point. "Consider me the greediest man on this fucking planet."

My hand slid from her neck to the base of her skull, grabbing her hair in a fist and tugging it back, exposing more of her soft skin.

"Trust me," she panted, her breath hitching before she added, "I always have."

My lips trailed down the V of her sweater, my tongue darting out to lap at the flavor of her. Something fruity invaded my senses, whether perfume or body wash, I didn't care. It was her I was developing a taste for. Or maybe I already had, and I was curving my craving. Either way, I wanted to sample every part of her.

"Then you won't be mad when I do this," I said into her skin, barely able to catch my own breath as she stole it from me by merely existing.

Before she could ask what I meant, my hand released her hair and slid to her sweater, tugging it down to reveal her breast. She wasn't wearing a bra, and my mind instantly wondered if she'd been like this around me before, other than at the wedding. Whatever the answer was, I was hard as a fucking rock at the sight of her piercing.

I kept her shielded at such an angle that if anyone were to walk down the hall, I could quickly cover her up. With the assurance that no one would glimpse her, I closed my mouth around her peaked nipple, my tongue flicking at the cool metal bar.

Her hands moved to my hair, tugging and gripping and tearing. It only fueled me as my teeth grabbed the jewelry and tugged. I could tell she was trying to be quiet as her moan came out restrained while her hips moved, grinding against my stomach.

This was only supposed to be a kiss, something to rile her up and make her come back to me, but I couldn't help myself. One taste, and I wanted to *devour* her.

Releasing the jewelry, my mouth closed around the bud again, my tongue flicking, lapping, caressing. All the while, little pants passed her lips, each one causing her chest to press against me harder, feeding her breast to me further.

Reluctantly, I finally released her nipple, doing my best to calm my breath but knowing there was no hope. Not with her legs wrapped around me and her looking like…that. All fucking worked up and beautiful. Her hooded eyelids, her bee-stung lips—it made me want to throw her over my shoulder and bring her to my truck and take her all fucking night.

She barely pulled her head away from the wall, my other hand moving to cup her ass again, holding her tighter.

Her hands loosened their hold on my hair before falling to my neck, her wrists draped heavily on my shoulders. "I can't stand you," she said between panting breaths.

My tongue darted out to dampen my lower lip, stealing another taste of her off myself. "I know."

I lowered her to the ground, angling my chin down as I fixed her sweater back over her breast.

Her back met the wall once more. "This is never happening again."

I didn't move away, my boots planted to the cement floor because I didn't think I could leave her here if I tried. "Never."

Eyes full of pure hatred stared up at me as I took in her mussed-up hair, the pout of her lower lip, the cherry stain on her cheeks.

I could almost smile seeing her look at me that way, knowing I was the one to cause all of it.

Fuck, I'd bite the bullet every time if it meant Brandy Rose was staring up at me afterwards, looking utterly and irrevocably ruined in the best way possible.

Her eyes narrowed once more, that venom she typically spewed nowhere to be found. Was she mad I'd kissed her or mad because she liked it?

"I'm going back out there," she stated, moving out from between me and the wall.

"Might want to fix your hair."

A little smirk formed on her mouth, her lips still red and swollen from our kiss. "Guys like messy hair. Might score me someone to bring home tonight."

Before I could respond, she turned and headed down the hall, leaving me standing there feeling both accomplished for bringing that spark back to life in her and pissed that it'd only resulted in her biting me in the ass.

29

BRANDY

Even as the road stretched on for miles and miles in front of me, I didn't *see* it. Not as my mind wandered back to last night and the way Reed's lips felt on me. He hadn't devoured just my mouth, but parts of me I never would've expected him to touch. Especially not with his tongue.

He'd lapped at my skin, leaving trails of moisture dotting me as he took. My body had never felt so alive and full of need, which had only made me feel guilty. Guilty for giving in and letting him kiss me, letting him touch me the way I craved to be touched. Desired. So I'd resorted to what I knew best with him—hate. My words and my body had been polar opposites, one pushing him away and the other pulling him in. When he'd come up for air, I wanted him to go further, to suffocate along with me in our moment of weakness.

Or maybe it wasn't debility, but rather finding the courage to try it out. And maybe that was all it was—a sample. One I'd wanted the entire helping of after one taste. But he'd said he was doing it to rile me up, and that was exactly what he'd done, just not in the way he'd intended. Whether he knew that fact or not, I wasn't sure, but all I was certain of was that every inch of my body had ached for him, and I had not a fucking clue how to feel about that now.

As I pulled up to the Bronsons' ranch and saw Reed's truck parked outside the white barn, I figured I might as well find out. Or apologize for last night. But the one thing I wouldn't do was cower or hide.

It was barely sprinkling as I slid out of the Bronco and closed the door behind me. As I walked up to the barn, a gust of wind blew my loose ponytail from my shoulder, indicating the storm was only beginning.

The door slammed shut behind me as I headed inside, out of the rain. In the short walk alone, strands of hair had come loose, framing my face. I shoved them away, the sleeves of my dark green crewneck covering my palms, nearly touching the tips of my fingers. I hadn't planned to do anything other than groundwork with the horses today, so I'd opted for black leggings and tennis shoes. But before I did that, I had to talk to Reed.

For the second time in a matter of days, I was purposefully seeking him out.

With the overcast sky, the barn wasn't as bright as it typically was, and I knew instantly where Reed was with the light from the tack room illuminating the hallway. Callan had taken the day off from riding lessons because of the weather, and Bailey finished his chores early enough that he was gone by now. Which meant Reed and I were alone in here, and that could either be a good thing or a very, very bad thing.

Keeping my steps light on the mats, I walked toward the tack room, taking a steadying breath. Why was I nervous? It was just Reed. I'd known him basically my entire life.

But I hadn't kissed him all my life, and that fact was now louder than a freight train horn blaring in my mind. I should get off this track of self-destruction, but instead, I only wanted to balance among them. Maybe see how far I could go.

No.

I had to get it together. Cut this off before it turned into something catastrophic.

Stopping right inside the doorframe, I found Reed facing away from me, changing a bit on one of the brown bridles. My shoe met the concrete as I took a step into the room. The quiet sound was enough for him to pause with his fingers on the leather, his broad shoulders going stiff under the black t-shirt he wore.

Reed hooked the bridle on the saddle horn in front of him, abandoning it to turn and face me. His deep hazel eyes held so much emotion in them, a contrast to how he typically walked around, hiding every feeling from sight.

We didn't say anything as we stared at each other. My fingers wove around the edge of my sleeves, nerves I'd rarely felt before taking root in the center of my confidence and spreading like a vine.

"What are you—" he started. At the same time, I said, "What did the—"

We both stopped, closing our mouths. He tipped his chin up, telling me to continue.

With a deep breath, I took one step back and leaned against the doorframe, needing something stable to keep myself grounded, as it felt like my entire world was knocked off its axis and trying to work overtime on a new one and utterly failing.

I wanted to ask what the kiss meant, if he had truly done it just to provoke me out of my depressive stupor. But now, with him staring at me like that, I didn't know what to say.

"We shouldn't have kissed," I blurted.

He arched a brow, saying nothing.

"Last night was a huge mistake, and I was upset, and really, I just don't like you at all, and that was probably overstepping—"

"Are you rambling right now?"

I snapped my lips shut, feeling my cheeks heat as if he took a flame to them himself. "No."

He took a step forward, his thumb rubbing a circle into his opposite palm. "The Brandy I know doesn't ramble."

"Well, I wasn't."

Another step. "Are you nervous?"

My brows pulled together, my eyes narrowing on him. "What? No."

Two steps, and now he was barely a few feet away. "Are you flustered because of me?"

My mouth popped open, but I quickly shut it and hardened my gaze. "No."

His hands dropped to his sides, brushing along his denim jeans as he closed in. I stayed planted next to the door, too afraid to lose its support. "I think you are. It's because of the kiss, isn't it?"

My nose scrunched, my mind reeling from the audacity of this man. What the fuck was he doing? "If this is another brilliant plan of yours to rile me up, forget it. It won't work."

I moved then, pushing off the doorjamb to walk away, but I barely made it a step before his hand wrapped around my arm and tugged me toward him. My back hit the doorframe, and he was suddenly towering over me, invading my space, my mind, my heart.

No, not my heart. Stop it, Brandy.

I tried not to look at the muscles in his arms flexing or the way his tattoos shifted with the movement as his arm braced against the doorframe above my head. His other hand still gripped my arm loosely, but it was very much there.

"Did you hate it as much as you hate me?" he asked, and the breath in my lungs punched out of me because fuck. No, I didn't hate it, but I hated him, and that's what mattered. Right? Or did I just not like being around him? Because right now, the latter seemed entirely more logical than the former with the way my mind was spinning. Was I even breathing?

What the fuck?

I blinked up at him, not knowing what to say. Should I lie or be honest? And if I was honest, would that only hurt me more when he told me it was the worst kiss he'd ever had? But was it? Should I ask?

"I—" My words cut off as I choked on my tongue. With a hard swallow and a deep breath, I continued. "I think you're just trying to distract me from—" But I didn't get to finish my sentence as he dipped his head and pressed his lips to mine.

The act was anything but gentle, his mouth rough as his tongue slipped into my mouth. Naturally, my lips parted for him, allowing him entrance. Just one more time to get whatever this was out of our systems, and things would go back to normal and he wouldn't keep having the nerve to kiss me. Maybe I was getting too soft and he was taking advantage of it. I should put my walls back up, shove him away, do *something*, but his lips were intoxicating and I was getting drunk off his taste alone.

My hands shot forward to shove at his chest, but instead of doing what I commanded, they fisted in his shirt, pulling him closer.

The back of my head pressed into the doorjamb, and as if he fucking knew, his hand slipped between the two, cradling the back of my skull with fingers tangled in my hair, my ponytail coming looser with the act. His teeth clashed with mine, our hunger for each other apparent, but even then, it wasn't enough.

He pulled my bottom lip into his mouth, sucking and nipping before releasing it and crashing into my mouth again. He tugged on my hair, I pulled at his shirt, and we were at war again, one neither of us would win because we wanted so much more than what was okay to offer.

Or was it?

Did we have to hold back?

I wasn't sure—not through this cloud fogging up my mind and heightening my senses with the feel of him.

His mouth left mine, his forehead pressing against my own as we both panted, unable to catch our breaths. I wasn't even sure either of us wanted to breathe in this moment if it wasn't mingled breaths and desperate hands.

"Drop your guard, Little Devil," he growled, his words breathless and starved.

My head shook on its own accord, my instincts telling me *no*.

His hand moved from the back of my head, gently brushing a stray lock of hair away from my cheek. He kept smoothing my hair, as if that was the only thing messed up in this moment.

"You don't have to keep this tough exterior up all the time," he murmured, his forehead still resting against mine, his other hand gripping the frame above my head. "Not around me."

My eyes closed as I willed my heart to steady itself and stop feeling like it was about to burst from my chest in a moment's notice. I didn't know what to say to him. Didn't know how to tell him I was scared because the second you let someone in, you allowed yourself to be vulnerable.

"You can let people take care of you, Brandy," he continued.

I shook my head again, this time by my own will. If I got used to someone—him—taking care of me, I feared I would only regret it later.

"That's how people get hurt," I whispered.

He cupped my cheek, angling my head up, but still, my eyes remained closed.

"Look at me."

I listened, my eyes opening to find him right there, anchoring me from falling off the cliff of my emotions. *This* was why I tucked them far away. What was I doing right now?

"I would *never* hurt you," he said, his voice stern with the purpose to ingrain the words into my brain.

My eyes darted between his, searching for what, I wasn't sure—but whatever it was, I found it.

"Let me in," he added in a whisper.

It took less than a second after the last word passed his lips for mine to meet his again, but this time, it wasn't full of hunger or starvation or craving. No, this kiss held us and all the things we wanted to say to each other over the last seven years but never did. All the reservations and hate and bickering melting away to an us I didn't know but wanted to become familiar with.

His other hand finally moved from above me, his warm palm meeting my cold cheek, snaking its way past my ear and to the back of my head again. He tugged me closer, but not with force. Rather like his intentions turned from feral Satan to savoring

Reed. His free arm snaked around my waist, pulling me flush to him so that I had to arch my neck.

Taking the opportunity, his lips left mine, trailing down my jaw to the sensitive skin on my neck, sending goosebumps up my arms.

"Tell me I can have you, Little Devil," he murmured into the crook of my neck. He sucked my flesh into his mouth, my lips parting on a small gasp.

"Do you want me?" I asked, feeling some sense of power come over me with the way he begged.

His mouth paused on the column of my throat before he pulled back, looking down at me. "Isn't that obvious?"

I shrugged. "This might just be another act of yours to rile me up."

"Let me know if you feel that way after this." Before I could ask what he meant, his hands fell to my ass, lifting me so I had to wrap my legs around his waist.

"You have three seconds to tell me to stop," Reed continued, moving us away from the door. He kicked it shut behind him, closing us in the room without a glance back.

"What?" I squeaked, watching as the door slammed shut.

"One," he started, carrying me across the tack room.

"Reed, we're in the barn."

"Didn't peg you for someone who cared about privacy. Two," he continued.

"It's not that—"

"One more second, Brandy," he warned.

My butt hit the edge of the counter, my eyes darting to his. He was utterly starved in this moment, the sheen to his hungry gaze silently begging me to let this continue.

I didn't want to stop. Didn't think I could if I tried.

"Please don't stop," I whispered.

A brief look of relief flashed across his features before some animalistic need took over him. He set me on the counter, his hands leaving my ass to skim down my thighs. "That's the good girl I was looking for." He crouched, placing a kiss to my knee as he hooked his thumbs into the waistband of my leggings.

"I'm not a good girl," I argued. Even in this, I was unable to stop pushing at everything he said. Despite that, my hips lifted on their own accord, giving him easier access for what he intended to.

He arched a brow up at me, pulling my pants down past my knees. He moved his hands to my shoes, taking his time unlacing them and placing them on the ground, along with my socks. He returned to removing my leggings, sliding them off the rest of the way. "No?"

I shook my head. "No."

A villainous smile pulled at his lips, one I'd never seen before but almost liked that it was aimed at me. "Not even when I do this?" His mouth fell to my inner thigh, his eyes focused on mine as he pressed a kiss to the sensitive skin. His hands moved to my panties, tugging them down.

I shook my head again.

He nipped my thigh, eliciting a little shriek from me. "Words, Little Devil, or this stops."

"No," I said quickly.

"That right there proves that you are," he teased, his voice low and rumbling against my skin. His lips moved higher, peppering kisses to my bare flesh. Rough hands glided up the outside of my thighs, the feeling intoxicating.

His mouth nearly reached my center, but he pulled away, looking up at me. "Fight it all you want, but I *will* make you come undone, and you'll love every minute of it."

I nearly rolled my eyes. "In your dreams."

"Been there for a long time, Brandy. But this is reality, and I'm making good on my promise."

"Promise to what?"

"To break the rules." He lowered his mouth to my pussy, dragging his tongue up my center as he gripped the inside of my thighs to pull them apart. A gasp ripped from my lips, and I grabbed the edge of the counter for stability as the unsaid rules between the two of us melted away with each flick of his tongue, breaking and shattering and obliterating into millions of pieces so small, they nearly never existed.

30

BRANDY

My head fell back against the cabinet behind me as Reed's tongue lapped at my clit, flicking the sensitive bud. He pulled back as I moaned, spitting on my pussy and sending a wave of pleasure through me. One hand left my thigh to rub circles on my clit before sliding down my center.

"I want to see your eyes when I'm in you," Reed growled, pausing at my entrance.

"You're not inside me," I stuttered, trying to catch my breath while he hesitated.

"Yet." He dropped his hand to his side.

I finally looked down at him, panting. "What are you doing?"

"Keep those eyes on me, Little Devil." His hand moved back to my center, sliding two fingers into my pussy. Instantly, my head fell back, my eyes closing at the fullness of just those two digits alone. He kept his fingers in me, but I felt some other part of him move right before a hand came around my neck, pinning me to the cabinet as he paused the movements of his fingers. My eyes flew open, finding him standing directly in front of me now.

"If you keep fighting me on this, I won't let you come." His hand tightened around my neck, but only enough to still allow me to breathe.

My lips pursed together as I inhaled through my nose. Removing one of my hands from the counter, I wrapped my fingers around his wrist, gripping hard as I shoved his palm harder against my throat. "Don't be soft now, Satan."

His eyes darkened as he cut off my air, instantly pumping his fingers inside me. He hooked them, moving in and out at a punishing pace, his thumb brushing my clit with each pass. I kept my grip tight on his wrist, my mouth parting on a silent moan as ripples of pleasure flowed through me. Never once in my life did I think I'd be bared before Reed Bronson with one of his hands between my legs and the other around my throat, remnants of me coating his chin, but here I was, and I was fucking *enjoying* it.

Not just enjoying—fuck, I was melting into a puddle of bliss at his hand and reveling in the fact that he was just as rough in this as he was in other things. It made me wonder what it'd be like if he thoroughly fucked me and ruined me for anyone else.

No, that would never happen.

Just this once, and I'd be satisfied.

He let up on his hold on my neck, allowing me to breathe as he watched his fingers move in and out of me, soaked and glistening in the light. He moved his thumb from my neck, gliding it along my jaw to pull at my bottom lip. I angled my head forward to pull his thumb into my mouth, sucking it while my tongue curled around the end.

He grabbed my jaw, leaving his thumb in my mouth as my cheeks hollowed around it. I wanted him to know what he was missing and couldn't have. Although, that was probably contradicting as his fingers were currently seated so far inside me, I'd likely feel him for days after this.

Pulling my face toward him with his grip on my jaw, he pressed his nose to mine as he added a third finger to my pussy. Another moan escaped me, the sound almost pained as I wanted more. Not just his fingers, but his cock. I was quickly realizing I wouldn't be satisfied after this. I'd need him again, and again, and again.

I'd fucking beg if I had to.

"So fucking naughty for me." Reed's voice was rough, like he, too, knew he'd need more from me.

My teeth grazed the tip of his thumb, nipping the end as I dropped the hand around his wrist to the counter again. A smirk crested his mouth, and the look alone made my core tighten around his fingers, his other thumb pressing harder against my clit as he kept pumping in and out.

"Come for me, Little Devil. Show me how you let go," he murmured before popping his thumb out of my mouth and stealing all the air from my lungs with a punishing kiss.

"It's not going to be that easy for you," I said into his mouth.

He pulled back, his gorgeous fucking eyes nearly making me melt. "I knew you were a needy girl, Brandy, but all you have to do is ask, and I'll kneel before you." Keeping to his word, he dropped to his knees, setting a hand on my knee to push my legs apart further. "Anytime," he murmured before wrapping his lips around my clit and sucking.

My mouth parted as a zing of electricity flowed through me.

He popped his mouth off. "Any day."

He flattened his tongue, licking from the base of his fingers seated deep inside me to my sensitive bud.

"Anywhere." His tongue speared me, flicking back and forth across my clit as I quickly lost it.

His words undid me as I clenched around his fingers. His free hand pried apart my thighs so he could continue his thrusts, eliciting moan after moan from me, my stomach pulsing, my mind spinning, and my world changing.

His tongue and fingers slowed as my orgasm ebbed, and he gently removed his fingers, running a wet trail up the inside of my thigh as I panted, my chest heaving.

Reed stayed on his knees, setting both hands on my thighs, almost like he was getting comfortable.

"What are you doing?" I asked, breathless as I looked down at him.

"Admiring what I did to you," he stated, like he was checking the fucking weather.

I tried to close my legs, but he landed a slap to my thigh, keeping them open. Before I could protest, he moved his hands to my pussy again, spreading it as he dipped his head between my legs. With a flattened tongue, he licked me clean, and I nearly wanted to combust at the sensation.

What the fuck was happening right now?

Once he was satisfied, he stood up, placing both hands on my cheeks to pull my head to him. He planted a kiss on my mouth, his tongue slipping past my lips. I tasted myself on him, and fuck, if that didn't turn me on.

Nearly breathless again, he took a step back, staring at me where I sat perched on the counter, bare from the waist down.

"I never would've thought it'd be like that with you," he said, his eyes roaming over me.

I didn't point out the fact that he was admitting he'd thought about this before. "Disappointed?"

He shook his head, his tongue darting out to run over his bottom lip, like he was savoring the taste of me still on him and already wanted more. "Hardly."

I hopped down from the counter, bending to grab my panties and leggings and pull them on. "Good. Because that's all you're getting." Even saying it fucking sucked. Why couldn't I just give in to what I wanted without feeling guilty for it?

As I straightened, Reed stepped in front of me, grabbing my jaw. "Let me make this clear. You can avoid your emotions all you want, run from your feelings for fucking miles, but you are not going to stop what's happening here."

His eyes darted between mine before he let me go.

"I can do what I want," I said.

He let out a half-assed chuckle. "Always so stubborn."

I crossed my arms. "It's what you're signing up for if you want this."

He shrugged, bending to grab my shoes and socks. He tapped my ankle, and against my better judgment, I lifted my foot.

"I'll fuck it out of you eventually."

My jaw dropped as he slipped my sock on. From his position, he looked up at me, smirking again. "Careful, Brandy. I'm hard as a fucking rock right now, and I won't hesitate to fill that hole."

I snapped my mouth shut, my cheeks flaming at the thought.

And the worst part was, I'd let him.

And I'd enjoy every minute of it.

31

REED

My fist pounded on the door for the sixth time. I'd been light the first few attempts, but after Beckham blatantly ignored them all, I was growing irritated.

I knew he was in there because his truck was sitting in the driveway and the light was on in the living room. Past the curtain, though, I couldn't tell where he was in the house. Knowing him, he was likely sitting on the couch, waiting for me to leave.

Lennon had texted me to come by and check on Beck after he drove him home drunk from the bar last night. I didn't know when the fuck this whole family started thinking I was on taking-care-of-Beckham duty, but I was starting to grow tired of it. My brother didn't typically act like this, but like Mom ingrained into me, I wouldn't be able to pry whatever was causing this out of him.

Len and Beck had gone back to Outlaw's Watering Hole last night, along with Bailey, Lettie, and Oakley. Lennon had said everything was fine until Beckham answered a call and came back in with bloodshot eyes and started slinging shots like there was no tomorrow. Hell, with the way his liver was being treated, it was quite possible there would be no tomorrow.

Which was exactly why Lennon wanted me to check on him.

I knocked one more time for good measure, and after another minute of being met with silence, I turned and headed down the porch steps to get back in my truck. After turning the key in the ignition, I switched the wiper blades on to clear the windshield of the light sprinkle that had started while I stood there. Reversing out of his driveway, I didn't spare a glance back at his double-wide as I pulled onto the road and drove away.

Frustration weighed heavily on my shoulders as I fought the urge to go back there and get Beckham to talk. It'd be no use, and I had better things to do. Better things that currently had my pants feeling too tight as I shifted on my seat.

Three days ago, I'd made Brandy come all over my hand, and for three days, it felt like my cock was in a perpetual state of hardness. I breathed, I thought of her. I closed my eyes, I saw her. I licked my lips, I tasted her. Right about now seemed like as good of a time as any to curb my craving. One more day, and I'd likely erupt.

I had no idea what the fuck we were doing, but I wasn't going to complain. She could fight it all she wanted, but we both knew that once this started, it'd likely never end. It wasn't in our blood to lose a fight, and that's all this was. Our bodies warring with each other for more, trying to satisfy a need we'd buried deep down for too long. Now that it was out to play, it wouldn't go back into hiding.

The bulge in my jeans was a testament to that fact.

I drove until I ended up in her driveway, my truck idling as I stared at her front door. My hand stayed firm around the steering wheel, gripping the leather like it was my last tether of restraint. If I let go, Brandy and I would touch for the third time. Three times seemed to be forming a habit, but something told me Brandy wouldn't let this continue for very long, regardless of my warning. Despite that, I wanted her. I wasn't blind to what was happening between us. Brandy might try to fight it—hell, she was good at that—but I'd get past her defenses.

Starting now.

Taking the key out of the ignition, I pried my hand from the steering wheel and got out. The rain had stopped for now, the chill in the air indicating it'd be snowing in a couple weeks' time.

Not bothering to lock the truck behind me, I headed to her door and knocked without hesitation. I stuffed my hands in my jacket pockets as I waited, listening for any movement behind the door. Silent as a mouse, she opened it. My eyes immediately fell to her hand wrapped around the top of her towel and her wet hair draped messily over her shoulders.

"Reed?"

With a heavy swallow, my gaze moved to her face. Tiny droplets of water rolled down her cheeks, one stuck to the tip of her nose. Her eyelashes were so dark, making her eyes pop. My body moved on its own accord, stepping over the threshold. She was a temptress, and I was stuck in her trance. I didn't know what overcame me, but there was no stopping myself. Not as my palms met her cheeks at the same time my mouth crashed into hers, lips and teeth already clashing as she hungrily met my pace. Her hands wrapped around my wrists as I backed her into the house and kicked the door shut behind me. As her back met the wall, she let out a small moan, her body going soft under mine.

Any question about whether she wanted more of this or not fled the room with her touching me. She may fight it, she may hate me, but deep down, she wanted this. And that was all I needed for now.

With her hands no longer gripping the towel, I felt it slipping between our bodies. Speeding up the inevitable, I put space between us, letting the towel fall to the floor at our feet. Our kiss never broke as her hands slid up my arms to my neck, tugging me closer. She smelled like mint, while the scent of rain clung to me like a cologne.

Letting go of her face, I shucked my jacket off, tossing it to the floor behind me. Her fingers tangled in the fabric of my shirt, pulling at it. I heeded her silent command by breaking the kiss for a split second to lose the shirt, throwing it somewhere along with the jacket.

Right before my lips were back on hers, she shoved on my chest, her eyes trained on my peck.

"What's that?" She kept her hand on my skin like she needed an anchor to keep her standing.

"What's what?" I questioned, though I knew exactly what she was referring to.

"This tattoo." Her finger traced the edge, exactly where mine had glided so many times.

"A flower." I tried to move closer again, but she straightened her arm, keeping me at a distance.

"What kind of flower?" She enunciated every word.

With a steadying breath, I said, "A rose."

"A brandy rose," she whispered, her finger moving to trace the horns peeking out from the folds of the petals.

Her eyelashes fluttered as she blinked, studying the ink etched into my skin.

"Horns because you call me Satan," I admitted, wanting to get this over with because all I needed right now was her.

Her gaze flicked up to mine. "When did you get this?"

I rolled my lips together, unsure how she was taking this. "I was drunk—"

"When, Reed?"

"The day after you called me Satan for the first time."

"But that—"

"Was almost a year ago," I filled in for her.

"Why?" The word was barely a whisper.

I shrugged. "To go with the rest."

She frowned up at me.

Dropping the act, I figured I had no choice but to tell her the truth. "Because you've always meant something to me, Brandy. Whether that be a lesson learned, or something more, I wasn't sure. But you have a permanent spot in my mind, so I figured a permanent spot over my heart wouldn't be too bad either."

She stared at me, and I couldn't tell what she was thinking, but she hadn't kicked me out yet, so I took that as a good sign. Then, her eyes took on a slight sheen, and I almost apologized—for a damn tattoo on my own body, for fuck's sake—but I didn't get the chance as she wrapped her arms around my neck and crashed her mouth to mine.

I met her stroke for stroke as her tongue danced with mine. My hands slid down her hips to wrap around the backs of her thighs, lifting her off the ground. Her legs came around my waist before I walked us down the hall toward her room. Once we were in there, I lowered her to the bed, unraveling her legs from around me. Standing straight again, I looked down at her. She was so fucking beautiful, every inch of her glowing and just so...her. Paintings, models, anyone—they didn't hold a candle to how breathtaking she was with her long, dark hair, that defiant spark always lit in her eyes, and those swollen lips.

Fuck, I was infatuated with the woman. Losing my mind over here, but for entirely different reasons now.

"Hang your head off the bed," I instructed.

Her forehead creased for a split second before she realized what I meant, and then she was moving into position, lying on her back with her head just barely off the edge of the bed.

My eyes scanned the arch in her back and the glint of the two bars going through her nipples. My cock twitched at the sight of them, and as if she knew, she trailed her hands up her stomach to her tiny breasts, cupping them before grabbing the jewelry and tugging ever so slightly.

I groaned, instantly working on my belt, zipper, and button. I needed to feel them, to touch them, right the fuck now. "You're killing me, Little Devil."

She smiled as she stared up at me, loving every minute of the torture she put me through. Though it was nothing compared to what I was about to do to her, I'd let her have her moment.

Tugging my jeans and boxers down, I left them on the floor along with my boots and stepped toward her. Her gaze moved to my cock as she played with her nipples, and instantly, her cheeks flushed.

"Don't get shy on me now," I said, my voice low.

As if that was a challenge, she smirked up at me. "Never."

Angling my head down, I let a drop of spit land on my cock, my hand rubbing it along the shaft. "Tongue out, and stop playing with those tits. They're mine."

I could tell she almost hated being told what to do as she dropped her hands to the bed, her eyes narrowed as she opened her mouth and stuck her tongue out. But for me, she'd do it. She was safe with me.

"If you need me to stop, tap my leg three times." I angled myself in front of her mouth.

She nodded, and not a moment later, I slid past her lips, her tongue lapping up the moisture at my tip and the saliva already coating my skin. I watched her jaw move as I slid deeper, her throat twitching as I hit the back of her tongue and kept going. She didn't gag once, and it made me all the more hard.

Once she was practically swallowing my cock whole, I pulled out, giving her a moment to breathe.

"Are you just going to stand there or are you going to fuck my mouth?" she asked, sass clear in her tone.

My tongue slid between my teeth as I let out a disbelieving chuckle. This woman.

Setting a hand on her throat, I slid back in, done with being gentle. I thrust in and out of her mouth at a steady pace, her tongue warm as it slid against the top of my cock. I reached forward, rolling one of her piercings between my thumb and forefinger. Her body moved in response, her foot trailing up the inside of her leg as a moan came from deep in her throat, vibrating against my length. With a hiss, I picked up the pace, tugging on the jewelry.

She tried to move her hand to that glistening spot between her legs, but I grabbed it, anchoring it to the bed.

"Not until I say you can," I warned.

Her teeth lightly grazed the underside of my cock in response, and I slapped her thigh in reprimand. Maybe it wasn't wise to trust her with my cock in her mouth, but there was no stopping now.

Sliding to the back of her throat, I admired the way her neck moved as my cock was inside her. How she took me so well, and how she'd only take me better when I was in between her legs. As if she was thinking the same, her thighs clenched together, rubbing along one another like she needed some way to ease the ache building there.

"You want to touch yourself?" I asked, sliding out of her mouth only to glide back in again.

She let out a small noise, and I took that as her 'yes.'

I ran a finger up the length of her stomach, watching her skin twitch under my touch. My other hand still played with her nipple piercing, tugging and twisting and soothing.

"You want to come with my cock in your mouth, don't you, Little Devil?"

She tried to nod, but it was futile.

My finger glided between her breasts to the column of her throat, feeling my cock sliding in and out of her mouth. Fuck, the sight of it made me crazy. *She* made me crazy.

"Then suck harder. I'm not convinced you deserve it."

The veins in her neck bulged as she hollowed out her cheeks, listening to my command because doing this alone made her ache with the need to touch herself. I fucked her mouth harder as I wondered if she'd ever touched herself to the thought of me before. Fuck, I'd be the first to admit that I'd come with her name in my mind in the past. Now today, I'd be doing the same, but she'd be here to swallow every last drop of what she did to me.

Her hands fisted in the comforter, her arms straining with the effort to keep from touching herself. I felt her craving for it, as all I wanted was to see her unravel again before me. My hand slid over her breast, cupping it before rolling the jewelry between my fingers, her peaked nipple grazing my calluses.

"I don't know if I should let you come. You've been a bad girl for a long fucking time, and this is exactly how I like to see you."

A small whimper sounded from her as I hit the back of her throat.

"Writhing," I said, pulling out only to glide back in all the way. "Aching." I slid my hand down her stomach, her body jumping at my touch. "Desperate for release." My fingers dipped between her thighs, her wetness coating my skin with just one pass through her center. "Soaked just for me."

I circled her clit with my two fingers, watching her stomach contract as she arched her back, my cock still sliding in and out of her mouth, my thrusts not missing a beat.

"Dip your fingers in your pussy," I commanded.

Her hand instantly moved, disappearing between her legs as she dipped two fingers in. With my free hand, I pried her legs apart. Then, I moved my other hand from her clit to her entrance, inserting two of my own fingers in with hers.

A gasp left her lips around my cock and I slid out, giving her a moment to breathe. Gently, I pulled at the side of her entrance, spreading her just enough. Angling myself over her,

I let a dribble of saliva drip down to her entrance, pooling in her pussy. With her fingers still deep inside herself, I shoved the saliva into her, then left her to it as I removed my hand.

Her free hand came up to grip my cock, angling it so she could wrap her lips around the head.

"So fucking needy, aren't you?" I said, the sentence ending on a groan as she sucked me hard.

Her wrist moved as she slid her fingers in and out of her pussy, her hand glistening with how fucking wet she was. I wanted so badly to fuck her into oblivion, but I needed her to come with her lips on my cock right now.

I felt my release coming as my stomach tightened, my thrusts picking up their pace on their own, but fuck, she needed to come first.

Reaching between her legs, I ran circles over her clit, and instantly, her back arched in response. "Fuck, you respond so well to me."

Her grip on my cock tightened as I thrust deeper, and then she removed her hand so I could hit the back of her throat. Still, she didn't gag. She was too fucking good at this, and I hated the thought of anyone else possibly experiencing this heaven from her.

"If you don't tell me to stop, I'm going to come in your mouth," I warned, not sure if that was what she wanted.

She didn't move to tap my leg, just sucked me harder, deeper, almost begging for me to ruin her from head to toe.

That was a promise I could deliver on.

I added pressure to her clit, my fingers quickening their pace as my other hand closed around her breast. Her thighs clamped together, her stomach twitching as her back bowed, and a moan came from deep in her throat, vibrating along the length of my cock. The sensation made it impossible to hold back, and I buried myself deep in her mouth, my cum spurting down her throat.

She swallowed every fucking drop as her orgasm wracked her body. Removing my hand from her clit, I slid out of her mouth, releasing her breast as I watched her breathing even out. Mine, on the other hand, was out of control, but only because I needed to do it again. And again. And again.

Once wouldn't be enough.

Fuck, I didn't think a hundred times would be enough.

She sat up on her elbows, tilting her head back to look up at me with big eyes and swollen, glistening lips. Her cheeks were flushed, her hair a mess, and she was...perfect.

Without a thought, I bent down, capturing her lips with mine, tasting the saltiness of my release on her tongue as I invaded her mouth.

Pulling away, I stared down at her, lost in the essence of this moment with her. Right now, there was no outside world. No jobs or families or responsibilities. There was only us, and fuck, that was enough for me. I just hoped it was for her, too.

"I should go," I said, not sure if staying was the right thing to do. I didn't know what the fuck we were doing, and while I wanted this to be more, I wasn't sure what she was expecting.

Would we always be push and pull, like two opposite sides of a magnet never being able to fully connect? Or could we get past that and be...normal? Was normal even in the cards for us?

She sat straighter, spinning around on the bed to face me. "You're leaving?"

The disappointment in her voice shot something through my body that nearly broke me. "Do you not want me to?"

She blinked, like she was unsure how to ask me to stay. Like doing so went against her very being.

"What are we doing?" she asked instead of answering my question.

"You tell me."

"You kissed me first," she pointed out.

"I think I kissed you first every time," I stated.

"Are you mad about that?"

"If I was mad, I wouldn't be standing here."

"What are you feeling, then?"

A chuckle rumbled from my chest as I pulled on my boxers. "We're talking feelings now?"

She threw her hands out, plopping them on the bed. "I don't fucking know. I don't know what we're doing, and it's clear you don't either."

I set my hands on the bed on either side of her, invading her space. She smelled so sweet and looked so sated. I feared I was growing an addiction for the woman, if I hadn't already. "I'm staking my claim, Brandy. Not sure what you're doing."

Her eyes popped. "Your *claim*?"

I nodded, my gaze darting to her lips. "Don't pretend you don't know what's going on here."

She scoffed. "If you think us fooling around puts us in some kind of relationship, you're twisted."

"You think this is fooling around?" I asked, bringing a hand up to trail a finger over her bottom lip. "Teens fool around, Brandy. This isn't some childish shit."

"I didn't say it was," she defended.

"Then stop trying to make light of something that isn't light. I want you, and you want me." I pulled on her lip, letting it pop back up before gliding my finger down her neck. "If this is just sex, or a relationship, or nothing, you decide that. But I'm not going to walk away. Ever."

Her breath hitched like that was the confirmation she needed to hear. I knew where the concern for that stemmed from, but I just didn't think she saw me as that kind of person. Part of me knew she didn't, that it was just her past rooted so deep in her brain she couldn't help but think everyone might leave her. But she didn't have to worry about that with me.

"I'm here to stay if you'll let me," I said, my voice dropping to a whisper as my hand slid up to cup her cheek. "So let me."

Her eyes darted between mine, like she wasn't sure what to say. She was warring with herself, wanting to let me in, but her instincts were telling her not to. Lucky for her, I was good at breaking down her walls.

"And if you hurt me?" she asked, vulnerability seeping into the question hiding in the back of her mind, one she never wanted to speak.

I shook my head, my thumb coasting over her cheekbone. "You're safe with me, Brandy. Life may not have taught you you can let someone be your safe space, but that's what I'll be. Fuck buddy, a warm blanket, a shoulder, whatever you want. Just give this a chance. Don't fight it. That's all I ask." My other hand came up to my chest, pointing to the tattoo. "I didn't get this for no reason."

Her gaze fell to the tattoo, her shoulders dropping with the sight of it, like she knew I was right.

After so long of her guard being up, it was hard for her to drop it. I didn't think it wouldn't be, but she never had anything to worry about with me. Her heart had always been safe with me, she was just too scared of the world to see it.

"Okay," she whispered.

I knew that one word took a lot of courage for her to say, but she was damn brave for giving me this chance.

Opening up wasn't easy, I knew that as much as her, but the two of us never had anything to worry about with each other.

And I secretly think she knew that, too.

32

BRANDY

Reed watched as I took a bite of my sandwich, the chips in the center crunching as I leaned over the plate sitting on the comforter of my bed. I sat closer to the pillows while Reed sat on the end of the bed, facing me.

"What is so interesting that you have to stare at me while I eat?" I asked after swallowing my bite.

He let out a burst of air, shaking his head. "Chips on a sandwich."

"It's delicious."

He raised his brows as if he hardly believed it before taking a bite of his not-so-crunchy turkey and cheese sandwich.

He was wearing only his boxers, his shirt now in my possession, as it was the only article of clothing I wore. It fell to my thighs, covering what it needed to. But I guessed that wasn't important after what went down not even twenty minutes ago. He decided to stay for lunch, even though I hadn't been able to muster the courage to outright ask him to. I was thankful he understood the words I was having a hard time speaking.

"Lettie and I always had these as kids. Did you Bronson brothers not get lucky enough to enjoy this type of delicacy?"

He rolled his eyes, taking a swig of his water. "We had finer things for lunch, like beef jerky and sunflower seeds."

"Oof, Lettie told me about the sunflower seeds," I said before taking another bite, a stray chip falling out the back and onto the plate.

Reed chuckled, and the sound stopped me mid-chew. That little glint of teeth, his mouth spreading into a smile he so rarely cracked. He was undeniably handsome with his dark hair and tattoos winding all over his skin, but he rarely grinned. And when he did... Well, the whole world stopped to look.

"Yeah, now that I think back on it, it was kind of fucked up of us to tell her the empty shells would grow." He put the last bite of his sandwich in his mouth.

"Why don't you do that more often?" I asked.

A crease formed between his brows as he finished chewing, then asked, "Do what?"

"Smile."

He cocked an eyebrow. "You're asking *me* why I don't smile more?"

I nodded confidently.

"Brandy, you're the grumpiest woman I've ever met. I think you should be asking yourself that question."

"I already know why *I* don't. I'm asking why *you* don't."

His tongue moved around in his mouth, thinking on his answer. Maybe he didn't have a reason, and this was just the kind of guy he was by nature.

"I save them."

"Save them?" I questioned.

He dipped his chin. "For moments when they really matter."

I frowned. "The whole town of Bell Buckle thinks you're an asshole because of it."

"What, all twelve people?"

"Our population is bigger than that, Reed," I stated before I finished off my sandwich.

"I don't need all of them to like me," he said, setting his plate on the nightstand. "Just the ones that matter."

"So that means you like me?" I asked, as if that wasn't becoming clearer each time we did…this.

But then he narrowed his eyes on me, and I knew I'd asked the wrong question, because I barely had time to move the plate out of the way before he was shoving me back against the pillows and straddling my hips. I let out a laugh as he grabbed my hands and pinned them above my head on the pillow.

"No, Brandy, I hate you," he said, looking down at me.

"Okay, good, I just wanted to make sure we were on the same—"

His mouth covered mine, cutting off my sentence with a kiss. It didn't last long before he pulled back, his nose ghosting against the tip of mine. "I hate the way you feel under my body." His gaze scanned my face. "How your cheeks flush that cherry red when you're wound up in all the right ways." His tongue darted out, running over his bottom lip like he was remembering a decadent meal. "I hate how your taste lingers on my tongue for hours, if not days, and all I crave is more." He shifted his hips, his fingers sliding in between mine where he still held me captive. His eyes darted between both of mine, like he needed to make sure I knew he wasn't serious. And I did. But why did that almost scare me?

"Does any of this make you think I still hate you?" he asked, his boner pressing right between my legs where I wanted it most. But if we went that far, was this solidified in the stars? Could I handle that?

"Well…" I contemplated, needing to make light of the heaviness this turned into.

"Seriously," he said, his tone losing that light it carried briefly.

I opened my mouth to reply, but my phone buzzed on the nightstand next to us and cut me off. Reed didn't take his eyes off me as he released my hands and straightened. I shoved up on my elbow to reach over and grab my phone, seeing that Lettie had texted me.

> **Lettie**
> Can you go to the Orsons' and help them set up their pumpkin patch? I told them

> Bailey and I would but we're both sick with the stomach flu now

I shifted to hold my phone in both hands so I could reply.

> This is what you get for swapping spit with that man

Lettie
> You'll understand once you finally lighten up that black heart of yours

> You're not being very nice for someone who is trying to convince their best friend to cover their ass

Lettie
> Oops sorry yacking all over my HUSBAND gtg

> That is in no way making me jealous of your relationship, just so you know

Lettie
> Are you going to the Orsons' or no

> Fine

Lettie
> Yay love you!!

> Love you too weirdo

She sent back a green puking emoji before I set my phone back down on the nightstand. Lying back on the pillow, I looked up to find Reed staring at me from where he was still straddling my hips.

"Are you ever going to stop that? This feels weird. I much prefer your scowl over"—I waved my hands around—"this."

He kept staring rather than responding, like he was waiting for me to tell him who I was texting.

I gasped, slapping a hand over my heart. "Is Reed Bronson jealous *again*?"

He frowned now, not giving in to my deflecting. He was too good at the blank face game.

"Lettie needs me to go help set up a pumpkin patch. I guess her and Bailey are sick," I finally explained.

"Is she okay?" he asked, ever the protective brother.

"Just a stomach flu, from what she told me. I didn't really have time to ask as I had this broody man staring at me over the top of my phone."

He ignored my jab. "At the Orsons' farm?" he asked. It was the only major pumpkin patch in Bell Buckle during the fall time.

I nodded.

"I'll come with," he said, getting off me.

I sat up, bending my knees. "She didn't tell you to go. She told me."

He grabbed his jeans from the floor, slipping each leg into them. "She didn't tell me *not* to go either."

He buttoned his pants before fixing his belt, and then my jaw fell.

"Is this because they have two sons?"

"No," he stated simply, but I didn't miss the deepening of his voice.

"*Reed*. They're, like, nineteen."

"It's not because of them," he reiterated, crossing his arms once he was done with his jeans. His eyes fell on his shirt I was wearing.

Slowly, I started to scoot away to the farthest side of the bed from him. "You can't go anywhere without your shirt."

"So give it to me," he grumbled.

"I think I'll keep it," I said before shooting off the bed.

He uncrossed his arms and darted for me, easily lifting me by the waist and tossing me back on the bed. Before I could right myself, he was tugging the shirt over my head, leaving me naked.

"Reed!" I shrieked, shoving my hair out of my face to find him already sliding the shirt on himself.

"Problem solved," he said, turning to leave the room. "Get dressed. We leave in five."

"Fucking men," I muttered, shoving off the bed.

"I heard that," he called from down the hall.

"I wanted you to!" I shouted back.

I yanked open the closet door, scanning my clothes for something I could wear to taunt him. If he wanted to be like that, I'd make him drool until he fucking exploded with need.

***

I kept stealing glances at Reed as he stacked hay bales in the formation Mrs. Orson instructed him to. I was working on sorting the pumpkins by size on their makeshift shelves made of the bales, but I kept getting distracted as the tattoos on Reed's arms flexed along with his muscles, the shirt I was wearing not even two hours ago fitting him like a glove.

I'd chosen to wear an open-back sweater solely for the purpose of watching Reed's jaw twitch with every male interaction I had. No one was looking—they knew I'd carve out their eyes if they did—but the statement still stood. If Reed wanted to be pushy, I'd shove right back.

"Hey, Brandy," Henry, one of the Orson twins, said as he approached from where he'd been setting up a separate display with his brother. He had blonde hair that swooshed down over his brows, the sides a bit shorter. His brother, on the other hand, had close-cropped hair.

I turned to face him with two pumpkins cradled in my hands, my back facing Reed.

"Hey," I said, holding the pumpkins closer to my chest.

"The pumpkins are looking good," Henry acknowledged, gesturing to the ones in my hands.

Behind me, a loud thud sounded, and we both looked to find Reed standing atop a bale next to the one he'd thrown down, brushing his gloved hands together as he stared down at us.

I ignored him and whatever display of possessiveness he was trying to show, turning back to Henry.

Henry cleared his throat, combing a hand through his hair. "Anyway, I just came over to let you guys know we can probably take it from here. We really appreciate the last-minute help."

I opened my mouth to respond, but I was cut off as Reed hopped down beside me, his boots kicking up dust. "Sounds good."

"Reed! Brandy!" Mrs. Orson's shrill voice came from the little makeshift shop as she emerged from between two wooden beams. "I have a little something for you two for your time!"

She held a large basket in her hand, the wicker filled with all sorts of fall goodies. She stopped next to her son, holding it out to us.

Reed pulled his gloves off and stuck them in his back pocket before taking the handle from her. I turned to set the two pumpkins on the bale behind us.

"You two were so nice for coming out in place of Lettie and Bailey. You really didn't have to," Mrs. Orson said.

"It's no problem at all, ma'am," Reed replied.

The way ma'am rolled off his tongue...

I swallowed, pasting on a smile. "Always happy to help. Thank you for this. You really didn't need to."

Mrs. Orson waved me off. "Please. It's no biggie. I always have extra every year anyway. Might as well not let it all go to waste." She peeked in the basket, pointing at a few items as she listed them off. "There's cinnamon streusel muffins, caramel apples, some extra homemade salted caramel. All the good stuff."

"Thank you," Reed said.

"Of course. And if you'd like, you can take home a pumpkin or two to carve," she offered.

"Will do," Reed replied. "If you need any more help during the season, let us know. I'm sure one of my brothers will be available if we're not."

She grinned. "You all are always so helpful." She set a hand on Henry's shoulder, but he shrugged it off like he was embarrassed by his mother.

"We try our best. I'm sure we'll see you around soon," Reed said, turning to grab two pumpkins from the bale. I could tell he didn't want to take them for free, but if he'd offered to pay, Mrs. Orson likely would've insisted we take them, along with more.

"Of course," she replied before turning with her son to head back into the little shop.

"I can take one of those," I said, eyeing the basket dangling from his hand as he held both pumpkins along with it.

Reed shook his head. "I've got it."

I let out a sigh as we approached his truck, stopping by the back tire on the passenger side. "Are you seriously going to go back to being stubborn now?"

He set the two pumpkins in the bed, pausing with his hands on the side. "You did, didn't you?"

He left me standing there with a frown as he got in behind the wheel. I supposed I should drop it, but this was typical for us. It felt a hell of a lot more normal than whatever domesticated dream we were living back at my house a couple hours ago.

I opened the passenger door and slid in, buckling myself before I grabbed the basket off the center console and set it in my lap. Reed started the truck, shifted into drive, and headed for the main road.

We were both quiet the whole way back to my house, the only sound the tires on the road as the heater warmed my legs. Within twenty minutes, we were pulling up my driveway.

"Are you mad at me or something?" I asked as he pulled to a stop.

"Why would I be mad?"

I rolled my lips together. As if the answer wasn't obvious. I'd worn a revealing sweater solely to spite him, and he'd clearly been jealous Henry had complimented my pumpkins. And yes, I was well aware he meant the pumpkin display and not my tits, but the insinuation stood.

"If this is about the Orson boys, I have no interest in them," I stated.

He stayed quiet, his hand still gripping the wheel.

I tossed my head back and forth. "Although, having a pair of twins—"

Before I could finish my sentence, he turned off the truck and got out. A smirk crested my mouth as I shifted the basket so I could unbuckle my seat belt, the fabric retracting as Reed opened the passenger door.

He lifted the basket off my lap, setting it on the ground next to him before his hands lifted me under the armpits and pulled me out.

"Reed," I warned, unsure of what he was doing.

He remained quiet as he set me down, then turned me so my back was facing him. Before I could question his actions, he set a hand between my shoulder blades and forced my breasts to the warm seat.

"What are you doing?" I asked, looking over my shoulder at him.

But still, he kept his mouth shut. His fingers came around my front, quickly undoing the button and zipper on my jeans before shucking them halfway down my legs.

"Reed!" I shrieked. "What the fuck are you doing?"

"You want to be a tease, Brandy?" Something popped behind me, but whatever it was, he held it from view so I couldn't see. "Flaunt your pretty back for a bunch of boys when the only man you need is five feet away?"

"I was only—"

"I know what you were doing. I know you wanted a reaction out of me. We've been doing this for years, Brandy. I'm not blind to the game you play."

"I'm not blind to yours either," I snapped before he yanked my panties down.

"Good." He gripped my sweater before ripping the bottom, and my mouth fell open. "I wasn't trying to hide."

"You just tore my sweater," I stated, almost in shock but silently writhing over wherever this was going.

"I did." He moved my hair over my shoulder, and then something cool hit the top of my spine, oozing its way down the center of my back.

"What is that?" I asked, trying to look over my shoulder to see, but he forced my face forward again.

"Caramel."

My eyes widened. "Your punishment is dripping caramel on me?"

"Nope." He landed a hard smack to my ass, his palm blissfully stinging my skin. "That was."

My teeth clamped down on my bottom lip as the sticky substance trailed a path down my spine, going lower, lower, lower.

Soon, it reached my tailbone, then continued heading south between my ass cheeks.

"Reed..."

"Yes, Little Devil?"

"How are you planning to—" But my words were cut off as he got to his knees and set his hands on my ass, spreading the cheeks. His tongue met my center, and then he dragged it up through the stream of caramel as he drizzled more over my hole.

I sucked in a breath, the sensation more than I was expecting. He took his time lapping his tongue gently over my hole, thoroughly cleaning it before he continued upwards along the sweet path.

"Holy fuck," I whispered as his hands coasted up the sides of my body as he made his way north.

My spine lit like a Christmas tree, every nerve in my body reacting to the feel of his tongue. I was almost sad he was nearly done cleaning his mess. Maybe I'd convince him to make another.

Once he reached the top of my spine, his tongue disappeared. With a light smack to my ass, he stepped away, the warmth of his body leaving mine. "See you later, Little Devil."

My head whipped around as I straightened. "I'm sorry, what?"

He was already heading around the front of the truck, back over to the driver's side.

"You're leaving me with this sticky mess?" I asked when he didn't reply.

"Yep."

"Are you kidding me?"

He looked at me over the windshield. "This is what punishment feels like, Brandy. Don't like it? Be a good girl."

But that was a challenge in itself.

Reed Bronson knew I'd never be a good girl.

And he fucking loved it.

33

REED

"He hasn't answered his phone in two days," Lettie said on the other end of the line as I drove toward Beckham's place. Her voice was rough from getting over the flu. Bailey was already better, but Lettie's immune system always took a little more of a hit due to her anemia.

"Did you call anyone else?" I asked, keeping my focus on the road through the downpour.

"Just you."

Despite her being sick herself, Lettie worried about her brothers just as much as we worried about her, so when Beckham wasn't answering her texts, concern grew in her gut like a weed on a spring day. I already felt bad they'd gotten sick. They were meant to be on their honeymoon this week, but they had to postpone it until they felt better.

"I can go check myself. I don't want to bother you—" she started.

"No. It's fine. I'll just swing by on my way back from the feed store." I paused to let her respond, then thought better of it. She was resting at home. Last thing she needed to be doing right now was worrying about her family. "I'll text you an update. Now quit worrying and watch some gossip show or something. I don't need Bailey showin' up to the ranch this week all pissy because he's worried about you." I knew the feeling all too well.

"I don't think he's the grump we have to worry about," she mumbled. "Thanks, Reed."

"Yep." I hung up the phone, tossing it in the cup holder as I turned toward Beckham's double-wide. Pulling up the driveway, I shifted into park and killed the engine, adjusting the brim of my hat before getting out and shutting the door behind me. I walked up the muddy gravel path to his porch, climbing the few steps before pounding a fist on the door loud enough to be heard over the rain.

I waited a moment before knocking again, and seconds later, the door swung in. I didn't wait for him to invite me in as I shoved past him, choosing not to acknowledge the beard he was growing and the trash littering every countertop.

"Lettie's worried about you," I stated, eyeing the mess of his house. What the fuck was he doing with all his spare time to be okay with his place looking like this?

The door clicked shut, and I turned to face him, taking in his messed up hair, stained t-shirt, and baggy sweatpants.

"Don't know why," he grumbled, moving to the kitchen. "Beer?"

"It's eight a.m.," I replied as he opened the fridge and ducked his head inside.

He reemerged, beer in hand, and shrugged. "Five o'clock somewhere, right?"

"The fuck is wrong with you?" He had our mom concerned, and now our sister. Before we knew it, the whole goddamn town would be on his case.

He popped the tab on his beer, taking a swig. "Don't need people worrying about me, if you couldn't guess as much."

"That's real fucking clear, Beck. But naturally, when you act like you don't give a shit about yourself, people are going to fucking care."

He leaned back against the counter, drawing my attention to the beer cans lined up behind him.

"Are you drunk?" I asked, taking a step forward.

He took another casual sip of his beer. "I can do whatever the fuck I want."

If defensive was how he wanted to be, maybe that'd get him to open up. Talk about whatever the fuck was going on with him. This closed-off broody shit wasn't working.

"Yeah, that's real mature. Rotting away at home, getting wasted every damn day. Do you even see the state of this place? It's a fucking mess."

He shrugged again, eyeing the space as if he was seeing it for the first time. "Ain't too bad."

"Are you depressed or some shit?" If emotions were what he was battling with, he needed to talk to Callan. I wasn't anyone's first choice to be their therapist. I could get Brandy to open up, but my brother? There was a reason siblings didn't always get along, and ninety-nine percent of the time, it was because of fucking emotions. That's why I never talked about mine with them. Fuck, half the time, I didn't know what the fuck I was feeling to begin with. To try and voice it would be a goddamn shit show. I didn't need my brothers witnessing that.

Beckham simply stared at me, looking bored, as if he couldn't wait for me to get the fuck out of here so he could go back to chugging beers and passing out on the couch alone.

What the fuck would make him quit this act? Snap out of whatever mood he was stuck in for good?

He didn't have a dog, a best friend, a girl—

Or did he?

There was only one way to find out.

"Man, Parker would fucking *love* to see you like this," I muttered.

I knew bringing her up was a line I shouldn't have crossed, and yet, for some fucking reason, I didn't expect the punch or the pain that stung after. My head snapped to the side, Beckham's fist connecting with my jaw with a loud *pop*. My teeth vibrated in my skull, the metallic tang of blood coating my mouth. My tongue slipped out to run along my lower lip as I stared at the wall, barely moving.

It wasn't the first time a Bronson brother got physical with another. Hell, we all had our fights growing up. It'd just been a while. But now I had an idea of what might be bothering him. Or at least, that he hadn't let that girl go.

My fingers ran along my jaw, dabbing at the liquid on my bottom lip. Pulling my hand away, I stared at the blood before wiping it on my jeans and shaking my head.

"Whatever you've got going on, Beck, I don't need to know. But you have a lot of people worried, and you might think whatever this is is killing you, but think about what it's doing to them. And now what it's done to us." My eyes fell to the ground. "This isn't you. I know that, you know that. So find some way to cope that doesn't involve digging your own grave."

I looked at him, but he refused to meet my gaze as he stared at the kitchen floor. Regret shone clear in the way he stood, but I wouldn't get an apology. Hell, I didn't need one. I would've done the same if someone had brought Brandy up in that way. Unfortunately for the both of us, that just meant we cared about them. And for Beckham, sometimes that care was wilting. It consumed him the same way it did our brother, Callan. Difference was, Callan wouldn't let himself waste away over it. Beckham was just overly sensitive in some topics, but I couldn't change that.

I could be there for him like our mom said. Wait for him to open up and not force it out of him. But that wasn't like me. And this wasn't like Beckham. The fact of the matter was—nothing was going to change here. Not today, not tomorrow, and likely not next week.

So after this, I'd drop it. My family could put the burden on me all they wanted, but Beckham wasn't mine to take care of. I loved him because he was my brother, but that didn't equip me with the mental tools to change who I was because he was struggling. Whatever was going on with him would have to be solved at the source, and his problem didn't include me.

Without another word, I turned and left, leaving him standing in the kitchen to think about all of this.

Maybe punching his brother was what he needed to snap out of it, or maybe I only made it worse. Whatever it was, I got a reaction out of him instead of a shrug or a grunt.

That had to count for something.

34

BRANDY

I hung up the bridle Callan's student had used on Butterscotch for their lesson in the indoor arena and moved to the opposite wall to reorganize the halters. We were all pretty good at keeping it neat, but it didn't prevent the ropes from getting caught up in one another from time to time.

Callan had to leave right after his lesson to go to a doctor's appointment with Sage, so I offered to untack Butterscotch and put everything away. I already finished what I needed to do for the day with desensitizing some of the rescue horses, so at this point, I was looking for things to do to pass the time. I didn't want to go home and sit in my feelings about my mother or Reed, and Lettie was still home sick. This ranch was always my safe space growing up, and it continued to be to this day.

I was thankful I had the Bronsons to go to when things were tough. Without them, I didn't know how I would've gotten through a majority of my childhood—seeing my father put his hands on my mother and having such a poor example of what love should really look like. Charlotte and Travis did more than just take me in as one of their own. They taught me things my parents never thought to—that love didn't have to lead with arguments and getting physical. It could be nice. Enjoyable, even.

But for the longest time, I didn't think I'd ever feel remotely close to that. I kept myself guarded from heavy emotions because I knew that if I let my walls down, I was opening myself up to the possibility of getting broken. Hurt. And I'd seen my mom hurt more times than I could count. Heard her sobs in the shower, or saw her flinch at sudden movements. It wasn't the sort of life I ever wanted to live, so I didn't allow myself to grow feelings for people. Sure, I dated, but it never got past the second or third date.

I used to excuse it to the fact that I just didn't like them, but as of lately, I figured out it wasn't that at all. They just weren't who I actually wanted. And the one person I did want was the person I'd shut out for years.

But Reed didn't get violent that night *at* me. He got violent *for* me. Because he wanted to keep me safe, and make the man who disrespected me pay for how he treated me. He likely would've killed him if given the chance. Hell, he was three punches away from doing so. But he also stopped because of me. Led me outside because he couldn't bear to see me sitting there, defeated and humiliated. Drove me home because he cared about me.

It took me so long to see that there were different types of violence in people, and not everyone was the same. The rage in my father wasn't the same rage I saw in Reed that night. It'd never be, and I hated that I isolated Reed because my mind couldn't comprehend any of it. Why would a man hit the woman he loved? Why was I dealt the hand of a shitty father who should've been there for me that night, but instead, it was Reed?

And that's when everything shifted. When I realized Reed only bickered with me to see me be less of a shell of a person. How he knew what clouded my mind every day, so he found ways to distract me. All this time, I was so blind to what was really happening between the two of us, all because of one fucked up night.

I was done with all of that ruling my life.

I left the tack room with the intention of grabbing my phone from where I'd set it on the wall of the indoor arena, but I stopped in the middle of the aisle when I heard a truck engine rumbling in the distance. Changing my direction to the door of the barn, I paused inside the threshold, out of the rain, as Reed turned off his truck and got out. He hung his head as he walked through the downpour in my direction, his black cowboy hat shielding his face from view.

My body hummed with the anticipation of seeing him, not sure if it was okay for me to hug or kiss him in greeting. All hope of either vanished as he walked right past me, wet boot prints following in his wake on the concrete.

"Reed," I said, hurrying after him.

"Not now, Brandy," he grumbled, not bothering to turn around or lift his head.

I grabbed his arm, tugging him back so he'd stop. "What's wrong?"

But the answer was all too clear as he spun to face me, revealing the split on his lip. My eyes widened at the sight of it. "What the fuck happened?"

"Nothing," he muttered as I dropped his arm.

My hand moved on its own, dabbing at the cut with the tip of my finger. It was no longer bleeding, but it wasn't scabbed over yet. "This isn't nothing."

He turned his head away, his eyes downcast on the ground. "I have shit to do."

"Oh, no. You don't get to tell me to open up to you and then you show up here with a cut lip and not tell me what happened. Who the fuck hit you?"

He shook his head, his lips rolling together. "Let it go."

My mouth opened and closed, at a loss for words. Was he serious right now?

He didn't wait as he turned, making it barely two steps before I blurted out, "I love you."

He froze, his back to me as I watched his shoulders stiffen, then relax under his black Carhartt jacket.

My heart raced like a thousand horses were galloping across the plains of my feelings, laid bare and ready to be trampled down by the hooves of his rejection. We'd shared moments, but what did any of that even mean? He wanted to be more than just my…enemy, and yet, he didn't want to open up to me. I was beyond confused, but I knew one thing for certain. Whether he rejected me over it or decided to continue whatever this was, I'd be ready.

Slowly, he pivoted to face me, the sound of the storm drowning out as my blood pumped through my veins at an alarming rate.

"What did you say?" he asked, his voice so quiet that I barely heard him. The question fell flat, and I couldn't tell if he was mad or happy or straight irritated with me for reasons I didn't know.

I blinked, trying to remember if I'd said what I thought I did out loud, or something crazy that was making him stare at me in disbelief.

"I love you." I swallowed, forcing a breath of air into my lungs. "I think. I don't know. I don't know how to do any of this, but I love you, and I don't want you to shut me out. Not now." Tears welled in my eyes, my throat suddenly feeling like a brick was dropped into it. "Please don't shut me out."

A tear rolled down my cheek, then another, as all I wanted to do was sink in on myself with the weight of the emotions threatening to crush me into pieces. I had blocked them all out, never wanting them to be seen or heard, or hell, half the time, even felt. But here I was, laying out this four-letter word to a man I thought I hated but really, I was just confused how to feel about him because I wasn't taught how to love. Right now, in this moment, though, I knew love wasn't something that even could be taught. It could be displayed, versions of it to be seen by others—but none of that prepared anyone for how they'd love when the time came.

And I thought all this time I wasn't capable of it because of the things I'd seen. It was never that. I just wasn't ready for what we could be, and now, I think I was. Ready to let him in, ready to love him and let him consume my every waking thought.

I just hoped he was ready, too.

Reed stood there staring at me, the look on his face so heavily guarded that I had no idea what he was thinking. Before I could let myself feel the humiliation of him not loving me back, he stormed forward, not stopping until his hands were on my cheeks, pulling my face up to his and crashing his lips to mine. My hands fisted in his shirt, parting his jacket to feel his warm chest and tug him closer.

My hands trailed over his chest, to his shoulders, his neck, down his arms until I was gripping his wrists as they held my face firm. I couldn't stop touching him. Our mouths spoke silent promises to each other with each caress, each pass of his tongue over mine.

Eventually, the kiss slowed, and he pressed his forehead to mine as he swiped my remaining tears away with his thumbs.

He pulled his head back to look down at me, brushing a stray strand of hair away that was stuck to my face. "You love me, huh?"

I nodded.

"I've been waiting to hear you say that."

I rolled my eyes, grabbing his wrist to try to get him to release his hold on me as I attempted to spin away. He held firm, not letting me get anywhere.

"I love you, too, Brandy."

I froze, staring up at him. Just in his eyes, I could tell he was being honest. I didn't think he'd lie about something like that, but my mind had a hard time wrapping around the idea of this being…good. For so long, I fought against him, and now that I didn't have to keep my guard up around him, I could let myself fall into him knowing he'd catch me.

All along, I knew that he would. I was just the one who needed to take the jump in the first place.

With no words to embody how I felt in this moment, I leaned into him, wrapping my arms around his waist and burying my head in his chest.

Reed Bronson loved me, and I loved him back.

I felt safe.

"Are you going to tell me what happened now?" I said into his shirt.

He ran his hands up and down my sides slowly. "We can't enjoy the moment for a little bit longer?" he asked, clearly trying to dodge the question.

I pulled away, crossing my arms over my chest as I looked up at him.

"I take that as a no," he said on a sigh. He reached up to take his cowboy hat off, running his hand through his hair before plopping it back on. "Beckham punched me."

My eyes went wide, my arms dropping to my sides. "Why would he do that?"

"I brought up something I shouldn't have," he admitted, sounding a bit ashamed.

"What was it?"

He gave me a sad puppy kind of look, like he didn't want to be forced to tell me what he did.

I popped a hip, waiting.

With another sigh, he leaned a shoulder against the wall beside us. "You're already putting me through the wringer. Maybe I should take it back—"

My mouth popped open on a gasp.

"I'm kidding!" He reached forward, pulling me to him so his back was to the wall now, his arms around my shoulders as he held me to his chest.

"You said you love me *and* you made a joke? I don't know if I like this new Reed," I teased.

"Well, get used to it. I'm not going anywhere."

The statement made the corners of my mouth curl up as warmth coiled through me.

"I brought up Parker," Reed went on, and I tried to hide my reaction as I cringed.

"Oh."

"Yeah. Not my brightest moment, I'll admit. But he's just been so...not himself lately, and I can't stand seeing him like this."

"You think it has something to do with her?" I asked.

He shrugged. "I'm not sure. I think I should just let it go. Wait until he comes around and wants to talk rather than trying to force it out of him."

"If he's anything like me, you know that's probably the best way to go about it," I told him.

"I just hate seeing my mom worry, but I'm not good at this, Brandy."

I pushed off his chest to look at him. "Good at what?"

"Feelings, I guess. Don't really talk about my own, so I don't know why I expect my brother to either. I guess we got that from our father."

Travis wasn't much of a talker to begin with, and when he did, it wasn't typically about his feelings. Callan took after their mom in that department, but the others were working on it.

"He'll be okay." I reached up, cupping his cheek. "Beckham didn't get through years of riding broncs to let some emotions bury him. We'll be here when he's ready." My thumb brushed over his injured lip. "But in the meantime, probably don't bring up sensitive subjects, yeah?"

He nodded. "Yeah."

With a smile, I dropped my hand to his chest. "Say it again."

He gripped my hips. "What?"

I frowned. "You know what."

"Hmm," he hummed, tossing his head back and forth. "You'll have to remind me. My memory's not too good after that hit."

I narrowed my eyes at him. "He hit your mouth, not your temple, smart-ass."

Reed grinned, aiming all his happiness straight down at me. "I love you. Even if sometimes, you're a little mean."

I faked a gasp, pressing a hand to my chest. "Me? Mean? No way."

He shook his head as he chuckled before leaning toward me and pressing his lips to mine.

Love with Reed felt pretty good.

35

BRANDY

Lighting the sixth candle on the edge of the tub, I turned the light off in the bathroom as the water finished filling. I wasn't much of a bath person, but my muscles were aching from moving a load of hay with the Bronsons before winter hit in full force. With Lettie still recovering at home, we didn't have as many hands, so like always, I tried to go above and beyond. Reed hadn't been too happy that I'd been doing so much, Mr. Protective and all, but it'd been cute to see him all grumpy about me overworking myself. Usually, it irritated me, but I was learning to accept he had only been looking out for me, especially now that we had admitted our love for each other.

The word felt foreign to think when it came to him, and I didn't know if I'd ever get used to it. It was a good thing I had a lifetime with him to do it.

We weren't married or even engaged, and I had a feeling that wouldn't come for a while, but with Reed, it felt right now that we'd finally gotten over our feud. For as long as we were together, I didn't think there'd ever be a dull moment in our lives, and that was the kind of life I wanted. Between the bickering and the way he almost knew my body better than I did, I knew we'd be okay.

Stripping out of my clothes, I sank into the tub. The room lit up as a burst of lightning struck in the distance, which was soon followed by the low rumble of thunder. The storm was far enough away that I wasn't worried about being in the tub for half an hour, so I sat back, resting my head on the ledge, and closed my eyes.

Steam filled the room from the scorching water, dampening my hair and making it curl around my face. On the stool beside the tub, my phone buzzed. I reached out of the water, drying my hand on the towel under my phone before picking it up.

> **Reed**
> How's your body feeling after today?

My teeth sank into my bottom lip at his question. Before, I would've told him to fuck off, but now, all I wanted to do was play.

> Pretty achey

> **Reed**
> Need anything?

My eyes moved to the bubbles floating on top of the water as they swished around my body. I needed a lot of things from Reed right now, and my core heating was a testament to that.

> Something to get my mind off the pain

Reed
What do you have in mind?

> Hmmm. A few things

Reed
What are you doing right now?

> Taking a bath

The three dots popped up on the screen before disappearing. It happened twice before he replied.

Reed
Making me think of you in there is cruel

> Did it do what I intended?

Reed
What was that?

> Make you want me

I bit back my smile, unable to believe I was on the verge of sexting with Reed right now.

> **Reed**
> I always want you, Little Devil. There's never a moment I'm not thinking of your body or the way your nipples look with those damn bars in them

> You like my piercings?

> **Reed**
> I fucking love your piercings and I want nothing more than to play with them every fucking day

> All I hear is empty promises

> **Reed**
> Is that a challenge?

Thinking there was no better time than now, I opened my photo album on my phone and scrolled to the photos I had taken in the field when Reed rudely interrupted me. I swiped through them, deciding on one I took from the side, arched forward on the horse with my hand on her withers. Tapping the icon in the bottom corner, I chose Reed's contact, hitting send before I could change my mind.

> You have a truck, don't you?

Those three dots popped up again, then immediately disappeared. Minutes ticked by before I got a response.

> **Reed**
> Is your front door unlocked?

Nerves hit me in the gut when he didn't acknowledge the photo. Maybe he hated it? He was mad that day, so I guess it wouldn't surprise me if he did.

> Yes... why?

I sat there waiting for a response, but when the phone remained silent after a few minutes, I finally put it back on the stool and sank deeper into the water.

My hand trailed over my thigh as the bubbles started disappearing around me. All I could think about was Reed's muscles as they flexed under his tattoos earlier today. How his t-shirt stretched across his chest, and the way his dark jeans hugged his ass.

That same man elicited orgasms from me like no other, worshiping my body like he could never have enough. I wanted nothing more in this moment than for him to do exactly that. To lick and touch and take and fuck.

Behind the closed door of the bathroom, I heard a creak and the familiar sound of my front door closing. Instantly on alert, I sat up straighter, careful to keep my breasts below the water.

"Hello?" I called out, gripping the porcelain edge of the tub.

The sound of boots on hardwood echoed down the hall, and my heart raced in my chest. Maybe it was just Reed. He'd asked if it was unlocked, so his showing up here wouldn't be out of the blue.

I should've locked the door, but no one ever came out here unless they had a reason. I guess murder would be a pretty solid motivation, though.

The handle on the door turned, and I shoved back against the opposite side of the tub, pulling my legs up to my chest. If it wasn't Reed, I was screwed and utterly vulnerable right now.

Slowly, the door opened, creaking on the hinge as the shadow of a man presented itself in the gap. With only the candlelight illuminating the room, it made it hard to see who it was, but once the cowboy hat came into view, I knew I was safe.

Reed stepped into the bathroom, one slow footstep at a time, making his way across the room to me. My chest was heaving as I tried to catch my breath. Fear had gripped me for moments before I'd known it was him, and now I was trying to calm down.

"You look scared, Brandy," he said, the candles casting a dim orange glow on his face.

"You came into my house unannounced. I have a reason to be scared," I retorted.

He stopped by the side of the tub, looking down at me. His eyes roamed over my body as if he could see through the bubbles, straight to my bare skin. Relaxing my legs, I let my back hit the tub again.

"Locking your front door could prevent that," he stated, lowering himself to the stool beside the tub. He tossed the towel to the ground, laying my phone next to it.

"No one comes out here. It's a small town."

He shoved the sleeve of his jacket up before trailing his finger through the water. "Small towns don't mean there aren't any creeps out."

I turned my head to the side as his touch met my skin. He glided his finger over my collarbone before trailing it down beneath the water between my breasts.

"What are you doing?" I asked.

"Why'd you send the photo?"

I inhaled deeply as he tugged on my jewelry. "Because I wanted to."

He pulled it harder, and I gasped. "Not the answer I wanted."

"Because I wanted you to come here and fuck me."

His hand palmed my breast before moving to the other, playing with my nipple like he could do this all day. "You're greedy, Brandy. Don't you think I've given you enough orgasms the past few days?"

I shook my head, my movements halting as he pinched my nipple in reprimand.

"You need to be careful," he stated, flicking the bar before pulling his hand away but keeping it under the water.

My eyes moved to his, finding him watching me. "Why? Are you going to hurt me?"

He trailed two fingers down my stomach, causing my belly to jump. "Is that what you want? A little pain?"

I let my body relax against the tub, not giving him a response as he moved lower. Then, without warning, he plunged three fingers into me. I shot forward, my hands coming up to grip the tub as he buried them deep in my pussy. Water splashed over the edges, soaking the floor. He curled his fingers, hooking them inside me. I let out a gasp as he pressed his palm against my clit, cupping me.

"Next time you're home alone, you're going to lock your door." When I didn't respond, he grabbed me harder, lifting me slightly. "Do you hear me, Brandy?"

I nodded, meeting his intense gaze. "I will."

He leaned over the edge of the tub, moving the tips of his fingers inside me. Pleasure shot through my belly, desperate for more friction. "And the next time you want to take photos of yourself looking the way you did, I'm the only one you send them to. Immediately. Before you even have a chance to glance at them, I want them on my phone."

I nodded again, needing him to stop talking and make me come.

But then he removed his hand, pulling it out from under the water. He grabbed the towel off the ground, drying his arm off before standing.

I sat forward, missing the feeling of him already. "Where are you going?"

"To the couch." He tossed the towel on the stool and turned for the door. "Enjoy your bath."

Then he closed me in the bathroom alone, leaving me gawking at the door. Did he seriously just shove his fingers inside me and make demands?

Fuck that.

Two could play that game.

***

I didn't bother to dry off after I stepped out of the bath and pulled the plug. I also didn't grab a robe as I opened the door and padded down the hall, my hair dripping behind me. If Reed thought he could edge me and walk away, I'd show him exactly how it felt.

Reed sat in the armchair facing the hallway, hungry eyes scanning my bare, dripping skin as I approached him. I took my time, sliding a finger along the back of the couch as I walked around it. My gaze never left his, confidence strumming through my veins with the knowledge that he was completely, utterly obsessed with me. I knew damn well what I did to him, as if the bulge in his jeans wasn't evidence enough of that.

He sat with his legs spread, his elbows propped on the armrests while his fists flexed.

"Mad, Little Devil?" he asked, restraint evident in those three words.

"Furious."

He tipped his chin in my direction. "That why you're out here looking like that? To take your anger out on me like you're so good at?"

Fully facing him now, I prowled toward him. Each step, I swayed my hips with the intent to make him absolutely feral. "That's exactly why."

He tipped his head back as I approached, looking up at me where I stopped before him. His jean-clad knee touched my thigh, but he made no attempt to move it. "You think you can come into my house uninvited..." I set my hands on his legs, leaning into his space. "Interrupt my bath time..." Pressing my breasts together with my arms, I dared to get closer, leaving less than an inch of space between our lips. "And leave?"

He cocked his head to the side. "I'm still here, aren't I?"

I grabbed his hand and forced it between my legs. He cupped me instantly. "But you're not *here*."

As he reached forward to position his fingers at my entrance, I shoved him away, forcing his hand back to the armrest. "Nuh-uh," I tsked. "You lost that privilege."

He arched a brow, waiting for what I was sure he wasn't prepared for.

I undid the buckle on his belt, then moved to pop the button on his jeans before pulling his zipper down. Our eyes were drawn to each other like magnets, wanting to look away but too compelled by the other to do so.

Tugging the waistband of his boxers down, his cock sprang up, hitting the fabric of his t-shirt stretched over his abs. I wanted him naked, completely bare like myself, but I also wanted him fucking begging for more, and keeping him on that edge was where he needed to be to get there. Which meant he wouldn't feel my skin against his when I did what I planned to do next.

Wrapping a hand around the base of his cock, I stroked up, down, before tilting my head. With my eyes still on his, I let a trickle of saliva fall on the head, dripping down the side of his length. He hissed in a breath when I captured the spit with my palm, rubbing it along his cock.

"Are you clean?" I asked, knowing the answer but still feeling it necessary to ask before I took this further than we've gone before.

"Of course, I'm clean," he replied. "You're worried about that now?"

I pursed my lips. "I've been kind of distracted, okay?" I gave him a moment, then added, "Aren't you going to ask me if I am?"

"Oh, I know you are."

I narrowed my gaze, pausing my strokes on his cock. "You're so sure?"

He leaned forward in the chair. "I am. Because if you said you weren't, I'd kill the fucker who made that your answer, and I think we both don't want murder on my hands tonight." His lips were close to mine now, his voice dropping. "I'd much rather it be your body under my hands as you scream my name while you ride my cock."

My breath hitched as he sat back in the chair, tipping his chin for me to continue. For a brief moment, I was stunned in place, utterly confused how we got here but loving every fucking minute of it. This entire time, I thought I was the one making him feral, but I was beginning to think it was the other way around. I was in a complete trance just from the things he said, and it was one I never wanted to wake up from.

Blinking out of my haze, I tightened my grip on his cock, eliciting a sharp breath from him. I smirked, resuming my strokes as I set a hand on his thigh. Lowering myself to my knees, I stared up at him, spreading his legs farther apart.

I dipped down, but rather than going for his cock, I went straight for his balls, pulling them into my mouth and sucking hard.

"Holy fucking hell," Reed hissed, his fingers digging into the chair as I picked up my pace on his length.

I worked his balls with my tongue as I sucked on them, tugging and pulling. A groan fell from him, somewhere deep in his chest, and I fucking loved the sound.

Releasing his balls, I dragged my tongue up his length, lapping at the bead of moisture collecting at the top. He stared down at me in awe, his eyes glazed over with pure, unfiltered need.

Setting my hands on his thighs, I stood up, lifting my leg to straddle his lap. He stared up at me now, finally loosening his hold on the armrests to grab my hips. I shoved his hands away, forcing them back to the chair.

"No touching."

He sucked on his teeth, running his tongue over his bottom lip as a challenge lit in his eyes. "I guess the sass doesn't ever leave you."

Instantly, my hand wrapped around his neck, forcing his head back against the cushion. I left enough pressure off his throat so he could breathe. "Keep talking like that, and this will only get worse."

His cock twitched against my thigh, and I used every ounce of my control to keep from reacting. "For me or for you?"

"Just you," I answered, running my thumb along his sharp jawline. "I'm perfectly capable of pleasuring myself."

Something between a growl and a groan rumbled up his throat, vibrating against my hand. He sealed his lips shut in a display of obedience, and I couldn't help the smile that pulled at my lips. "Good boy."

Adjusting myself over his length, I let go of his neck, setting one hand on his shoulder while the other disappeared between my legs to grip his cock. He let out a breath when my skin came in contact with his, staring down between us with a fixation that would have brought any girl to their knees.

With that look in his eye alone, I didn't trust him not to listen. Hell, I didn't think I could hold back much longer either. I wanted him to completely ruin me, and I was holding him back from what we both wanted.

I lifted up to rub my clit along his length before letting him go. Grabbing the flaps of his jacket, I tugged it down to his elbows, forcing his arms back.

"Behind your back," I commanded, and he looked up at me with something close to loathing. He could hate me all he wanted for keeping him restrained. I didn't want him to go easy on me when I let him free, and hate was a feeling we both knew so well when it came to each other.

He shifted so he could put his arms behind his back, the jacket keeping them mostly restrained. For now.

It'd take him seconds to get free if he wanted to, and if by the way his cock twitched against my clit was any indication of how desperate he was to have me, I knew it wouldn't be long.

Satisfied with his mostly helpless position, I returned my one hand to his shoulder and the other to his cock. His lips were a thin line as he stared up at me like he knew just as well as I did that torturing him was my new favorite hobby.

But fuck, it wasn't just him aching for more.

My clit throbbed, and I needed some kind of reprieve before I came just looking at him like this.

Using his shoulder for support, I lifted higher, positioning him at my entrance. His jaw clenched as he waited, and waited, and waited.

"I'm on birth control," I whispered, not knowing why I needed to say the words out loud. He had enough confidence in me to know I wouldn't be stupid about sex.

But I was hesitating, and I didn't know why. I wanted this—wanted to feel him inside me and never anyone else again. Reed and I were set in stone, whether we had sex or not.

But this...this would solidify all of it. It wasn't just a blowjob or him fingering me. It was more. I'd never given much thought to sex in the past, but doing this with Reed felt like so much more than just a quick fuck.

It felt like writing our names in the stars and knowing there was no going back from the permanence this put on us.

"I want this, Brandy," Reed said. My eyes flicked to his at his words. "I want you."

As if his voice was the only thing I needed to spur me forward, I sank down onto his cock. I sucked in a breath as his cock stretched me, his length sinking deeper and deeper as I lowered myself until I was seated on him. His head fell back on a moan as my other hand flew to his shoulder for something to hold on to.

"Please," he begged. "Let me touch you."

I shook my head, digging my fingers into him through his shirt as I lifted, just to slide back down a moment later. I ground my hips forward, the tip of his cock rubbing against something so blissfully intoxicating inside of me. I moaned, repeating the motion.

"Fuck, Brandy. Use me, then. Ride my cock. Because once you let me out of this, I'm going to completely fucking ruin this tight little pussy to the point you can't walk."

My lips parted as I continued grinding my hips against him, lost in his words and the way his cock was so fucking deep inside me, I saw stars.

Finally, I lifted again until his tip was barely resting against my entrance. I watched his mouth fall open as I slid back down, taking every last inch of him.

"God, I love how that feels," I whispered, looking down between us to watch as I rode him.

He sat forward, pressing his forehead to mine so I'd look at him. "There's no one else here, Brandy, so the next time you want to say someone's name, it better fucking be mine. God isn't saving you today."

My breath hitched, my insides turning to complete mush. I couldn't do this anymore. I *needed* him.

"Touch me," I murmured, the words nearly ending on a sob. My body hummed in anticipation.

His arms were out of the sleeves in the blink of an eye, his hands coming up to grab my hips in a painful grip. I reveled in the feeling as he shoved off the chair, lifting me with him. I sucked in a breath as my legs quickly wrapped around his waist.

He spun us around and bent me over the chair, laying me so that my back was to the seat. With my legs still around him, he let go of my waist and straightened, pulling his shirt off and chucking it behind him. My eyes fell to the tattoo over his heart, my core heating with the knowledge that he got it for me.

Gripping my thighs, he unraveled me from him, bending them so my knees nearly touched my chest. He thrust deep inside me, his cock having not left my pussy. I screamed out, my nails digging into the edge of the seat cushion.

"Hold your legs," Reed commanded.

I grabbed the backs of my knees, and Reed pushed them farther so my legs were touching my shoulders. "Keep them here."

He didn't give me a chance to nod as he grabbed the armrests and slammed into me. My neck arched as I moaned, his cock deeper than I thought it could possibly be.

The man had me bent in half and wanting him to break me. Fuck, I think I'd thank him if he did. *That's* how fucking gone I was for him.

His abs flexed as he fucked me, pounding my body into the cushion as his grip nearly tore the leather.

Prying one of his hands off the armrest, he reached between my legs and rubbed circles over my clit. A curse passed my lips, his name right behind it, and it only spurred him on. He picked up his pace with his thrusts, adding more pressure to my sensitive bud.

The sensations became almost overwhelming as my nails dug into the backs of my thighs, and then I was screaming, my back arching as ripples of pleasure tore through me like a hurricane.

"What a good fucking girl," Reed praised as he kept endlessly fucking me.

My stomach tightened right as my orgasm started to ebb, but then something wet landed on my clit, and Reed rubbed it into my skin. I registered that he'd spit on my clit, and with the thought alone, my core spasmed as another wave of intense pleasure ran through my entire body. This time, his name was on my lips.

As soon as the word left me, he seated himself as deep as he could, his groan filling the room as he held onto my legs for stability. I felt every spurt of his warm release as he emptied himself inside of me, and I fucking loved it.

As we both caught our breath, he slowly pulled out of me. I went to lower my legs, but he kept them up. I looked up to find his intense gaze trained between my legs.

"You're so fucking sexy with my cum leaking out of you." He let go of one of my legs to trail a finger up my center, sliding the digit inside of me. A quiet moan fell from me as he shoved his release back inside me.

The man left me fucking speechless.

Once he removed his finger, he helped lower my legs. My back was stiff from the position, but nothing terrible. Before I could sit up, he leaned over me, pressing a kiss to my lips. "You're pure torture, you know that?"

I smiled against his lips. "That was the purpose."

He threaded his fingers through my hair before sliding his palm to the back of my neck. Lifting me from the chair with my ass propped against the edge of the seat, he brushed a strand of hair from my forehead.

"I love you, Brandy Rose," he murmured, hazel eyes shining with the intensity of his words.

"I love you, too," I whispered before pressing my lips to his in a kiss that sealed us in this moment, together.

It may have taken years, but my heart was fully opened to him, beating against my chest like a whisper of his name with mine.

Because that's what Reed Bronson was.

Mine.

36

BRANDY

Two days after Reed bent me in half on my living room chair, I called my mom.

Texting her didn't seem safe anymore, knowing that my father was most likely checking her phone. If I had to bet, he most likely wasn't even trying to hide it, which was why she was barely talking to me. He was controlling, manipulative, and I needed to talk to her if I was ever going to make her see the light in all of this.

When I was young, she was alone through his abuse. What parent wanted to drag their child through the hardships of a relationship, especially when it was physical? She did her best to keep me hidden from the worst of it, but even so, I saw it all. She was my best friend before anything, and I couldn't let her be treated like this any longer. I wouldn't let her be alone through this again.

The thought of friends hit me like a rock to the chest, knowing I'd neglected Lettie the past few weeks. She'd just married the man who'd been pining after her for years, so giving her space was the nice thing to do, but with all of the drama with my father being back in town, and my feelings for Reed demanding to no longer be shoved aside, I'd left little time to spare for Lettie.

As the phone rang on speaker, I pulled up Lettie's text thread.

> Miss you lots

Almost immediately, her response came through.

> **Lettie**
> I miss you more

> Lunch tomorrow, maybe?

She reacted to my text with a heart before replying.

> **Lettie**
> Coffee at Triple B?

Bell Buckle Brews was our favorite coffee shop in town. She knew I'd never pass up the opportunity to grab a drink and some food there.

> Meet you there at noon

She sent another heart as my mom picked up the phone right when I thought it'd go to voicemail.

"Brandy?" Her voice was soft, almost like she was trying to keep quiet.

"Don't sound so surprised to hear from me." I attempted to joke with her, but it fell flat as she let out a small sigh into the phone.

"Are you okay?" she asked.

I shook my head, staring out the front window of my Bronco at the field in front of me. I was already dressed and ready to meet her somewhere if she was free.

"Of course, I am. I actually wanted to talk to you about something," I said hesitantly, testing to see if he was listening in the background.

She was quiet a moment before saying, "I'm okay, honey—"

"About a boy," I cut her off, knowing she'd automatically jump to me checking in on her. Using my new relationship with Reed as an excuse to see her alone worked perfectly in my favor. "Can I see you?"

She let out a small chuckle before it dropped off.

Before she could reply, I said, "Please. Maybe at the diner?"

Silence filled the cab, not a sound coming from the other end of the phone. My knee started bouncing on its own, anxiety blowing up like a balloon in my ribs.

All of a sudden, faint static filled the line. The telltale sign that she'd had it muted. "I can do that. When?"

"Now?"

She inhaled, likely weighing her options here. If he was there listening, she was probably waiting to see his answer. He hopefully wouldn't care about boy talk, and he couldn't keep her away from me forever. At some point, he had to loosen the leash.

"Sure. I'll meet you there."

"Sounds good. I love you, Mom."

"I love you, too."

I hung up the phone, hoping like hell he didn't tag along. If I didn't talk to her about this now, I feared she'd be stuck forever.

And I couldn't let that happen again.

***

My mom slid into the booth across from me, setting her purse on the seat next to her. Her brunette hair hung in her face, more so on the left side, and when she lifted her head and tucked her hair behind her ear out of habit, my jaw dropped.

"Mom," I started.

"Hi," she said, thinking I was greeting her.

No, I was fucking shell-shocked over the bruise under her left eye, making her hazel eyes appear more gold than usual. It was obvious she had tried to cover it up with concealer, but she'd always been bad with makeup. She'd gotten better with it the more she had to hide, but it was clear she was out of practice from the years of him being gone.

I shook my head. No one should have to practice how to cover up a fucking bruise with drugstore concealer.

"Did he do that to you?" I asked, all emotion gone from my words. I felt like a robot, seeing only red through my lens and knowing exactly who my fucking target was.

"Do what?"

She was seriously acting *oblivious*?

I shook my head again. "Don't play dumb. You've never been good at hiding them."

Them. Because for her, it wasn't just once. Or twice. It was dozens and dozens of hits she had to get creative with covering up. Wearing long sleeves in the summer or sunglasses indoors on a cloudy day.

"Brandy—"

I held up my hand to stop her. "You don't have to try to make up some bullshit excuse."

Her eyes fell to the table, neither of us having opened our menus. I didn't think I could eat even if I forced myself to. I loved my mom—loved her so damn much that I'd do anything for her. If she wouldn't fight her demons, then I'd have to for her. It wouldn't be the first time.

"Can we not talk about it? Please?" Her plea came out in a whisper, and it nearly tore my heart in half.

My shoulders fell as a long breath escaped me, tension aching to leave my body but having no desire to let it until I made him feel even half as bad as he made her feel.

"Okay," I seceded, not wanting to make her feel any worse. If an hour of lunch with her daughter would brighten her day in the least amount, I'd set aside everything to make her smile.

Thankfully, it'd be much easier without my father here.

"So, you're seeing someone?" she asked, her attention focused on me.

I opened my menu, needing to do something with my hands. She was the first person I was really telling about Reed, and even though she was my mom, it wasn't making this any easier.

My feelings were kept tightly locked behind an impenetrable wall for a reason, and admitting I'd opened my heart to Reed felt like giving someone ammo to hurt me, even if I knew my mom would never do that to me. My entire life, I didn't have a father I could go to when I got hurt, or wanted to cry, or to tell him how my day was. Instead, I hid from him, never showing when I had a good or bad day. For my mom, I was an open book, and after he left, I felt more safe to be myself in that house, but now that he was back, my body was acting on instinct, wanting to reconstruct those walls even higher so the brunt of his fist couldn't tear my happiness to dust.

"I am." I couldn't help the smile that formed with the admission.

A glance at my mom showed she was mirroring my look. "Well"—she waved her hands in front of her—"tell me about him."

My teeth dug into my bottom lip as my eyes scanned the menu, not really seeing any of the words. "You sort of already know him."

A crease formed in the center of her forehead. "Who is it?"

I sucked on my lip before setting the menu down and forcing my hands into a ball on my lap. "Reed Bronson."

Her eyes went wide, her mouth parting in surprise. She blinked, almost like her thoughts were stuttering, trying to process whose name I'd just said.

"Reed. Charlotte and Travis's boy?"

"He's not so much a boy anymore, but yeah."

Her gaze moved to the table, her mind spinning behind her eyes, before she looked at me again. "But you hate him."

"It's...complicated." I had no idea where to start. How to explain that between the trip to Salt Lake City, the wedding, and every moment since then, my eyes were opened to a new side of Reed. One I'd come to love. Hell, I think I loved him all along, having always seen parts of him he didn't let anyone else catch even the slightest glimpse of. In a way, our feud opened us up to sides of each other most didn't see for years into a relationship. Even through the bickering and his overprotectiveness, he grew on me.

"I guess you've always had issues with men for a reason," she mumbled as she finally picked up her menu.

Her comment struck me. "What?"

She glanced up at me, doing a double take as she saw the look on my face. "I'm just saying, you never had a great father figure growing up, and that probably explains why you've never stayed with any guy."

My brows pulled together. "Are you saying I've butted heads with Reed because of dad? Or that you just figured none of my relationships would work out because you allowed him to be the man I had to look up to?"

She laid her menu on the table. "Brandy, that's not what I mean. Don't get defensive."

"I have every right to be defensive because you're right. Dad *is* the reason Reed and I hated each other for so long."

That spot on her forehead deepened. "What do you mean?"

"I went to a party one night because I was so tired of the yelling. How you'd let him treat us like shit and then turn around and make him dinner like nothing was wrong."

She shook her head. "That doesn't explain your problem with Reed."

"A guy tried to sexually assault me that night. Hell, he probably would have raped me if given the chance, but Reed showed up."

Her expression softened at my words, but I wasn't done. "Honey—"

"No," I interrupted. "Reed nearly beat a guy to death because I went to a party alone to escape the home you raised me in. You were supposed to keep me safe." My voice broke on the last word, tears pooling in my eyes.

She sucked in a shaky breath, her own eyes glassy from the tears she held back.

I'd held those words in for seven years, wanting so badly to tell her about that night but knowing it'd be no use. My dad was still in our lives, still tormenting our home, and she wouldn't have done anything about it. She'd have comforted me as a mother, held me while I cried, but she wouldn't have kicked him out. In the end, it wasn't really his fault how that night went. I'd shown up to that party on my own, decided to go up to that room with that guy, and I'd had to pay the mental price for it for over half a decade.

I was done letting that night hold me back.

She deserved to know all of this, whether it hurt her or not, because it was ruining me trying to protect her feelings. She was supposed to be protecting mine, and yet—

"I didn't know," she whispered, and the hurt in her voice killed me. This was why I'd kept it inside. I didn't want to hear anyone else devastated over me. Feel sorry for me.

But it was time. I was so tired of hurting.

"Of course, you didn't know. You were too busy catering to that monster instead of the daughter who loved you despite the circumstances. I could have left, run away or lived with the Bronsons like they offered so many times, but I stayed because I love you, Mom. I couldn't abandon you to that man, but I don't know how much longer I can do this."

She nodded, her eyes falling to the table as a tear streaked through the caked concealer, revealing the deeper blue of her bruise. "I'm sorry."

With a sniffle, I slid out of the booth, my appetite and ability to sit through this completely gone. "I know. And I'm sorry, too. But I have to choose me, in a healthy way this time. I will always be there for you, no matter what. You're my mom."

She looked up at me, so much sadness in her gaze. "I know. It's not fair to you. I understand."

I wanted to hug her, to take back every word, but this had to be done. I shouldn't have daddy issues or trauma from attempted sexual assault. I shouldn't have to deal with any of it. So I was choosing to work through it, and if that meant giving my mother the wake-up call she needed, I had to do it.

None of this was okay.

"I love you, but I have to go," I said, trying to swallow the rock in my throat.

She nodded, more tears falling as she looked back down at the table.

Then I left her sitting there, walking out of the diner as regret sat heavy on my shoulders.

But it didn't feel so suffocating anymore.

Because the words that weighed me down for seven years were voiced, and while it hurt, it was progress.

Didn't matter how long it took to get here.

It just mattered that I did it, and kept my heart intact while I did.

37

REED

I wiped my hands on the towel, staring at the small scab on my lip in the mirror. Avoiding Beckham wasn't hard to do, especially with my mind—and now, body—so wrapped up in Brandy that I didn't have time to care.

It wasn't that I didn't want to worry about my brother's struggles, but they weren't mine to battle. Beck was always carefree growing up, never overthinking the what-ifs, and now that he was handling something hard for once, he didn't know how to navigate it. He knew our family was here for him, but he chose not to confide in us. There'd be no changing that.

So for now, I'd sit by and wait. For an apology or a smile, I didn't care. As long as he snapped out of whatever dark place he was in, I'd be happy for him.

I headed out of the bathroom, planning to make a quick bite to eat when a knock sounded on the door. I wasn't expecting anyone, but I figured it couldn't be a stranger since I lived in the middle of my parents' property. Changing direction to the front door, I unlocked the handle, opening it wide.

Brandy stood there, sad eyes gleaming up at me before she threw herself at me, wrapping her arms around my neck and crashing her lips to mine. I met her pace, curious why she was here but quickly not caring with the way the feel of her clouded my senses and made every nerve in my body home in on her. I walked backwards enough to kick the door shut, all the while Brandy clung to me like I was a lifeline she needed to stay alive.

Her palms met my neck, and immediately, I felt the tremor in them. I set my hands on her cheeks, pulling her face away from mine. She fought my effort, but I didn't let her get her way.

"What's wrong?" I asked, already breathless.

She shook her head, trying to kiss me again. "I want you."

I craned my neck back, staring into her glassy eyes. "And you can have me right after you tell me what's bothering you."

Hazel eyes found mine, devastation coursing through every little line in her irises. "Please, Reed. Not now."

My lips pursed. I didn't want her sad or upset, and most of all, I didn't want her to hide her feelings behind closed doors any longer. But if a distraction was what she needed, I'd give it to her, and after, she'd tell me what was causing those eyes to lose their fire.

"Fine," I grunted, releasing her cheeks and scooping her up under her thighs.

She moved with me fluently, easily wrapping her legs around my waist. I walked us down the hall, nudging my bedroom door open with my foot before walking in and tossing her on the bed. She bounced slightly as she propped her hands behind her. I didn't miss a beat as I shucked my shirt off and to the side, then moved to my pants.

"I want you naked and on your hands and knees by the time I get back." I slid off my belt, tossing it to the ground before moving into my bathroom. I opened the cabinet and grabbed a container of lube. After shutting it, I walked back into the bedroom to find Brandy had obeyed. Her ass was facing me, her back arched as she waited.

"So obedient, Little Devil. I'm surprised."

Coming up behind her, I planted my feet on the ground, running a hand over her perfect little ass. I gripped her cheek before letting go and landing a slap to the plump flesh. She jerked a bit, then perked her ass higher, begging for more.

"You like when I spank you, don't you?"

She swayed her hips slightly, humming her agreement.

"You want something to distract you from your feelings, so you came to me," I said, spreading her ass.

She nodded, letting out a breathy, "Yes."

"How much of a distraction are you really looking for?" I asked, running a thumb over her puckered hole.

"Anything." She sounded so desperate, but I heard the undertone of sadness. I'd give her what she wanted, but then I'd get what I wanted in return. Answers.

Bringing my thumb to my mouth, I slid it past my lips, coating the skin in saliva before bringing it back to her ass. I ran circles around the hole, watching as she flexed.

"Is this okay?" I asked, wanting to make sure she set boundaries if she wanted them.

She nodded. "Yes."

I opened the cap on the lube with one hand, holding it a few inches over her hole and letting it drizzle down her crack. She hummed at the cooling sensation as it traveled, clearly enjoying the anticipation of what was to come.

Collecting as much lube as I could with my thumb, I ran it in circles over her hole before adding a bit of pressure. She let out a gasp as the tip of my thumb slid in, the tightness of her ass unreal.

Giving her a moment to adjust, I set my knees on the bed, positioning myself behind her. I set my other hand on her shoulder blades, lowering her chest to the bed so her ass was perked high in the air. My thumb slid in to the knuckle before I stopped again.

Using my other hand to unbutton my pants and slide down the zipper, I freed my throbbing cock. I wanted her so badly it hurt, but I also hated that this was what she wanted to distract herself rather than to talk to me about what she was feeling. Out of all of it, though, I was glad she came to me, regardless of what she wanted out of this right now. She used to shrink in on herself when emotions got the best of her, but now, I was her outlet. These were baby steps, but steps nonetheless.

Slowly, I slid my thumb deeper, seeing her body tense, then relax, as she adjusted to the feeling.

"Does that feel good, Little Devil?"

She nodded, her cheek pressed against the bed. "Yes."

"Good. Because it's about to feel a whole lot better."

Dragging the head of my cock through the lube, I slid into her pussy seamlessly, burying myself as deep as I could go. Her hands fisted in the sheets, her mouth opening on a moan as my thumb disappeared inside her ass.

At the same time and pace, I slid both out nearly all the way, then thrust back in, repeating the motions as her breathing picked up and her body pushed back against me, aching for more.

"Fuck, you're so perfect like this, Brandy. Laid out and begging for me with your body. Is this what you wanted?"

She nodded again as I picked up the pace, fucking both her ass and her pussy. I felt her tighten, her orgasm growing near as I filled her. My fingers dug into her ass cheek as I hooked my thumb. My other hand reached underneath her, rubbing circles around her swollen clit. She cried out, instantly clenching around me as her release took over, consuming both me and her.

The moans, the cries, the screams that passed her lips were all I needed to let go. I lost myself in her, mind, body, and soul, as I groaned, her pussy milking every last drop from me.

As her body relaxed, I slowly slid my thumb out, careful with my movements. Once it was out, I pulled out of her pussy, watching as my release followed. Dragging my finger through it, I shoved it back inside her, pumping her a few times for good measure. After I was done, I grabbed her hips and flipped her onto her back.

She let out a squeak as I climbed over her, grabbing her hands and pinning her to the bed.

"Talk."

She blinked, attempting to clear the fog of her orgasm as reality set back in. She was upset. I was concerned.

"We said no more running from our feelings, Brandy," I warned.

She nodded, inhaling deeply. "I know."

I softened my posture, loosening my grip on her hands but keeping them locked in mine. "I want to help you. To be that shoulder you need when you feel like this."

She tried to give me a small smile, but it fell flat with the look in her eyes. "Can we take a bath?"

I hesitated, wondering if this was another tactic of hers to avoid telling me what was wrong. I quickly decided it wasn't. I'd give my girl what she wanted to be comfortable. Even if that included taking a bath. Something I hadn't done since I was a kid.

"Of course."

Leaving her on the bed, I went into the bathroom to start filling the tub. Once it was nearly to the rim and steaming, I led her in there. With my pants now off, I settled in with my back to the porcelain. She stepped in after me, lowering herself with her back to me. Wrapping my arms around her chest, I scooted her back until she was pressed against my front.

I peppered soft kisses to the soft spot between her neck and shoulder, moving her hair away for more access. I let her take all the time she needed to say what she wanted to say.

Finally, she spoke. "I saw my mom today."

My body instantly tensed, worried that her dad had done something.

She set a hand on my arm, running it up and down my skin in soothing strokes. "He wasn't there. Don't worry."

A fraction of the tension left my bones as I stayed silent, waiting for her to continue.

"I told her about that night at the party. I kind of just...let all my emotions spill out. All the things I'd felt over the years and hadn't told her. It felt good, but I can't help but feel bad for upsetting her with all of it."

I tightened my hold around her. "Sometimes, we have to tell people hard things, because in the end, the only ones who can truly protect ourselves is us. If getting that off your chest helped you, don't feel guilty. Feel proud." My thumb ran circles under her breast in a small attempt to soothe her. "You held that in for years, and while it may have hurt her to hear it, no one can do better if they don't know what they did wrong in the first place."

"Yeah, but now *she* feels guilty. I know she does. That's the last thing I want her to feel. She did her best raising me, despite the circumstances. Now I just...failed her by basically telling her things I'd kept locked inside for so long."

My lips moved against her skin as I spoke. "I'd hardly call that failing, baby. You may not see it right now—hell, she might not either—but she's proud of you for speaking up about how you feel. We don't go through life simply feeling okay about everything. We're allowed to be upset or mad or get angry when things aren't fair."

Her head fell back against my shoulder. "But I never was. I—" Her voice broke, and she swallowed before continuing. "I bottled it up for years, and now I laid it all on her and left."

"That's what we have to do sometimes, baby. That's growth."

She shook her head. "I wouldn't call that growth."

I cupped her cheek, turning her to face me. "It is. Whether you leap a mile or take one step, you told her how you felt, and you came to me. You didn't keep quiet and stuff it inside that locked box in your head. You voiced how something made you feel, and you came to me when you were upset."

"But if I'm supposed to feel good about letting that out, why do I feel so bad?"

I ran a hand down her hair. "Because you care."

She stared at me a moment before she let out a long, pent-up breath. She brought a wet hand up to my wrist, running her palm along my arm. "Thank you."

Warmth flooded my chest as a small smile pulled at my mouth. "No matter what it is, you can run to me. I'll always catch you."

Tears welled in her eyes before she pressed her lips to mine, sealing my words between us like a spoken vow.

Fuck, I loved Brandy Rose with my entire fucking soul.

38

BRANDY

"But why would she say you have a problem with men? What even brought that up?" Lettie asked after taking a sip of her iced caramel coffee.

The temperature was in the high forties today, but the cold never stopped us from enjoying an iced latte.

"About that..." I was hesitating, putting off what I needed to tell her. That her brother and I were...together. Were we boyfriend and girlfriend? Dating? Hooking up? I really wasn't sure. I guess I should've had this conversation with Reed before I decided to tell his little sister about us, but I was starting to think Reed didn't care about a label, so long as I let my walls down and let him in.

Lettie and I had met up this afternoon as planned, and I'd been skirting around the topic for an hour now. There was only so long I could avoid it while also telling her about my conversation with my mom. The question was bound to come up.

Lettie stared at me from across the tiny table against the wall in Bell Buckle Brews, waiting for me to continue. Her brows were raised, her caramel-colored hair tied up in a messy bun to pair with her oversized sweater and baggy jeans. She was trying to find a style that fit her, given she typically only wore Kimes jeans, old t-shirts, and boots. This new look was cute on her.

And giving me a reason to ignore what I needed to tell her.

Ugh.

"Did I tell you you look cute today?" I asked, setting my elbows on the table as if I was so infatuated with her getup that I couldn't get close enough.

She rolled her eyes. "Only ten times. Now spill. I know when my best friend is avoiding telling me something."

Sitting up straight, I sighed. Sometimes having a best friend wasn't all that great. She could read me like an open book, which was both a blessing and a curse.

"Fine. I'm just going to spit it out, and if you give me some kind of look or blow up or get mad—"

"Brandy!"

"Reed and I are together," I spit out, slouching in my chair and bracing for the criticism.

I thought you guys hated each other.
Do I need to plan a funeral?
Is it the end of the world?

Please don't claw my brother's eyeballs out and feed them to the fish.

Okay, that last one was a threat I made ages ago. It totally wouldn't happen.

Unless he pissed me off, then supper's ready, fishies.

But instead of what I feared most to come out of her mouth, she shocked me to my damn core.

The biggest toothy smile lit up her face, and she burst out laughing.

When she didn't say a word and sat there giggling like a maniac, I sat forward.

"Are you okay?" I asked.

She set a hand on the table like she needed to steady herself, and all I could manage to do was stare. My best friend had to be having a heart attack. I checked behind me, maybe hoping a doctor or a nurse was in for a bite to eat. With no such luck, I faced Lettie again.

She was out of breath, nearly wheezing as she keeled over the table, then sat straight again. "Oh my gosh, I'm sorry." She fanned herself. Seriously *fanned* herself.

I blinked, waiting for her to get her shit together. This was *not* the reaction I was expecting. Honestly, seeing her mad about it would have been more comforting than this. This was straight weird.

She took a sip of her coffee, as if she was parched from all the giggling, then inhaled deeply to compose herself. "I never thought this day would come."

My brows furrowed. "Yeah, me either," I said hesitantly. Was that a good or bad thing?

"You two have been dodging the obvious for *years*. Literal years. This is such a relief." She fanned herself again, her cheeks red from the fit of giggles.

I processed her words twice before confusion hit me harder than a freight train barreling down the tracks with no brakes. "I'm sorry. Did you say *relief*?"

She nodded. "Oh, yeah." She reached up to tuck a strand of hair that had come loose back into her bun. As if this conversation was casual. "I was beginning to wonder if you two would ever quit the act."

"*Act?*"

She pinned me with a look. "Don't bullshit me, Brandy. You two have liked each other for ages."

My jaw nearly dropped to the floor. "You mean we've *hated* each other for ages."

She shook her head. "I know what I said. All that bickering"—she waved a finger at me—"was just foreplay."

"Foreplay," I repeated blandly. "Is there something in your coffee?"

She tried to smother her smile but failed miserably. "I'm happy for you! Is that so wrong?"

"I'm dating your *brother*." I emphasized the last word, as if it wasn't clear the first time.

She plucked an egg bite off the plate between us. "So you said."

"And that doesn't bother you?" I asked as she took a bite.

She shrugged, chewing before speaking. "Not at all."

I sat back in my chair, staring at the ceiling like it might be able to grant me answers to what the fuck was going on.

"Brandy." I faced Lettie again. "It's okay to be happy for yourself, you know. Be glad you're not fighting with him all the time now."

I gave her a blank stare. No, we were no longer bickering all the time. We'd just traded that for giving each other orgasms.

"So your mom made that comment after you told her you were with Reed?" she asked.

I picked up an egg bite, turning it over in my fingers. "Yeah. I mean, I don't blame her. She's obviously going through something because my dad is in town. I wanted to talk to her more about that, but she clearly didn't feel the same. I guess I just need to let her figure it out on her own." I looked down at the egg bite, my chest aching with the words I said next. "I can't fix my dad being in town. I can't make him leave, can't make him stop hurting her. He has his battles, and she has hers. I just hate that hers makes her feel like she has to put up with this."

Lettie reached across the table, covering my fidgeting hand with her own. "She'll come around."

I looked at her. "When? The only reason she did before was because he left." But I didn't expect an answer. My entire childhood, there wasn't one. That wouldn't change today.

"And he'll leave. He'll get bored and ditch town again." She sounded so sure. I wished I shared the same confidence.

"I doubt it. He's got her right where he wants her. I'm not living there anymore, so he can do whatever the fuck he wants." I shook my head at myself, looking down at the egg bite again before tossing it on the napkin and wiping my fingers on the edge.

Lettie pulled her hand back to her lap, attempting a smile. "Invite her to dinner at my parents' next week. If anyone can talk sense into her, it's my mom."

I let out a sigh. "I don't know. It was hard enough getting her to come out to meet me. A whole family dinner..."

"You never know unless you try." Lettie gave a small shrug in an attempt to lighten the heaviness of the conversation.

"Plus," she added, "you can tell everyone about you and Reed then, too."

I pointed a look at her. "Just what we need. An announcement like that on top of an intervention."

"Everyone is going to be so happy!" she squeaked, squeezing her hands together in front of her like she couldn't contain her excitement over it.

"Or pass out from shock," I muttered.

"Either way, you're coming, and you're inviting your mom," Lettie ordered.

"Okay, fine. I can't promise she'll come, but I'll try."

Because I knew if I didn't, Lettie would do it herself, and she'd give my mom no choice but to show up. Hell, she'd probably bring Bailey as backup to try and intimidate my dad if he tried to intervene, and the last thing I needed was my best friends dealing with him.

I didn't know what I'd do without the Bronsons in my life.

They truly made me a little more complete.

Made me feel a little less ruined.

I guess that's what family did.

Held the pieces together when all they felt like doing was breaking apart.

***

I decided to hell with a text or call to my mom and went straight to her house. Was it the brightest idea? Probably not. But at this rate, I didn't know who was listening on the other end, and I was tired of second-guessing everything I said. Plus, asking my mom if she'd come to the Bronsons' family dinner next week in person would give her less of a chance to say no, and an even lower possibility of my dad stepping in with his own answer before she had the ability to decide for herself.

After pulling up to the curb, I noticed the kitchen light was on, but other than that, the house was dark. It gave me hope that maybe she was inside prepping for dinner while my dad was elsewhere.

I pulled the key from the ignition and exited the car, walking up the path to the front door. I took a deep, steadying breath before rapping my knuckles on the door. As if breathing exercises could prevent the anxiety that bloomed in my chest from showing up here.

I waited a minute at least before the door finally swung in, and the last person I wanted to see crowded the doorway.

"Hello, Brandy," my dad greeted, those two words sounding anything but welcoming.

A chill broke out across my skin, despite the wool sweater I wore. "Is Mom here?"

He wiped his hand on a rag, drawing my attention to his red knuckles. Flames licked at my muscles, urging me to run away or storm inside, I wasn't sure, but I didn't feel right standing here. Unease crawled under my skin like a snake unable to find its hole.

"That's no way to greet your father, now, is it?"

I nearly rolled my eyes at the predictability of this, but the slight fear of what he'd do if I showed such disrespect had me keeping them still. My head almost ached with the effort. I was so tired of the act.

"I'm not here to talk to you, so yeah. We don't need to pretend pleasantries are in order." I crossed my arms, needing something to do with them before I decided to shove my way past him.

"Is that what your love for me is? Pretend?" He feigned hurt, but I knew the knowledge made him fucking gleam from the inside out. He didn't need love to be able to control. He did it anyway.

"Yep," I clipped. "Where is she?"

"Busy." He leaned a shoulder against the doorway, his eyes roaming over my body before landing on my face again. Judgment shone in his gaze, but I didn't give a shit. He wasn't in the place to have an opinion.

"If you don't tell me where she is—"

"You'll what?" he interrupted before I could continue.

I leaned closer, though all my instincts screamed to back away. "I'll tell everyone in town what you did to her face."

He fisted the rag in his hands, crossing his arms with a smug fucking smile. What an asshole. "So she didn't lie, then. She really did go see you the other day."

My jaw clenched, aggravation at his avoidance digging a grave in my chest. I needed to make sure my mom was okay. By the look of his hands, who knew what he'd done to her since? And especially if he thought she lied about where she was?

"If you touched her again—"

Before I could finish my threat, I was shoved against the wall in one swift movement by a grip on my throat. My head slammed into the stucco, pain ringing through my skull. But it was nothing compared to the pure rage on my father's face as he held me against the outside of the house.

"You'll what, little girl? Go tell on me? Your mother *loves* me. No one is going to believe the bullshit you spew about us."

My heart raced in my chest, pumping blood through my veins at an alarming rate. I couldn't get my tongue to work, my muscles, my lungs. All of it was frozen. In shock or fear, I couldn't tell. A combination of both, probably.

I couldn't look at him, not as he held my life in his hand, holding me against the house I grew up in. The house that was supposed to protect me from the boogeyman, not harbor him in the next room over.

He waited for me to speak, but I couldn't. Words evaporated on my tongue like a mist, tangible, but not graspable.

"That's what I thought," he spit, letting me go. I stood frozen with my back ramrod straight against the rough stucco, too scared to move.

"Don't come back here," he warned as he headed back inside the house, leaving me there like I was nothing but trash on the wind. "Your mother doesn't want you anymore."

The door slammed, causing me to flinch. He was lying. Trying to get under my skin. But the threat still stood.

I needed to get out of here.

Forcing my legs to move with every ounce of will in my body, I ran to my Bronco. After nearly missing the small step into the car, I finally situated myself in the seat. As soon as the door was closed, every limb on my body vibrated with a violent tremor. I felt stiff, cold, and every bone in my being shook to the core.

Reed.

I needed Reed.

It took me six tries to finally get the key in the ignition, then I eased my foot onto the gas, trying to control the pressure I added because even that part of me was shaking.

My dad was a scary man, typically making true on his threats, but with his hand around my neck and his face in mine, true fear hit me like a bullet to the heart. I shouldn't have come here alone. I should have known better. I should have called my mom and asked her over the phone, but instead, I walked straight into the lion's den and expected not to get bit.

My brain felt foggy the whole way to Reed's house, and once I pulled up, I barely had the ability to get out of the car on my own.

He'd be so mad seeing me like this. I knew he'd be. All my life, Reed was the most protective brother to Lettie, and in return, to me, too. It just came naturally to him. So showing up on his doorstep a complete and utter mess after he'd told me not to go there alone...

I'd be lucky if I got out of this without having to bury a body.

But fuck, I needed him.

39

REED

I was already at the door by the time Brandy was stepping out of her Bronco. She hadn't texted before she came over, which meant something had to be wrong.

I nearly ripped the front door off the hinges before running out to meet her in the driveway after I'd seen her pull up through the kitchen window. Her chest was rising and falling too fast as I approached, her whole body shaking in the cold, despite wearing a sweater.

"What's wrong? What happened?" Before she could answer, I wrapped my arms around her, pulling her to my chest. Her hands fisted in my shirt, but it did little to ease the tremor.

"My d-dad," she stuttered, and the sound broke my fucking heart. Shredded it to pieces and stabbed it a hundred times.

I could handle anything other than broken Brandy. *Anything*. "He g-grabbed me."

She didn't have to tell me where. I was already moving.

But I didn't make it far as her hand wrapped around my arm, stopping me in place. "No. Stay. *Please* stay. I need you."

I looked down at her, into eyes filled with unshed tears. Fuck, I couldn't do this. I wasn't built to choose. I wanted to rip him apart, then hold her for eternity. I couldn't do both at the same time.

But over the course of the last few months, I realized maybe I could.

Brandy came first.

Always.

I knew it took a lot in her to admit that she needed someone other than herself. I couldn't abandon her right now. Not like this.

"Okay." I moved back to her, wrapping my arms around her again before pulling back and scooping her up. She didn't even attempt to fight it as her head fell against my shoulder while I carried her inside. I headed straight for my bedroom, pulling back the black sheets once we were in there. I laid her on the bed, scooting in next to her and covering us with the blanket.

I pulled her close as she nuzzled her head into my chest, and finally, she let those tears fall. A sob wracked her, her fingers digging into my skin through my shirt as she let it all out. All the pain, the years of fear that lived deep inside her. She let it all fall like water out of a ruined dam, feeling every emotion she tried to keep carefully tucked away. Today was the last straw, for her and for me. I wouldn't let him do this to them anymore.

No woman should ever have to live in fear, and if I had to be the bad guy to ensure they felt safe, I would be. I'd be anything Brandy needed me to be, so long as she was okay, mentally and physically.

Once she calmed down and her breathing evened out, I stroked a hand down her hair, mustering up the courage to ask the question I didn't know if I wanted the answer to.

Swallowing the rage that threatened to consume me, I finally asked, "Where did he grab you?"

She nuzzled her head deeper into my chest, as if she could dig a hole there and bury herself away from the pain of today.

"My neck," she answered, her voice muffled in my shirt.

My entire body stiffened, her answer the last choice I was imagining. I expected an arm, a wrist, but her *neck*?

"I'll kill him," I promised, no other option acceptable.

She shook her head, gripping me tighter. "You can't."

"I can." And I would.

"Reed." She shimmied away from me slightly, looking directly at me. "You have to promise me you won't do something that lands you in jail."

I kept my mouth shut because I couldn't promise her that. Imagining her helpless with his hand around her throat... Fuck. Why the fuck was I still lying here?

"Please."

"We have to do something, Brandy. He can't just get away with touching you." Her eyes fell, and devastation hit me in the gut. "What?"

With a heavy breath, she said, "He hasn't only touched me since he's been back."

My head fell against the pillow as I rolled to my back, my hand coming up to drag down my face. She had to be fucking kidding.

"He touched your mom again and you didn't tell me?" I was no longer able to keep the anger out of my tone. But I wasn't mad at her. Fuck, I could never be. It was him I wanted to rip apart.

"I didn't want you to get involved. What if you go to jail? What if he hurts you?"

I sat up, looking down at her beside me. "*Me*? He's been hurting your mom your whole life, fucked with your head, and now he could have killed you today, and you're worried about *me*?"

Her bottom lip trembled, and guilt instantly crept in, dwarfing my frustration.

"Come here," I murmured, reaching for her. She scooted over, laying her head on my lap. I ran my fingers through her hair as I rested against the headboard.

And as her breathing evened out and she fell into a deep sleep, I knew we wouldn't have to come up with a plan once she woke up.

I already had one.

And it didn't include him making it out of this unscathed.

***

Once midnight rolled around, I carefully scooted out from under Brandy, where she still lay sleeping on my bed. I'd nearly woken her to make sure she ate dinner, but I figured she wouldn't be in the mood to eat. As soon as I got back from what I was about to do, I'd make her the best damn breakfast she ever had. But first, I had an agenda I needed to take care of.

Quietly sliding her mother's house key off her key ring, I pocketed it before grabbing my gun from my safe. I didn't plan to use it, but I was bringing it as a precaution. Her father was clearly unpredictable, and the last thing I wanted was to walk into the fire unarmed.

After sneaking out of the room, I headed out the front door, trying to be as silent as possible as I got in my truck, started it, and headed toward the road. Once I made it to Brandy's mother's house, I decided to park up the block in case her father wasn't home. By the looks of the empty driveway, I figured he wasn't, so this was the safest bet to remain discreet. Last thing I needed was him to see my truck out front and instantly grow suspicious before I had the chance to say my piece.

Hooking my gun into the waistband of my jeans, I got out, locked the truck, and walked the rest of the way. Using Brandy's key, I let myself in, making sure to lock the door behind me.

Then, I sat at the kitchen table in the dark for two hours before finally, the deadbolt clicked.

I didn't move an inch as Brandy's father entered the house, clearly inebriated as he swayed on his feet. His hand slid along the wall, searching for the light switch before finding it and flicking it on. As soon as he did, he froze with frightened eyes pinned on me, alarm clear in his posture.

Like the switch itself, his body slouched slightly as he realized it was me, his guard dropping. That was his first mistake.

"Oh, it's just my daughter's boy toy," he muttered, dismissing me with the wave of a hand. "What do you want?"

I kept my calm, reaching into my jeans to pull out my gun and set it on the table. I didn't try to be gentle about it, hoping it'd send a message that I wasn't here to make small talk.

His gaze moved to the gun as he swayed again. He set a hand on the wall for support, moving his focus back to me. "This some kind of threat, boy?"

"Does using such demeaning terms make you feel powerful?" I asked, my tone flat, reserved, lethal.

He blinked as if the question took him off guard.

"Does putting your hands on women give you some kind of power trip?" I folded my hands in my lap, like I had all the time in the world to wait for his answers. Truth was, I didn't give a shit what bullshit response he might try to spew.

"This some kind of joke?" he questioned, leaning into the wall.

I shrugged. "If you want to live, I wouldn't take it that way."

His eyes narrowed. "That's definitely a threat if I've heard one." He started to move forward, and my hand went for the gun. He froze, knowing if he made another move, I wouldn't hesitate to use it. Maybe he had a brain after all.

"Here's what's going to happen," I said, lifting the firearm off the table and studying it like it was the most interesting thing on the fucking planet. Really, I just needed to get my eyes off him before I put a bullet in his damn skull. "You're going to take your ass to the station and turn yourself in."

"And if I don't?" The man had balls to ask questions with a loaded pistol not ten feet from him.

I looked at him now, letting every ounce of hatred come to the surface and shine in my gaze. "Then this chamber will be empty in less than five seconds."

Fear widened his eyes, and it only satisfied me. Good, the man was starting to realize I wasn't fucking around.

"They'll give you a light sentence for confessing," I went on. "But those men in prison? They don't take kindly to cowards who put their hands on women. So if I were you, I'd be real fucking careful the moment you step into that building." I stood from the chair, my finger a hair's width away from curling around the trigger. "But if I'm being honest, it's not those inmates you should be scared of." I looked at the gun again, turning my wrist to eye the other side of the pistol before pinning him with my eyes. "It's me."

His throat bobbed as he swallowed, and I wanted to fucking revel in the pure terror that shone on his face. After scaring his family for years, he was finally feeling an ounce of their fear, and I wanted nothing more than to let him suffer in it. But even then, that wasn't enough. Hell, prison wasn't enough. But I needed to be here for Brandy. I wanted to see our future together, and landing my ass in a jail cell wouldn't get me there.

He stepped forward, nearly missing his footing as his face contorted in rage, the alcohol giving him the confidence he needed to override his fear. "You think you can come into my house and threaten me?"

I shrugged, knowing I had the upper hand here if he wanted to get any closer. He was drunk, unbalanced, and pissed. The combination wouldn't get him far.

But then the door behind him opened, and the last fucking person I wanted to see here right now barged in.

Brandy stopped in her tracks as she saw the gun in my hand, her eyes moving to her father as he spun around to face her.

Fuck, fuck, fuck.

He was directly between us, and I had no way of getting to her before—

He was already moving, knowing exactly what I was thinking. I started running, but he was too fast, even drunk. Brandy was frozen to the spot as he grabbed her, and before she could register the scene before her, she screamed as he put her in a headlock and faced me.

I already had my gun trained on him, but fuck, I couldn't take the shot without risking hitting her. And I would never risk her life. He knew that.

He tightened his hold on her, and she pressed her lips together, her eyes pleading with me to do something. But I had no fucking idea what. Would he kill her? I didn't fucking know, but I didn't want to find out.

"Threaten me now, boy," he yelled, spit flying from his mouth.

"Let her go," I said through gritted teeth, trying to keep my voice level so I wouldn't show him how truly fucking screwed I felt. "Let her go and do what I told you, and this will all be over."

"You won't fucking shoot me," he said confidently, the sentence ending with his laugh. The man was really fucking *laughing* with his arm around his daughter's neck. "Although, maybe if you try and miss, that bullet will teach her a lesson."

Despite the helpless position, Brandy's eyes rolled the slightest. But clearly it wasn't subtle enough, as her father flexed his arm, squeezing harder. Her hands came up to his arm, fingers clawing at them as her face turned red.

"Drop your fucking arm or I swear on my life, I will put a bullet through your foot before I put a second through your heart." I shifted the aim to his legs, but he quickly shuffled them to hide perfectly behind Brandy's. I internally cursed.

"Oh, come on, Reed. You're just like me. That anger would've ended in this anyway," her father said, a sardonic smile on his face.

I shook my head as Brandy choked out, "No. He wouldn't."

He brought his face closer to hers, his body practically vibrating with rage. He opened his mouth to speak, but all sound was cut off as a shot rang through the air, and my whole world tipped on its axis.

40

BRANDY

My ears rang from the shot as I dropped to the floor, not sure where the bullet had come from. Did it hit me? My dad? I hadn't seen Reed lift his gun, so if it wasn't him who fired, then who?

Strong hands grabbed my arms, pulling me up and away from where my dad lay on the floor. As the ringing in my head subsided, his angered shouts filtered in.

"Fuck! You fucking shot me!" my dad screamed.

Reed finally stopped once we were back where he was standing before, his gun in his hold and pointed to the floor, finger off the trigger. My gaze moved to my dad, and I froze when I saw blood gushing from the bullet wound in his leg.

Right as I opened my mouth to ask if Reed shot him, my mom came out from the hallway with a gun trained on my father.

"I should have done that a long time ago," she said, eyes trained on where he lay writhing in pain.

His face was redder than I'd ever seen it before, and I knew his ego was hurt. The woman he did his best to instill fear in, the one he always took the upper hand on, fought back. And she fucking won.

"You two okay?" she asked, nudging her chin in our direction while keeping her eyes on my dad.

I nodded as Reed said, "We're fine."

"Police are on their way," she stated, not moving the barrel of her gun away from him.

"You're a fucking bitch," he spit, barely able to catch his breath through the pain of the wound. "They better be bringing a goddamn ambulance."

My mom crouched, her hair swinging to reveal the bruise over her eye. It was clearly healing, but still looked swollen and painful. "Oh, are you in pain, sweetie?"

He stared at her, nostrils flaring. Reed's arms tightened around me, his body fighting the urge to protect her, too. He'd do it in a heartbeat, and it only made me love him more, if that was even possible.

"Sucks when all you want is to not feel that pain, and it just keeps fucking coming. It's a bitch, isn't it?"

He ground his jaw, his face somehow getting even redder. "Just you wait. Once I'm healed, I'm not going easy on you anymore."

Reed moved, leaving me standing there alone as he stormed over and landed a punch right in my dad's face. For anyone else, I would've felt bad, but he had that coming.

Reed stood over him, flexing his fist. "You ever even think about touching my family again, and I'll remove every fucking organ from your pathetic body and feed every last bit to you, including your fucking tongue."

My heart clenched with the use of the word family. No matter what I felt or how much we tried to avoid these feelings, Reed and I were endgame.

Five minutes later, the police showed up and took my father away in an ambulance. He was being admitted for his wound, and then he'd go straight to the county jail. My mom wanted to go in for a statement of all the things he'd done in the past, to which I agreed to do the same. It was time to stop being scared of the man that tormented us for so long and put an end to this cycle.

After tonight, he'd never come back.

As she talked to the officer, I found Reed sitting at the kitchen table after getting done with his questioning of the events that took place. I'd already given my statement, though it was much shorter than his.

I approached him, taking a seat on his lap and draping my legs over his. I wrapped an arm around his neck, resting my elbow on his shoulder as he set a hand on my waist.

"You left me," I said quietly.

His thumb stroked my side. "I know. I'm sorry. I just— I had to do something."

I bent to kiss him, quieting him before he had the chance to come up with some excuse. I knew why he did it. I didn't have to agree with everything he did to understand that he'd do anything to protect me. I pulled back, meeting his gaze. "I know. But the last thing I want you to do right now is apologize."

His brows furrowed. "Really?"

I nodded. "Really. If you hadn't come here tonight, I don't know if any of this ever would have stopped."

He frowned, tugging me closer. "As risky as it was, I'm glad I did it, then."

I leaned into him, resting my forehead against his. "I'm glad you did, too."

"He'll never hurt either of you again," he murmured, his fingers digging into my side.

I nodded against him. "I know." I pulled back, trying to harden my gaze. "But if you ever scare me like that again—"

"Scare you?"

"You left me in the middle of the night," I reminded him. "I thought you were going to get yourself hurt, or worse." My throat constricted, hating even the thought of something happening to him.

He pressed his forehead to mine again, closing his eyes. "Never again, Little Devil. I'm yours for the keeping."

I choked out a laugh, the sound ending on a sob. I set a hand on his chest, gripping his shirt and tugging it. Words wouldn't form on my tongue, but I knew he was telling me the truth. Tonight proved how far he'd go for me, and while he didn't have to do what he did, he did it anyway.

Reed Bronson was my big, broody protector, and I was finally accepting that. But even more importantly, he was mine.

41

BRANDY

I spent the entire next day with the horses on the Bronson ranch, desensitizing some of the more frightened rescues and working with some of their personal ones, too. Now that my job with them was done, I had one more task to do before the sun disappeared behind the horizon.

Finding the gray rescue horse in his stall, I slid open the door. His head perked up, but instead of his typical defensive stance and moving away from me, he stayed put, watching as I stood in the doorway.

"Today's the day, big fella," I said, grabbing the lead rope off the metal bar nailed into the door. "You're a free man."

His ear twitched as he swatted a fly with his tail. I stepped into the stall, my boots digging into the shavings as I kept my eyes on him. "Are you going to fight me today?"

I figured talking to him couldn't hurt, just like Lettie suggested. When that gunshot rang out in my childhood home, I could've folded in on myself. Lost myself in the chaos. But instead, Reed's voice kept me grounded. Calm.

Maybe that's what this horse needed all along. Someone to listen to when things were scary. When he didn't know what'd happen next. But he'd had enough of trying to be tamed. He was wild at heart, and I didn't want to change his spirit. Much like Reed didn't try to change mine, he accepted me.

Perhaps me and this horse were more alike than I'd once thought.

Mustering all the confidence I had, I stepped toward him and clipped the lead rope on his halter. He'd been wearing it for a while, and it was time he lost it.

For likely the last time, I led him out of the stall, keeping my shoulders straight and my mind clear. He followed like he'd been doing this for years, but he knew what this meant.

It wasn't another walk to the round pen or the cross ties. He was going home.

The cotton candy clouds cast a pink hue over the ranch as I brought him to the pasture gate. As we came to a stop, his ears perked up, his nostrils flaring as he took in the crisp air.

"You like that?" I asked, keeping the lead rope firm in my grip while I unlatched the gate. "Smells like freedom, huh?"

He stepped closer behind me, turning his head in the direction of the other horses out in the pasture. It was a mixture of personal horses and others we'd set out to retire, and I got the feeling he'd fit right in with them.

"All twenty acres of this pasture are just for you," I told him, draping the chain over the metal rung and swinging the gate inward. It was a small portion of the Bronsons' ranch, but plenty of space for the gelding to roam.

Truthfully, I was surprised he was being so calm standing this close to me, but maybe he felt the weight taken off my shoulders with my father now behind bars.

Horses felt a lot, and maybe he felt my trauma like his own.

I led him inside the pasture, swinging the gate shut behind us. Turning to face him, I reached up to the halter to unbuckle it rather than just take the lead rope off. As soon as it slid off the back of his head, he took off like a bullet—galloping with his tail high in the air and his neck extended confidently.

Rather than head back to my Bronco to go home, I lowered myself to the grass, watching as he ran off into the sunset, the other horses turning to join him in his victory gallop.

The metal gate creaked behind me, and seconds later, Lettie plopped herself in the grass beside me, leaning a head on my shoulder as we both watched the pink sky fade behind the mountains in the distance.

"You ever think of a name for him?" she asked, wrapping her arms around my bicep.

I tilted my head to the side, leaning my cheek on the top of her head. I hadn't thought of a name since that day she brought it up, getting too caught up in life.

But I didn't hesitate as I watched his form grow smaller and smaller in the distance.

Really, only one name could embody everything that horse was.

Everything that caused my shoulders to feel a little less heavy, and my heart a little less weighted.

"Bullet."

42

REED

A week after Brandy's mother shot her dad, I pulled up to my parents' house wearing a black long-sleeve button-up and my cowboy hat to match, ready for yet another family dinner. After shifting the truck into park, I stared at the bouquets of flowers on my passenger seat. It'd been difficult to find a bundle of brandy roses without picking them straight from Brandy's bushes, but after driving four counties over to some town in the middle of the valley, I finally found the combination I was looking for.

Brandy had picked her mom up on the way here, so I was waiting for the two of them to arrive before heading inside. It'd been raining earlier, but thankfully it'd stopped for now, though the chill in the air hadn't left with the clouds. It'd be winter before we knew it, which meant we had a lot of preparation to do around the ranch in the coming weeks. Fall never lasted long in the west, so at least we were familiar with the workload.

After the incident last week, the three of us had given our statements regarding what transpired that night and the abuse her father dealt to not only his wife, but his daughter, too. Though Ms. Rose took the brunt of the physical behavior, Brandy went through a lot of mental trauma, and the police wanted to know about all of it. The more evidence they gave them, the more they could use against him in court.

One of the officers had confided in us that he was more than certain he'd be convicted of his crimes, so that wasn't to worry. The tension I saw visibly lift from Brandy's and her mother's shoulders was a small mercy with everything they'd gone through. A part of me had hoped he'd succumb to his injury, but he'd come out fine. Knowing he'd rot in prison for years to come was enough for now.

My brain was still trying to wrap around the fact that her mother shot him in the entryway to their house, but not because I was shocked she did it. It was a miracle she waited so long to finally take the reins. She'd admitted that seeing him touch her daughter and physically hurt her in that way was enough for her to pull the trigger.

Parents could handle a lot of pain, but when it came to their children? They'd walk through the depths of hell for retribution. And that's exactly what her mother did that night.

Every night since, I held Brandy in my arms as she fell asleep, that soft side of her coming out in full force now that she had no reason to hold her guard up. She was still her typical snappy self, but she'd learned to be okay with being taken care of. No longer having to look over her shoulder for the impending judgment and critique from a parent, she seemed lighter. More carefree. Happy.

And that, in the end, was all I wanted for her. Whether that was with me or someone else, so long as her demons no longer haunted her every step, I'd be happy for her. Thankfully for the both of us, though, she'd chosen me.

And I was never letting her go now that I had her.

Headlights lit up the driveway in the early night sky, shining through my window with their approach. With fall quickly turning to winter, there was no longer long, sunny days, but rather dark skies and bright moons by the time dinner rolled around.

I expected Brandy's Bronco, but instead, Beckham's truck pulled up next to me. He killed the engine and got out, to which I did the same. It was time we talked, especially before this family dinner. Last thing I needed was another punch being thrown my way in front of Brandy's mother.

"Hey," he said, coming around the back of his truck with his hands tucked in the front pocket of his sweatshirt. He'd shaved his beard since I last saw him, leaving only a bushy mustache behind.

I leaned an elbow on his tailgate. "If you're gonna sock me again, might as well get it over with now. Preferably on the other side of my face, though."

He reached up to rub the back of his neck, an apologetic look passing over his face under the brim of his baseball cap. "About that. I've been meaning to call, I've just... I've got a lot going on. I'm sorry about punching you."

I waved him off. "It's nothing I'm not used to from growing up with three brothers and Bailey."

He dropped his hand, stuffing it back in his pocket. "Yeah. I guess we did get a little rough growing up."

I shrugged, glancing at the house because truly, I didn't know how to go about this. Beckham was my brother. We disagreed about things at times, but in the end, we all came out together. He was family, and family stuck together, no matter what one another was going through. So I did the one thing I think we both least expected—I stepped forward and pulled him in for a hug.

His body went stiff against mine before he pulled his hands out from between us and hugged me back. I patted his shoulder, holding him a little tighter.

"Whatever it is, Beck, you'll get through it," I mumbled over his shoulder, closing my eyes against the sting of the cold. Definitely not because of the tears that threatened to build. "Hard things are meant to be overcome. Don't give whatever this is the power to break you."

I felt him nod, his fingers gripping my shirt for a moment before he let go and pulled away. He turned his head to the side, muffling his sniffle as he ran a hand down his face.

"I'm working through it," he said, facing me again.

I gave a quick nod before another car turned down the driveway, headlights lighting us up where we stood. "I know. I'll always love you, despite you socking me in the face."

He cracked a smile, though it didn't really reach his eyes. "Just don't think about trying to get any payback."

I chuckled, glad he was attempting to joke in some way. "I wasn't planning on it, but now that you mention it…"

His smile widened slightly before he shook his head, glancing at the ground before patting my shoulder. "I'll see you inside."

With a dip of my chin, he walked off as a familiar Bronco rolled to a stop on the other side of my truck. As Brandy turned off the engine, I came around to her door and opened it for her.

"Ever the gentleman," she teased as she got out of the vehicle.

"Funny. Just a little bit ago, you were giving me shit for this," I reminded her.

She smiled, leaning in to pop a kiss on my cheek. "Don't tempt me to resort back to my more violent ways."

I closed her door, taking in her red skirt that flowed to her ankles and the white knitted sweater she wore over top. She had a wool jacket over her shoulders to fight against the fall air. "Remember what I said about violence being a turn-on?"

She sent me a devilish smirk, and my cock stirred with the look. My girl never left, despite the shit show she went through the past few weeks, and I was damn glad for it. If anyone broke my Brandy, I'd return the favor and break their fucking spine. She was a force to be reckoned with, and I chose to poke that fire any chance I got. In the end, it worked out for me, but for anyone else? I was sure Brandy would put them in their place before I even got a chance to see what they looked like. She was strong, beyond resilient, independent, and it was no secret she could handle herself just fine.

I was the backup to the woman who made men cower with a simple look. But for me? Those narrowed eyes and pull of her lips only made me want to get on my knees and worship my little devil. Now I had a free pass to do so whenever I pleased.

Was there even anything better than this?

I opened the passenger door of my truck to pull out one of the bouquets, then pivoted to face her, holding it against my chest.

Her brows raised at the sight of them, a look of shock passing over her features. "Where did you manage to find these roses?" She gave me a skeptical look. "Are they from my bushes? Reed Bronson, if you took sheers to my—"

I smiled, placing a palm on the back of her head to bring her lips to mine. She melted into me, her hand folding over mine where it held the bouquet. The sound of a set of tires crunching over gravel was the only thing that made us pull away from each other. But still, I kept my focus on her.

"I'd never touch your rose bushes. I want to keep my dick attached, thank you very much. I drove a couple hours to some small town up north. Guess they're the only ones that had that type of rose in stock."

Something in her expression shifted, like a softness overtook her.

My brows pulled together. "Is something wrong? Are you melting?"

She laughed, the sound seeping into the dark crevices of my heart and warming me up from the inside. "No, I'm not melting, weirdo. That was really sweet of you to go out of your way to get these for me."

I ran a thumb over her cheekbone, a small blush blooming on her skin. "It was nothing, really."

She leaned in, kissing me again. I'd never get used to this—kissing her. I went from never expecting to know the flavor of her to being addicted to her taste overnight, and now I couldn't get enough.

"I love you," she murmured against my lips.

"Say it again," I murmured back, threading my fingers into her hair and pulling her closer, careful not to crush the flowers.

Our lips got lost in each other, our tongues exploring, dancing, savoring.

"I love you," she repeated, fisting my shirt in her hand like she didn't want me to back away. At some point, we'd have to.

I set my forehead against hers, breathing her in and enjoying the feel of her being so openly mine. "I love you, too."

"I don't think I'll ever get used to you saying that," she whispered.

"I guess I'll just have to say it all the time, then."

She rolled her eyes, pulling away from me before I tugged her right back and sealed her protests with another kiss. Fuck, we were being cheesy, but I didn't give a shit.

"I don't know if *I'll* ever get used to this," her mother's voice announced as we parted.

"Yeah, me either," I admitted, facing Ms. Rose to find her shoving her lip gloss in her tiny purse.

"I'll leave you two alone and head on in to say hi to Charlotte," she said, waving us off. She was wearing a deep purple dress with long sleeves and a maple leaf pinned right over her collarbone.

"I have something for you." I kept Brandy's bouquet in my hand as I reached into my truck to grab the second one. It had orange carnations and a few irises for a pop of color, and it was clearly to her liking with the way her eyes beamed at the bundle as I held them out to her.

"Oh, Reed, you didn't need to get me flowers."

I shook my head. "After the last week, I think you deserve them."

She let out a choked laugh, clearly trying to keep herself together as she took them from me. "Thank you so much. They're beautiful."

I offered a closed-lip smile. "Of course."

She dabbed a finger under her eye before waving us off again. "Alright. Before I cry over some other surprise gift, I'm going in. I'll see you two inside."

"See you in a minute," Brandy said, leaning into my side as she watched her mom walk off.

"You guys are just so cute," came a high-pitched voice from the end of my truck.

Brandy straightened, finding her best friend coming around the corner.

"What's going on h—" Bailey's voice dropped off as he saw the proximity of me and Brandy. "Uh. What *is* going on here?"

Lettie elbowed her husband. "They're dating, duh."

"Dating?" he repeated, testing the word on his tongue, as if it was impossible for that to be the case. Technically, he wasn't too far off. I wasn't even sure if what Brandy and I were doing *was* dating. We'd never really talked about the official term for what we were, but either way, she was mine, and we loved each other. Boyfriend, girlfriend, whatever it was, it didn't matter. This was official.

Brandy hesitated, like she was thinking the same thing, so I filled in for her. "Yep." I grabbed her hand, still holding the bouquet at my chest. "We're dating."

Bailey's brows nearly shot up to the moon. "Really?"

I nodded.

He rubbed his forehead, turning to Lettie. "Do I have a fever?"

"Oh, quit being so dramatic," Brandy scolded, taking the bouquet from me before she led me toward them.

"Does the family know?" Bailey asked.

"We were planning to tell them tonight," I answered, stopping just a few feet from the two of them.

He tried to hide his grin, but the attempt was futile. "Good luck with that." He stepped forward to pat my shoulder. "You're gonna need it."

I shook my head as Bailey and Lettie walked toward the house, leaving the two of us alone once again.

"Dating, huh?" Brandy said, turning to face me as she dropped my hand.

I tried to gauge her reaction, hoping it was a good one. "That too much for you?"

She shook her head, the apples of her cheeks round with the pull of her smile. She reached up to drape an arm over my shoulder. "Never with you."

"Good," I replied. "I guess that makes you my official girlfriend."

Her grin only widened. "I guess it does, even though you haven't formally asked me."

I teasingly rolled my eyes. I should've known that even in this, she would let her sass shine. "Shall we go inside?" I asked, happy with...everything. Life, Brandy, tonight. If someone told me months ago I'd be standing outside my parents' house with this woman, about to tell everyone we were dating, I'd have never believed them. But fuck, was I glad this was real.

She inhaled deeply, dropping her arm from me and facing the house with a determined look on her face. "I suppose we have to." She turned back to me with a grimace. "You're sure we can't just sneak away and fuck in the barn?"

I smiled, setting my palm on the crook of her waist. "Don't entice me. That sounds a hell of a lot more fun than sitting through this dinner with all the stares and questions."

"It's not too late," she said hopefully.

I slid my hand around to her lower back, pulling her close again. "One hour, and then we'll leave."

She let out a dramatic sigh of relief. "Thank fuck."

"Come on, Little Devil. It won't be too bad."

I grabbed the last bouquet from my passenger seat and closed the door before we headed toward the house. But as we walked toward the lit-up house, the smell of home-baked casserole and impending hell wafting from the cracked windows, I think we both knew I was wrong about how smooth this dinner might go.

43

BRANDY

Reed and I walked into the Bronsons' house, hand in hand, and braced ourselves for the inevitable shock. No one could've seen this coming, so their surprise at the news was to be expected, but I wished we could skip past this part and have everyone already in the know. Though I did enjoy me and Reed being a little unspoken secret for a while, this would be nice. His family would know, and we wouldn't need to sneak around the ranch like two teenagers.

Reed paused once we passed the threshold, his eyes roaming over me as he rolled his sleeves up to his elbows, buttoning them to keep them in place as he shifted the bouquet from hand to hand with the act. My gaze followed the action, my thighs clenching on their own accord.

He leaned in, tucking my hair back before brushing his lips over the shell of my ear. "If you think that skirt is hiding anything from me, you're sorely mistaken."

"Then maybe don't look like *that*, and I won't have to try to hide how you make me feel," I murmured a little aggressively.

"One hour, and you can show me just how wet you really are. Until then, be a good girl and be on your best behavior." He straightened, looking out past the wall to the buzzing kitchen.

I internally smirked, knowing I was about to have the time of my life making him squirm for the next hour. At least, after we got this small announcement over with.

He laced his fingers through mine before giving me a quick glance to make sure I was okay with what was about to happen. It was almost like we were preparing for an uncertain war, not sure if we were going to be berated with questions or clapped on the back in congratulations. The unknown was stressing me the fuck out, to say the least.

I gave him a small nod of encouragement, thinking maybe he needed it as much as I did. Though, Reed didn't let things bother him if he could help it. I used to not either, but after the last couple months, my heart opened up, shining a new light on a side of myself I hadn't been familiar with since a young age.

It was cute seeing him so nervous over something like this. Reed was typically hard as a rock, never cracking a smile, rarely offering anything other than a grunt or warning, but this side of him, though new, was still so him.

We rounded the corner of the front entry, into the dining area that connected to the kitchen. With the old farmhouse being an open floor plan, there was no taking this slow. The way every person in the room quieted and turned to look at us was proof of that.

Reed didn't miss a stride, leading me over to the kitchen, where he poured me a glass of red wine and grabbed himself a beer from the fridge, all while keeping his hand in mine. He'd set his mother's bouquet on the counter, clearly seeing as the two of us would be addressed first. Everyone in the Bronson family was here, significant others in tow. Even Avery was staring at us from where she sat on the living room floor, toy horse poised in one hand mid-gallop.

I took a slow sip of my wine, acting as if I was savoring the flavor but really not tasting it at all. This was...weird.

Reed cleared his throat, leaning back against the counter in the kitchen as he faced everyone. "Got something you all want to say?"

From the dining room where she'd been setting up the table, Oakley shrugged. "I knew it'd happen eventually." She gave me a look of encouragement, and I mouthed my thanks in response.

Travis was standing in front of the crockpot, not looking up from whatever he was stirring. I was sure he probably thought the world had ended. That, or he didn't want to get involved in yet another of his children's relationships. He let his grown kids do what they wanted, doing his best to keep himself out of whatever they were up to. Charlotte, on the other hand, was always in the know, even if they tried to keep something a secret from her. So when she opened her mouth, it didn't surprise me in the least with what she said.

"I can finally say how happy I am that you two got together," Charlotte said with a gleaming grin from where she stood near the couch with her glass of wine, my mom by her side with her own glass. She gave me a sweet smile for support, which I returned.

"Thanks, Mom," Reed grumbled, taking a swig of his beer.

"You two sure you're not gonna bite each other's heads off?" Lennon asked, passing us in the kitchen to grab himself a water from the fridge.

I tossed my head side to side. "I haven't decided yet."

Reed shot me a frown, to which I squeezed his hand.

"It's probably their version of foreplay," Bailey teased from the couch, where Lettie had her legs thrown over his lap.

Callan grimaced from where he sat in the chair with Sage perched on his knee. "There's children in the room."

Bailey tossed a look at Avery, who was staring at him in question. "What's foreplay?"

Bailey coughed as Lettie barked out a laugh.

"It's when you prep to play," Oakley answered.

Sage shot her a look, a hand resting on her belly.

"Like when I get all my toys out?" Avery asked.

Sage cleared her throat, sitting forward slightly to lean closer to Avery. "Exactly. When you set up all your ponies to start playing pretend."

Avery shot her a smile before returning to her galloping horse. Callan released a breath, as if he was relieved that was over.

"Well," I interrupted before this could go any further south than it already had, "Reed and I are dating now, if you couldn't tell."

"The whole state of Idaho felt the world tip off its axis the day you two quit bickering," Beckham said from his seat at the table.

"We can go back to that if that's what you all prefer," Reed said.

A chorus of no's came from everyone in the room.

"That's what I thought," he muttered before sipping his beer.

Finally, Travis looked at the two of us, stopping his stirring and setting the spoon on the holder. Reed waited, unsure what reaction to expect from him. I was in the same boat. Out of everyone, I had no idea what Travis would think of the two of us together. And though everyone's opinion in this family mattered, Travis accepting us was almost like a right of passage. Reed looked up to his dad on a lot of different things, but getting his approval of the two of us meant a lot to him. And after our past...I wasn't sure what to prepare for.

"It's about damn time," Travis said, his voice low and full of gravel. "I was getting to the point I thought one of you was itching to burn the other's house down."

I pretended to contemplate the idea. "Hm. I don't know. I still might." I looked up at Reed. "Might add a little pizazz to the honeymoon phase."

Beckham shook his head disapprovingly. "Great. Violence really *is* their foreplay."

Travis's mustache twitched before he wiped his hands on the dish towel. "As long as it isn't on my ranch, and I don't have to hear about it."

He went to walk past us, but before leaving the kitchen, he paused, setting a hand on Reed's shoulder. Travis didn't show much affection, but when he did little acts like this, it meant more than anything else in this world.

He approved of us, no matter how much he tried to act like he didn't.

By the light in Reed's eyes, that was exactly what he needed.

For me, I was just damn glad this part was over.

***

After being peppered with at least a hundred questions of how we ended up like this when just during the wedding, we wanted to rip each other's throats out, we moved from the dinner table to the living room. It was difficult to explain, to say the least, but we got through it. Now, as everyone sat around with their bellies full and smiles on their faces, I leaned into Reed's arm where I sat beside him on the couch, listening as everyone talked and joked with each other. The Bronsons were always a second family to me, my home away from home, and now being with Reed, I felt even closer to them, if that was even possible.

My mom was sitting next to Charlotte on the couch, the two of them chatting away, likely about what transpired with my father that landed him in jail. His next stop would be prison for the foreseeable future, depending on the sentence the judge decided to give him. I hoped it'd be a long, grueling couple decades, but a girl could only dream.

I watched as my mom laughed at something Charlotte whispered to her, and I couldn't help the smile that crept up on me at the sight. I loved seeing her like this—so carefree, not looking over her shoulder like she might get scolded at any time. Just a woman having fun with a friend, as it always should be.

In the end, my mom and I were never really alone, even if some days it felt that way. We always had the Bronsons here to lift us up, to offer refuge not many people had in bad situations. I could never repay them for the sanctuary they offered, even if they did so unknowingly.

Half an hour later, my mom stood from her spot, giving me a look before hiking her thumb toward the door. I went to stand, but she waved me back like it wasn't necessary. I wanted to talk to her anyway, so I excused myself from my warm cocoon under Reed's arm and followed her out. She grabbed her coat on the way, but I left mine inside, thinking this wouldn't take long.

"Dinner was nice," she said as we descended the porch steps.

I wrapped my arms around myself to save some semblance of warmth against the bitter night air. "It was delicious," I agreed.

"Thank you for coming." I knew it probably felt weird for her to be able to make the decision to come tonight on her own without my father over her shoulder dictating what she could and couldn't do. Even though he was only back for a short amount of time, I could tell she'd gone back to that dark place mentally.

She stuffed her hands in her jacket pockets as we walked toward the Bronco. I'd told her earlier she could take my car if she wanted to leave early and Reed would drive me home later. Thankfully, she knew how to drive stick.

"Are you doing okay?" she asked, studying my reaction, as if she thought I'd put up my walls like I always did.

Tonight, I'd kept them down. I wanted to be able to be vulnerable with topics like this because otherwise, I'd never work through them and move on, but it was instinct to hide behind a mask. It'd take some getting used to, but there wasn't a better time to start than the present.

"It took a few days, but yeah, I am. Now that he's likely not coming back, I feel like I don't have to worry so much about it anymore," I admitted.

"It being..."

I inhaled, bracing myself for speaking the words out loud. "His manipulation, the anger. How he'd blow up at the drop of a dime. Waiting to hear if he was in a good or bad mood, or for the sound of his fist." It all played through my mind like a movie, the way he'd look when he was mad or the sound of doors slamming making me jump.

"I'm sorry I made you go through that for so long, Brandy," Mom said, stopping so she could face me.

"It's not your fault."

She shook her head, taking my hands in hers. "His anger may not have been my fault, but I had the power to leave. I was"—she searched the ground as if it held the word she was looking for—"lost. Stuck. Helpless. I thought there were no other options than staying comfortable with him. That if we left, we'd end up in a motel, or a women's shelter, or homeless. I didn't have a glamorous job or a bunch of resources or a family to take us in." She glanced at the house behind me. "But we had somewhere to go all along, and I just didn't want to burden them." She looked at me, making sure I met her gaze. "It's okay to be a burden sometimes, okay? Don't be scared to speak up or tell people you're struggling. Because if you don't, your mind will never quiet. You'll destroy yourself from the inside out and convince yourself there's no option other than to stay put." She gripped my hands tighter, her throat working on a swallow. "There are always options. They may not be obvious, but they're there."

"I don't blame you, Mom," I assured her, hoping she didn't think I hated her for any of this. She didn't make him a bad man, he was that way on his own. I knew how easy it must be for her to point the blame at herself, but even if she was the woman who was supposed to keep me safe, that didn't mean she was taught how. She did what she thought was best, and while it may not have been the number one option, she kept me alive. Fed. Loved—even if it was just by her.

"I know you don't, sweetie. That day in the diner, we were both upset. But those are things we have to talk about, no matter how hard they are to discuss."

I nodded, my throat stuck as I struggled to find words that could express how strong I thought she was. She fought back against the monster that plagued us for decades. Even if it took her years to finally do it, it didn't make her any less of a warrior.

So instead of saying the positive words we both knew we wanted to speak, I pulled her toward me, wrapping my arms around her as she did the same.

"I love you, Mom," I murmured into her shoulder, hugging her tighter.

"I love you, too, Brandy."

Before tears could make their way down my cheeks, she pulled away, looking at something over my shoulder. I turned to find Reed standing there, my coat in his hand.

"You take care of her. And if you don't, I know where you live," my mom warned, though the statement held no threat. She loved him almost as much as I did.

"Hurting her has never been on the agenda," Reed said, his eyes meeting mine. So much warmth and love was held in that gaze alone, and all I wanted to do was melt into it. Into him.

My mom squeezed my hand before stepping away. "You two have a good night." She looked at me. "Text me when you get home."

"I will. You do the same." I handed her the keys to the Bronco, then she walked off, getting in the car.

Reed approached me, wrapping the jacket around my shoulders and tugging it together in the front. He used the fabric to pull me close to him, and I tipped my head back to look up at him.

"Everything okay?" he asked.

I leaned closer to him, wanting nothing more than for his lips to be on mine. "Everything's perfect."

Then I reached up on my tip toes and closed the distance, taking him in as he wrapped me in his arms and forged the word "mine" on my heart.

Epilogue

Reed

Day before Halloween...

"What are those?" Brandy asked as she lowered herself beside me on the porch.

"Gloves," I answered as I slid the tools out of the pumpkin carving kit. I made sure to set the sharper ones closer to me. I didn't put it past her that just because we were together, she wouldn't take the opportunity to stab me if I made fun of her carving. Which, given our track record, some teasing was in order. I was glad our dynamic hadn't changed much, aside from the perks of being in a relationship. Dating or not, I liked Brandy's flame. Never wanted her to lose it.

"Gloves for carving pumpkins?" she questioned with a furrowed brow. We were sitting on my parents' porch, carving pumpkins on the day before Halloween. We'd put it off for so long, not able to take our hands off each other long enough to complete the activity. But even after all those orgasms the past couple weeks, my cock was swelling in my pants at the sight of her in that black crewneck with a little ghost stitched on the front, and those skintight leggings to match. The woman made me as horny as a fucking teenager.

"You tend to get wounds when you even think about a knife. Or shears," I replied, trying to hide my smirk. I knew the comment would rile her up. I *wanted* that. But she needed to wear gloves when she pruned those bushes out front of her house. I never missed the little cuts she'd have the next day.

"I'm extremely proficient with a knife, thank you very much." She reached across me to grab one of the sharp carving tools, her ass perked high as she did. I couldn't help myself as I reached up to cup her ass and squeeze. "Don't make me show you just how well I can use this." She lifted the tool for emphasis.

As she lowered herself back, I grabbed her chin with my thumb and forefinger, stopping her from plopping back down. "I'd love nothing more."

"Gross. Are you guys doing that 'foreplay' thing again?" Avery announced as she hopped out of Beckham's truck. He'd been babysitting her this morning while Sage and Callan went to a doctor's appointment, and had texted me that he had somewhere to be but her parents weren't back yet. I'd offered for her to join us for carving some pumpkins until they returned. Beck was doing a bit better, getting his shit together for the most part, and Avery had become attached to him at family dinners now that he was around more. But still, something seemed...off.

Brandy's lips flattened into a line as she held back a laugh and sat back down beside me. "No. I was just warning Reed that women know how to stand up for themselves."

Avery's curious gaze darted between us before she lowered herself into a criss-cross position across from us on the red plaid blanket. "But isn't he your boyfriend?"

"He is," Brandy answered confidently as she set the hand holding the tool over my knee. It was her quiet way of reminding me that the threat remained.

Avery plucked the smaller pumpkin off the blanket, setting it in front of her. "How can you be boyfriend and girlfriend if you fight all the time?"

"We have a special kind of love," Brandy answered as Beckham got out of his truck. Her explanation faded into the background as I stood. Beck never wore a suit.

I left the two girls to discuss boys and all the things about love I was sure Sage and Callan didn't want Avery knowing about yet, and crossed the distance to Beck, making it down the porch stairs to meet him halfway.

"You're sure it's okay if you two watch her for a bit?" Beckham asked, shoving his hands in the pockets of his pants.

I gave a quick nod. "Yep. Despite popular belief, we're responsible. She'll be okay with us." We'd, of course, made sure it was okay with her parents before we swapped, and while Callan had been hesitant at first, Sage was more than happy to let us watch her. Thinking back on it now, it may not have been the brightest idea. For all I knew, I'd go back to Brandy telling Avery about the birds and the bees. It wouldn't be the first time the conversation nearly got to that point.

"Thanks." The toe of his cowboy boot dug into the dirt as he looked over my shoulder at the two of them talking. "Pumpkin carving will be fun for her."

"Yeah." I eyed his suit. "Going somewhere special?"

His lips rolled together before he rubbed at his chin, his hand coasting over his five o'clock shadow, which paired with his mustache. "If you'd call a funeral special."

Instantly, I stiffened. "A funeral? Whose?"

His Adam's apple bobbed as he swallowed deep. "I don't, uh— I don't really want to talk about it right now."

I nodded in understanding. If it had been someone the family knew closely, we would've known there was a funeral. Whoever it was that passed was close to Beckham. I wouldn't weasel my way into his business. I'd learned my lesson the last time I tried to do that.

"Alright. If you need someone to talk to about it when you're done, I'm always here, Beck."

He nodded, but his eyes were vacant with the act. "I know. Thank you."

Avery and Brandy let out a chorus of laughs from behind me, and I glanced over my shoulder to find Brandy bent over and Avery's face red as a tomato.

"I should probably get back to them before Brandy says too much," I said, studying Beck for his reaction. I didn't want him to be alone in whatever he was going through, but he was an adult. He knew now that drowning in alcohol wasn't the answer. He'd be okay, and our family would be there for him in the meantime.

"Yeah, I should get going anyway. Thanks again for watching her."

I dipped my chin. "Of course. See you later."

"Later." He turned and headed back to his truck, hesitating a moment before getting in and driving off.

Dirt kicked up around his tires as his truck disappeared down the driveway, and once it was out of view, I headed back to Brandy and Avery.

"I'm gonna be a cowgirl," Avery said as I approached.

"A cowgirl? But you already are one!" Brandy exclaimed, clearly having fun with her.

"Well, yeah, but I want to be one all the time. So Mama said I can wear my cowgirl hat and boots and the chaps Daddy got me."

Emotion hit me in the chest at Avery calling Callan her dad. He had always wanted kids, and it was no secret he'd make that house of theirs as full as he could in the next few years. I looked at Brandy as she got lost in her conversation with Avery, the two of them going on and on about costumes Brandy dressed up in as a kid.

But I didn't hear any of it. Not as my entire being got lost in the sound of her voice. My heart skipped beats just thinking of having a family with her one day. Only if she wanted kids, of course. And if she didn't, that'd be okay, too. We'd be the best damn aunt and uncle in the entire state of Idaho.

"What's wrong?" Brandy asked, interrupting my trance.

I flashed her a smile before leaning forward and pressing a kiss to her lips. "Nothing, Little Devil."

"Promise?"

Before I retreated, I moved closer to her ear so Avery wouldn't hear and murmured, "Other than wanting to be buried inside your pussy while you're wearing that pink lingerie set? No, nothing." I straightened. "This is perfect."

Her cheeks tinged pink as I looked at Avery. "What do you wanna carve?"

"A castle!" Avery answered.

I grabbed the pencil from beside the tools. "A castle it is, Princess."

Avery let out a gasp. "A princess cowgirl! I can wear my dress!"

Brandy cleared her throat. "That'd be perfect, Aves."

That was the only way I could describe any of this, with my girl and my brother's daughter, carving pumpkins on my parents' porch.

Perfect.

The End

ACKNOWLEDGEMENTS

I want to give the biggest thanks to you, the reader, for having so much patience. Reed and Brandy needed their time to go through what they did, and showing that on page, in both this book and the first three, was important to me. That, and Reed's dynamic with Beckham after he returned. Sibling relationships aren't always sunshine and rainbows, as most of us know. Reed may seem closed off and grumpy, but he still has a heart. Sometimes it just takes a little while for that part of someone to feel comfortable coming out. So thank you. For getting through their hardships with me. For loving them as much as I do. And for sharing these characters. Reed and Brandy... they're messy, complicated, and challenging. But they fit. They both don't always make the best decisions or the smartest choices, but that's what makes them human. Flaws are not a bad thing.

Next, I have to thank my editor and best friend, Bobbi. I'm sure there's typos in these acknowledgements, so ignore them please. I like to surprise you with this part. From the beginning, you helped make this story what it is. When I constantly complain, "My characters are just doing things," and you say, "That's what a story is," and put me in my place, I know it's because you care for Bell Buckle, and all my other stories, just as much as I do. I'm so hard on myself some days, nitpicking my stories to no end, and you're always there to lift me up and shoot that negative voice in my head down. So thank you for the help with the wedding errands in this book, and some of the tropes, and giving me the confidence to make Reed and Beckham a little complicated. I can do hard things, I just have to try.

Shaylee, my wonderful and beautiful PA and best friend. I truly couldn't have made this release as amazing as it was without you. Between content and ideas and everything else, you've helped me tremendously, taking so many tedious things off my plate so I can dive into these worlds I create and be in my happy place. I can't express enough how much I appreciate you. You deserve the world.

Thank you to my wonderful fiance for always talking me off a ledge and reminding me my stories are worth it. You pull me out of my head on the worst days and lift me up when all I want to do is sink. This story was incredibly difficult to write because I felt so much pressure to make it perfect, but you reminded me that no matter where I go with it, it will be good, and it is. And also, if you read this, ignore all the similarities between me and Brandy. I swear I try to not be so stubborn but I just can't help it.

My baby, I love you beyond words. Thank you for continuing to nap at least once during the day so I can write. This is all for you, buddy. (and all the toys, but we won't talk about that.)

Thank you to my amazing beta readers for always helping perfect my stories. You all have the best ideas my brain likes to skip over. I appreciate the heck out of you all.

To my cover designer, Ali Clemons. You put a face to the stories that live in my brain, and I'm so damn grateful to have you a part of this Bell Buckle journey. I'm so in love with your work and the time you put in to make everything perfect. Thank you for being the best.

Kate Crew, of course I'm going to put you in here. You've been here with me from the beginning, and I'm so damn happy to call you my best friend. You seriously give me the strength to keep going despite whatever is thrown at us. You mean so, so much to me, and I can't even put it into words, so just thank you. Thank you for being the hand I can hold, even when it's dark.

Lastly, thank you to my wonderful ARC readers for hyping this book up to no end and getting the word out. Your edits, your love, all of it brings me so much joy and happiness. I don't think I'll ever not cry on release day seeing all your love and positivity. You all are the reason I'm able to do what I do. Every post, every like, every share, it all means so much to me. I love each and every one of you.

About the Author

Karley Brenna lives in a small town in the middle of nowhere out west with her fiancé, son, and herd of pets. Her hobbies include writing, reading countless books heavy on romance, and listening to country music for hours. If she's not at home, she's either at a bookstore or getting lost in the hills on horseback. She enjoys writing contemporary romance, dark romance, and fantasy. To stay up to date with Karley's future projects, follow her on social media @authorkarleybrenna.

Printed in Great Britain
by Amazon